Sarah com

sculpture. And Cookie spoke perceptively of the facial expressions captured in several century-old portraits. They reminisced about their after-school sketching classes and how unique these had been.

"Sarah, you really should take more art courses. I can see how much you still love it."

"I do love it. I've even taken out my sketchpad again." She thought back to a couple of pages she'd added the other night—the inside of Gianni's intriguing shop as well as a humorous drawing of Edgar with a huge batch of files about to topple off his desk. It had been fun.

"You're going to tell me everything about the job soon, right?" asked Cookie before they parted. "The stuff you didn't tell me today?"

"Absolutely," said Sarah with a smile. "The job stories will keep. Insurance isn't the most exciting game in town." *Unless it's peppered with behind-the-scenes intrigue and murder.*

To Sketch a Killer

by

Caryl Janis

To Sketch a Killer

Cover Art by *Kim Mendoza*

The Wild Rose Press, Inc.
PO Box 708
Adams Basin, NY 14410-0708
Visit us at www.thewildrosepress.com

Publishing History
First Edition, 2023
Trade Paperback ISBN 978-1-5092-5192-6
Digital ISBN 978-1-5092-5193-3

Published in the United States of America

Dedication

In loving memory of my mother--with gratitude always.

Acknowledgments

Deepest thanks to wonderful fellow writers, Katie Ferriello and Marketa Forstova-Horton, for their valuable comments and unwavering support throughout several drafts of this book. Heartfelt appreciation to Ann Marie Frissell, my fantastic beta reader. Sincere gratitude to my superb editor, Dianne Rich, and to everyone at The Wild Rose Press for making this book a reality. As always, many thanks to my husband Richard and daughter Daria for their continuing encouragement.

Chapter One

There was no avoiding the woman, wrapped in a faded blue coat and huddled on the steps outside the old church. She wasn't far from passers-by on the sidewalk or those heading inside for a moment of quiet prayer, as Sarah often did before work.

But a chill gripped Sarah whenever she hurried up those church steps as the old woman gestured toward the pastel flowers embroidered on the black velvet panels of Sarah's scarf—all the while humming a nameless tune.

"She's harmless," said Kelly, the young secretary, greeting Sarah on her first day at the Butler Insurance Agency. "Which is more than I can say for a lot of others out there." She shut the aging door with conviction.

Some days the woman lingered for a few hours, and others, not at all. It was anyone's guess where she vanished otherwise. She was as much a part of things as the church bells that had chimed daily for almost a century.

"Don't worry about her." Mr. Butler ran a hand over his thinning hair. "Just watch out for that guy. He's been hanging around for a few days." He nodded toward a man in a soiled tan jacket across the street, crouched low and tossing crumpled wrappers from a trash container. "This whole city's going to hell." He let out a sigh as worn as the lapel of his overcoat.

The elegant scrollwork and tall windows of the street's older brownstones and buildings hinted at days of bygone charm. But some were empty and only a few small businesses remained, the Butler Agency and the old-fashioned shoe repair shop among them. Residents of the walk-up apartments kept to themselves, intent on minding their own business, whatever that business might be.

Newspaper headlines echoed Mr. Butler's words, and the summer of 1977's massive blackout, with costly lootings and fires, left New York stunned. Despite the arrest of the .44 Caliber Killer, an uneasy aftertaste lingered. Everyone had a crime story, and people were moving to where the air was cleaner and the streets safer.

"Be careful," cautioned an elderly neighbor in the working-class Manhattan building where Sarah now sublet a tiny apartment. "This isn't the way it used to be, especially since the '50s. Twenty years and the city's gone downhill. Watch out for yourself, young lady."

Sarah thanked the woman for her concern. But she was all too aware that things had changed—and not always for the better.

Now, Sarah slipped into her dark gray coat, pulling her collar up and snugly wrapping the scarf over her long chestnut curls.

"Stay warm." Edgar raised his head as she walked by, pushing up the glasses that forever slid down his nose. Edgar was always there, head bent over a desk piled high, deciphering some complex policy, claim, or client report.

Sarah had also stayed to finish some paperwork, eager to do her best. The employment agent called the position a steppingstone to the future. "*This* job," he'd said, waving a cheap ballpoint pen in the air, "will be a real asset to your résumé." For Sarah, though, *this* job simply came at the right time.

Outside, the darkening sky held the lingering vibration of the church bells next door. She pressed a fold of the smooth velvet scarf closer to her face—the scarf that once belonged to her aunt and captured the attention of the old woman on the church steps.

The woman was still there, the cool breeze catching scattered strands of faded gray and red hair as they escaped from beneath her old woolen hat. Again, she hummed. The same handful of notes in a repeated pattern, not quite a discernible melody.

A teenager just then swaggered down the sidewalk, tossing his stringy, copper-colored hair.

"Hey, lady!"

Common sense urged Sarah to continue. But she turned.

The teen stared at the old woman. "Quit singin'. It's lousy!" His cruel snicker followed.

Sarah's shout rang clear, piercing the chill air. "Leave her alone!" Choking back a breath, she forced her eyes to lock with his.

The teen's face twisted with insolence.

The moment was ripe with something ugly until the low rumble of an approaching cab broke the spell. Its lights mingled with those switched on in a nearby window.

He raised a tattooed hand in a theatrical gesture. "Bitch."

Taking one last drag on his cigarette, he pitched it into the gutter and swaggered on, again tossing his stringy, copper-colored hair.

Sarah froze until his form grew smaller, finally disappearing around a distant corner. Taking an enormous breath, she turned to the old woman who'd finally raised her head. Her moist eyes met Sarah's with gratitude.

Sarah nodded and walked away, the teen's angry, contorted face still burning in her mind.

Chapter Two

Sarah tossed the contents of her shopping basket onto the conveyor belt. Colorful fresh vegetables and a small package of chicken tumbled after two pints of strawberry ice cream.

"How's the new job?" Hilda, the motherly cashier, captured a green pepper before it rolled out of reach.

"Still feeling pretty new." Sarah tried for a light tone, still shaking off her earlier encounter with the teenager.

"You like it, though?" Concern crept into Hilda's question.

Sarah dug through her purse in search of her wallet. *Did she like the job?*

"It's a good change," she said. "I needed that."

Sarah said a weary goodbye to Hilda and trudged home to her tiny apartment. She'd been lucky to sublet this place from her college friend, Gen, just when it'd been time to move. Now, closing the door behind her, she breathed in the warmth of the snug and comfortable space. *But where did the old woman go at night? Was it as warm as here? As warm as the nursing home where Sarah's aunt had been?*

Tossing her coat on the chair, she turned on the radio and brought her groceries into the kitchen. "Welcome to your easy listening station," said the silky voice, "where you can enjoy almost a full hour of uninterrupted beautiful music." Her mother and aunt used to enjoy this station, humming along with familiar melodies. Now Sarah joined in with a Rodgers and Hammerstein tune while making dinner. *What was it the woman was trying to hum anyway?*

As she chopped the pepper and onion and swept them into the pan with broth and chicken, Sarah's appetite began to return. By the time she added a touch or two of spice, the welcome aroma of simmering ingredients filled the room. When she sat down at the small table to eat, the hot meal and soothing music combined to give her a sense of calm. After dinner, it was time for dessert in front of the TV—a chance to further unwind, to get lost in the latest episode of *All in the Family.*

As she savored the first creamy spoonful of strawberry ice cream, the Bunker family's opening theme song was just ending, Archie and Edith's reminiscences of the good old days ringing loud and shrill. Then came Archie's pronouncements from his favorite easy chair about his son-in-law Meathead, the neighbors, and daily events in Queens. It reminded Sarah of her old neighborhood.

Staring at her empty dish during a commercial, Sarah contemplated a second scoop. But the clang of the phone interrupted. She hesitated. It was late, and she loathed giving up even a few minutes of relaxation. But the ringing persisted. Setting aside her dish, she reached for the beige receiver, straightening out its long, tangled cord as she answered.

"Where have you been? Sarah, I'm worried about you."

Lorna never wasted time on unessential opening

pleasantries.

"Sorry, Lorna. I'm just getting used to the new job. Beginner's fatigue and all." Did a couple of months on the job still qualify her as a rank beginner?

"C'mon. Do you like it?"

The best thing about the Butler Insurance Agency was that it was a change—a change from her old job in the business office at Westervale Nursing Home where Aunt Addie spent her two final years. The place where Sarah worked during that time to be near her, to maintain that fading bond with her last close relative.

"Sure. Lots of excitement in the insurance game."

"I'll bet it's beyond dull." Lorna jumped in without hesitation. "No antics like we had today. Remember Cora? The lady in 512? She threw her wig into Mr. Ainsley's peach cobbler at the afternoon social. You should have seen the ruckus after that."

"Mr. Ainsley must have been less than thrilled," Sarah said.

Even non-medical workers got to know Westervale's residents, stopping to chat with them. After Aunt Addie died, Sarah found it increasingly difficult to stay there in an atmosphere where sadness and loss were underlying themes. And now Lorna, a well-meaning friend and former co-worker, wanted to keep her within the Westervale fold.

Lorna plunged ahead. "So, a few of us are getting together for a drink on Friday night. Want to come? We're trying a new place. Captain Neptune's. Word has it that the hors d'oeuvres can't be beat. A few drinks and you can make a meal of 'em."

"Thanks, but I've been wiped out lately. Maybe next time," said Sarah.

Lorna didn't give up easily. "You're not holding out on me, are you? Like maybe that new manager of yours, Mr. Butler, is cute and you're having a drink with him instead?"

Sarah's spontaneous laughter was a relief. "Cute? Maybe to Mrs. Butler or if you're ready for social security."

"Sarah, I still don't get it. Why did you have to go to work for that small insurance place anyway? You could have gotten a job at a big bank or something. Lots of cute guys there."

This was a well-worn path with Lorna. If she hadn't been planning her own wedding, Lorna would be gone from Westervale in a heartbeat and taking her own advice.

"Not in the market for cute guys now." Sarah grimaced at the old memory of a short engagement, broken by a fiancé angry at her for spending time with Aunt Addie and not enough out partying with him.

"Anyway," Sarah continued, "it's a tough market, and the Butlers offered me the job quicker than any of those big places would have."

Or so said Dave, the guy in the garish sports jacket at the employment agency. He knew his business, even if he did have the look and hustle of the used car salesmen in her old neighborhood. A year or less at the Butler Insurance Agency, he proclaimed, would add to her teaching and Westervale credentials and lead to bigger things.

Lorna sighed. "Okay, we'll talk soon. If you change your mind, it's Friday at five thirty. Captain Neptune's. Two doors from Fiddler's. And it's a quicker ride to midtown for you now."

"Next time," promised Sarah. "And please say hi to the gang for me."

After hanging up the phone, Sarah hugged the cheerful yellow crocheted pillow tight to her chest. It was the one that had decorated Aunt Addie's familiar chair by the window at Westervale. After she died, it was time to stop walking by her old room. Time to stop listening to the visiting entertainers Addie enjoyed so much. Time to stop spending Monday mornings on the way to work wondering who had passed away over the weekend. Meeting Lorna and the old work gang would bring back too many memories.

Sarah switched on the radio again, just as the five-minute newsbreak was ending.

"Temperatures plunging into the thirties tonight." The voice was relaxing. So was the lush orchestral medley of Gershwin songs that followed.

Sarah brought her empty ice cream bowl to the sink, its familiar leafy green pattern a reminder of her growing-up years when, after her mom passed away, Aunt Addie had cared for her. She'd dried her tears over the everyday problems of youth—from her disappointment over not making the school basketball team to her heartbreak when her first high school crush didn't ask her to the prom. And she made sure Sarah took the sketching lessons she loved.

Now Sarah grabbed several sheets of pale pink stationery and sat down at the small table. She penciled a few light strokes on the paper to create simple sketches of her desk at the Butler Agency, the old woman on the church steps, and the surly teenager. She owed Gen a letter and would include these sketches along with some newsy tidbits from work as well as an account of this evening's events. Gen loved Sarah's sketches, and Sarah loved creating them.

Sitting back, Sarah rubbed her tired neck. Then she added a finishing line or two, emphasizing the teen's twisted expression and the old woman's face, upturned toward Sarah.

A moment or two later, as she studied the finished sketches, a tear dropped onto the back of Sarah's hand. She suddenly realized why the old woman made her uneasy. She reminded Sarah of Westervale and Aunt Addie.

She'd avoided the old woman for no other reason than the sadness she represented, the sadness that Sarah was trying so hard to leave behind.

Chapter Three

Sarah left home early the next morning. She wanted to say a prayer at the church before work, craving peace inside the almost empty sanctuary with its warm wood trim and soft glow of stained glass.

Hiking up the final steps of the subway exit, she rounded the corner, taking in the aroma of the newsstand clerk's robust coffee as it punctured the air. A split second later, Sarah collided with a woman who had just grabbed the daily paper from the top of the pile there.

"I don't know why I even bother reading this," she said, ignoring Sarah's profuse apologies for bumping into her.

Sarah glanced down at the headlines, familiar battle cries in bold type—the city's ongoing fiscal crisis and crime on the rise. She shook her head and hurried on, the first peal of the morning bell sounding as she arrived at the church.

The old woman was settling in, brushing off her step with a gloved hand. *How cold it must be. Weren't there other places warmer than this? Was her coat enough protection?* It occurred to Sarah that she should bring her an extra sweater or blanket. Guilt stabbed at her heart for not making this small gesture already.

The woman glanced at Sarah and paused, not sitting down. She tilted her head toward the church itself, as if sensing something. At the same time, a sharp *crunch* made Sarah grimace. She'd been so careful of her new work pumps. But her heel snagged on a jagged piece of the concrete church step. She looked down, relieved that it wasn't totally stuck.

That was when she noticed a rusty splash on the right side of the stairs. Two more steps and she spied a dried rusty trickle. Shielding her eyes from the sun's cold, brilliant glare, she glanced up at the church doors, first straight ahead and then off to the far right.

Could the trickle have come from there?

From the man slumped in the far doorway, as if he'd wanted to take shelter?

But his coat was slightly open. Exposing a wound.

The man was dead.

Sarah's scream shattered the quiet morning air. Rising as high as the church's tower, just as the last of its morning bells faded into the distance.

Chapter Four

Three figures hunched shoulder to shoulder on the church steps. Sarah squeezed close between the old woman and Father Haney from the church, as much for warmth as for a feeling of security. Police cars and officers flooded the street, and the cordoned-off crime scene drew a crowd of residents and curiosity seekers. It resembled a surreal movie set.

Out on the sidewalk, Sarah's boss, Mr. Butler, wrung his hands as he waylaid some uniformed cops, pointing across the street to where the derelict had recently been foraging in the garbage. *Was he suggesting the derelict was guilty of murder?* Mr. Butler ran his hand over his receding hairline as a few of his random words carried through the air. "Mugging and store robbery. And now, murder." It had only been a matter of time.

"Lou. *Please* come inside. Get your coat!" Mrs. Butler appeared, clutching her tweed winter jacket close. Her voice rose high over the chaos as she tugged at her husband's sleeve.

At that moment, two plainclothes officers arrived. After exchanging a few quiet words with a uniformed cop, they approached the hapless trio on the church steps.

The older of the two men spoke first, not a flicker of expression on his face.

"Miss Quinlee. You were the one who discovered the body?"

Sarah bit her lip and nodded. "Yes."

"You work for that guy?" He jerked his head in the direction of Mr. Butler, still pacing on the sidewalk.

"Yes, I do."

"And why were you at the church?" He didn't give Sarah a chance to answer. "You here to meet the dead guy or something? There was no Mass for at least another half hour."

Sarah drew her slender frame out of its slouching position, resentful of the man's tone. "I come to this church sometimes before work to say a prayer for my dead mother and aunt."

"So, you didn't know the deceased?" His eyes bore into hers.

"No, I didn't." Her voice was a little louder now.

The old woman looked up at the detective as if something in his words resonated with her.

"Relax, May," he said. "I'll get to you next."

May? Her name was May? And the detective knew her? Of course. The cops probably knew all of the homeless people in the neighborhood.

The younger detective, silent until now, laid a hand on his partner's sleeve. "Why don't I take it from here? Look. Over there." He gestured to an official-looking duo marching up the steps toward the crime scene, a place already swarming with activity.

The older man dragged his paunchy form in their direction. "'Bout time."

The young detective turned to Sarah and her two companions. His deep blue eyes were kind. "I'm sorry. It's been a stressful week."

Sarah nodded, her shoulders tightening as she started to shiver.

"Father, would it be okay if we went into the church somewhere? Maybe your office? Then we could all talk where it's warmer."

Father Haney nodded at the detective's request and rose. "We can use the entrance on the left. It won't be near…" He faltered, with a slight acknowledgement of the crime scene.

The detective now spoke softly to the old woman. "It's all right, May. You come, too."

May turned to Sarah, almost as if for guidance. For the second time in less than twenty-four hours, Sarah met her gaze.

It seemed as if May was trying to speak but, instead, she started humming those notes, as if something important was contained in their simple pattern.

Sarah gently grasped May's gloved hand. "C'mon, May."

****

Father Haney's office reminded Sarah of the one her grammar school principal had occupied. A place where ancient books and beat-up desks absorbed the essence of the room's history. Along one wall was an old couch, a 1960s relic upholstered in hideous green plastic with tiny cracks and tears. Sarah sat there next to May. Father Haney and the younger detective, who'd introduced himself as Gil Rian, each grabbed a wooden chair.

Sarah leaned closer to May.

Could this be the same woman she had avoided for weeks on end?

Detective Rian turned to Sarah and asked for her version of events. "Whenever you're ready," he said, "just tell me whatever you can remember." His voice was as gentle as the waves in his brown hair.

It didn't take long for Sarah to tell her story. There wasn't much to say.

The same was true for Father Haney. He'd arrived earlier than usual that morning. The sexton was home sick, so Father Haney opened up and took care of things in his place.

"How long has he been home?" asked Detective Rian.

"Two days so far with the flu," said the priest. "And I always come in through the back entrance." It was easier, he explained, since it was closer to the residence where he lived. He then walked through the sanctuary to the front where he unlocked the main doors.

He paused. "That's when I heard the screams."

Several people nearby also heard Sarah's screams, and Father Haney yelled to them to run home and call the police. He stayed to comfort Sarah. No one else was in the church yet, of course, since Father Haney was just opening up for anyone who wished to come in and pray before he prepared for morning Mass.

"It was just going to be the normal routine," he said. But this morning's discovery had turned that normal routine into a very ugly business.

Detective Rian nodded, penciling brief notes from time to time.

Next, he turned to May, still sitting motionless, listening.

He leaned closer. "May, is there anything you

might have seen that could help us?"

She searched his face for a few seconds and then began singing a couple of the notes that Sarah had heard before.

But just then the door burst open and the surly detective entered with the force of a cyclone. Mr. Butler was close behind. He never retrieved his overcoat. Only his white shirt and vest, both a size too small, protected him from the chilly outside elements.

"Sarah!" Mr. Butler slid across the aging couch, its cracked green surface emitting a sound of protest. "Are you all right?"

"I'm okay." The thin tone of her voice said otherwise.

The older detective—Harry Cahill—skipped any expression of concern. Acknowledging Father Haney, he then glared at Sarah.

"So, I assume you told your story to my partner here." He paused to catch her brief nod. "And again, why were you at the church so early? You said saying a prayer for dead relatives?"

"Yes, that's right."

"And you do this often?" His eyes, underscored with dark circles, narrowed as he spoke.

"Yes, I sometimes go there before work or later on. It's just for a few minutes."

"But you don't go to Mass?"

"No, sir." Sarah clutched her hands in her lap.

"She has to be at work before Mass starts," Mr. Butler broke in.

"Yes, that's right," Sarah said. "But sometimes I find it comforting to meditate and say a short prayer in the quiet of the church before work. Not every day, but on occasion."

Cahill gave a hard stare while Father Haney looked on with interest. Sarah never met the priest before. She wondered if he'd ever noticed her in the church.

"Mr. Butler tells me you've only worked for him a short time." Cahill kept pressing.

"That's right. About two months now."

"So, you're new to the neighborhood and…"

"I never saw that man before!" Sarah clutched her hands tighter, her voice rising.

Was she going to be accused of something? All because of wanting to go to church?

"It's okay," Detective Rian interrupted, a look of distress crossing his face. "We only want to get as much information as we can."

Good cop, bad cop?

Mr. Butler broke in again. "Yeah, and it's not like violent crime is anything new around here." He turned to Detective Cahill. "Like the woman who was beaten in her building vestibule two weeks ago? And how about the guy knocked over for his wallet at the bus stop?"

Cahill seemed to deflate. A murder on the steps of a church wouldn't look good within the precinct area. He wasn't very young. *Shouldn't he have risen further in the ranks by now?* Then again, times were tough and, given budget cuts, maybe he was just glad to have a job.

"Okay, look." He addressed Sarah, more reasonable now. "You discovered the guy. And you're new around here. Maybe you noticed something— *anything* we can follow up on."

May began humming again. Just the same few

notes.

"It's all right, May," said Detective Rian.

"So, May," interrupted Cahill. "Anything you got to say?"

But she only hummed those few notes in response. Then she tried a word. It almost sounded like "aah." But nothing was distinct.

Cahill snorted. "Same's I figured."

"Give her a chance," shot back Detective Rian.

May hummed again.

"She's trying." Sarah patted May's hand, noticing her gloves. Worn, well past their prime, they were once of good quality suede. Had she found them? Had a Good Samaritan given them to her?

"What're you, a relative?" Cahill erupted once more.

Sparks radiated from Sarah's eyes. She leaned forward. She couldn't stop now. "No, I'm not. But she reminds me of my aunt. My aunt who died earlier this year. My aunt who died in the nursing home where I used to work. And that's why I left that job. To get away from all that sadness. My aunt who I was going to say a prayer for when I saw that…that poor man…"

Sarah choked on her last words, sitting back and covering her face with her hands.

It was suddenly still. Almost silent. Except for the faint sound of May humming.

Chapter Five

Friday night, and the murmur of after-work cocktail chatter rose as Sarah headed down the short flight of stairs to Captain Neptune's, a new watering hole just a stone's throw from the gleaming corporate centers of midtown. She paused to check her image in the stairwell's walls. Their reflective copper surface reminded her of material from an old school art project.

Sarah had replayed the events of the other morning a thousand times. She'd insisted on going back to work that day. At least in the office, there were diversions. She'd pocketed the names and numbers of the detectives, who urged her to call if she remembered anything more. But all she wanted to do was forget.

Tonight, though, Sarah decided to take up Lorna's invitation for drinks with the old work gang. Until only a few days ago, Westervale was a part of her life she also wanted to forget. But now the world had shifted.

At the bottom of the stairs, Sarah crashed into a full-sized statue of Neptune in a captain's hat, prompting laughter from those nearby. She joined in with them before threading her way through the youthful crowd toward the familiar Westervale faces at the far end of the room. Lorna spied her first. "Look who's here! Sar-ar-aah." Squealing, she almost knocked the breath out of Sarah with an enthusiastic hug.

"What a great outfit," shouted Christine over the

boisterous surroundings. She waved a tall gin and tonic in salute as Sarah removed her coat to reveal a stylish auburn, wrap-around dress. "The world of insurance must be good. You never dressed like that for us."

But she'd chosen the pretty dress to lift her own spirits.

Laughter and hugs followed as the others rushed to greet her. Why had she left them in the first place? If she'd stayed at Westervale, she wouldn't have discovered a dead body and have had to deal with all of the unpleasantness that followed.

But after a few sips of her white wine spritzer, she remembered why.

Julie's story was first. "Really, it was heartbreaking," she said. The sweet elderly man in Room 302 had tearfully wandered the hall in search of a half-remembered candy shop from his youth. All the while, two aides bickered while guiding him back.

"What were they arguing about?" Christine asked.

"Who was going to lose out on the next raise if they were blamed for some lost paperwork."

"Ha!" Christine gave a snort. "Raise? These days? They must have been dreaming."

Glen picked up when Julie's story ended, spinning yet another tale of the week's mishaps. He finished with the sad news of residents who'd passed away. Sarah remembered one woman, in particular, with soft white hair who sat alone by her window. Aunt Addie also loved her place by the window. *Yes, it had been time to leave Westervale.*

"So, Lorna." Sarah abruptly changed the subject. "How are your wedding plans going?"

Lorna took a gulp of her drink and smiled broadly.

"You can't imagine how many details there are! A million *little* details like which gifts are good for the bridesmaids, why this cousin shouldn't sit next to that cousin at the reception, should I march down the aisle to "Here Comes the Bride" or some stuffy trumpet tune. And that's just for starters."

"So do the guys figure in at all? Or are they just like props in a production number?" asked Scott. "Like Captain Neptune over there?"

The group roared with laughter.

"The guys are loving that they don't have to do any of the planning." Lorna grinned. "Everyone's happier that way. It'd only mean more chaos."

"Sarah." Julie turned to her. "Ever hear from that old boyfriend of yours?"

Sarah tried not to choke on one of the mini-meatballs she'd just speared with a toothpick. The overdone seasoning left a bad taste. Or maybe it was Julie's question.

Lorna jumped in before Sarah could answer.

"Ex-fiancé," Lorna corrected, unintentionally making it worse.

"I forgot," said Julie. "Any chance…?" Julie was ever ready to write a happy ending.

"Over and done with a million years ago." Sarah tapped the table for emphasis. "I'm *really* enjoying my unattached status right now."

A slight pause followed while everyone dug into their noxious little cocktail meatballs.

"How's the new job?" asked Glen as he accepted a plate of hot chicken wings from the waitress in her official Captain Neptune tee shirt. Meanwhile, Scott tried, and failed, to establish eye contact with her.

"Pretty good," Sarah said. "The agency is different than Westervale. More paperwork. And it's a really small company. But the people are nice, and I'm learning about insurance." She finished with a laugh, knowing they considered the industry and the neighborhood boring.

"Hey, I caught on the news that someone got killed around there," said Glen.

Sarah bit into a chicken wing and made an obvious show of fanning her mouth from the hot sauce, buying a moment before responding. Given the other pressing headlines, the mayoral election included, the murder had only gotten a brief mention. Obviously, not brief enough. Couldn't they go back to gossiping about Westervale or Captain Neptune's hat? Or anything?

"Yeah, but there's no real details on that," Sarah said, ignoring the look that Lorna shot her way. "But if you want the latest crime story, I heard that some guy waving a knife held up the card store around the corner from here this afternoon."

"You mean Smart Elegance?" Christine's jaw dropped at this news.

"That's the one," said Sarah. "I wouldn't have known except the deli clerk told me when I stopped in to get some mints on my way here." *And thank heaven for that twist of good fortune.* She'd run into the deli at just the right moment to hear this news flash.

In an instant, each person began with their own can-you-top-this crime tale. There was never a lack of material on the subject. But it cast a pall over their table.

A couple of minutes of this discussion was enough. Sarah grabbed a clean paper placemat and fished a pen out of her purse.

"Hey, how did you find this place, anyway?" she interrupted during a brief pause while smoothly drawing lines and shapes on the small paper's surface.

Scott chimed in first. "My roommate and I were heading for Fiddler's Grill two weeks ago when we saw the sign. The hors d'oeuvres are a lot better here."

"Sarah, what are you doing?"

Sarah clicked her pen closed. "Well, Scott, since you found the place, this is for you."

She handed him her quick sketch of Captain Neptune, his cap at a jaunty angle, as he harpooned a cocktail meatball. Underneath the picture she'd written: "Better than all the fish in the sea."

The group cheered as Scott passed it around. "We miss your sketches, Sarah."

"And we miss you, too," added Lorna.

Sarah grinned. She was glad her little sketch lightened the mood.

After two wine spritzers and as many cocktail meatballs and spicy wings as she could handle, not to mention a hefty amount of gossip, Sarah was more than ready to leave. She said her goodbyes and promised to keep in touch.

Making her way back up the stairs to street level, Sarah made a foolish face at her reflection in the copper-colored walls while brushing her hair away from her tired eyes. *What a ridiculous place.*

But the harsh overhead light bounced off those wall coverings, giving her chestnut hair a copper-colored glow. Sarah halted, stunned by a flashback to the hostile teenager who had taunted May. He'd tossed his stringy hair in defiance. And that hair was copper-colored, just like hers now appeared in the reflection from the crazy walls. Sarah had forgotten to tell the detectives about the teenager when they'd asked if anything unusual happened recently.

Maybe it wasn't important. But, then again, maybe it was.

Chapter Six

Although work at the Butler Agency appeared routine the following week, Sarah caught each person casting furtive glances out the window from time to time. There was tension in the air, a heightened fear in an already wary neighborhood. "Probably a drug deal gone wrong," said Kelly. "Just another random crime."

There had been no official word or any other recent information for that matter, making Sarah wonder if the incident with the obnoxious teenager really was important. There were lots of obnoxious people out there, and she didn't want to bother the cops with anything trivial.

What was not so trivial was the bond forming between Sarah and May. Sarah brought her a small, sturdy brown blanket of Aunt Addie's, offering it to the woman as she settled in on her step one morning.

"For you, May." Sarah spoke gently. The woman clutched the blanket close to her as if it might have been a dear friend.

Sarah now gazed at the church. She was determined to cast aside her anxiety and go back inside. Surely it was safe. Maybe within its peaceful walls, she might decide if she should tell the police about the teenager. Would they be angry she had forgotten about it or just laugh?

Father Haney waved as she climbed the church

steps. He was outside checking the announcement board. "Sarah, how are you?" The priest smiled. "I've been hoping you'd stop by for a few minutes to say hi and maybe come in for a quick prayer the way you used to." He had probably been aware of her presence in the church all along. More than she'd realized.

"I guess I've been a little worried." She cleared her throat. "Have you heard anything about the, um, poor man who was killed?"

Father Haney skipped a beat before replying. "No, nothing." He looked up. "I understand you're worrying that it might not be safe here. But I'm sure the police are watching. And I'd hate to see you miss the peace and uplift that our church can offer."

Sarah smiled, well aware that the murder, even though outside the church itself, had done nothing to enhance the already dwindling numbers of the congregation, not to mention occasional visitors such as herself. And she had been grateful on the day of the crime for Father Haney's offer of help or prayer anytime.

"Don't worry, Father," she said. "I'm going in for a few moments right now."

He nodded, his gaze kind behind the wire eyeglasses. "Anytime, Sarah. And I'll say a prayer for you and for the aunt you spoke of last week."

"Thanks." She was surprised he remembered. "I'd appreciate that."

In the church's familiar interior, Sarah eased into a smooth wooden pew at the back. Several other individuals were already deep in prayer and contemplation. Bowing her head, she said a brief prayer for her aunt and her mother. Then she studied the peaceful interior of the small sanctuary for a few minutes, focusing on the vivid colors of the stained-glass windows lining the walls.

When she rose to leave, she pulled Aunt Addie's velvet scarf closer, feeling the distinctive outline of its embroidered flowers. Starting down the steps, she saw May settling in. The woman looked up at Sarah.

"Hi, May." She knew that the woman couldn't, for whatever reason, greet her in a traditional manner in return. Then May again pointed to her scarf. Sarah smiled. She caught the sound of May humming once more. Those same few notes. The same pattern. *What was that melody? And why did Sarah's scarf always attract May's attention?* Sarah wished she could linger a few minutes and sit with May. Try to identify that fragment of a song. But she needed to get to work now.

The moment she pushed open the door to the agency, she was surprised to see Detectives Cahill and Rian in the outer office chatting with Mr. Butler. Kelly rearranged papers on her desk while leaning forward to catch every word of the conversation.

Sarah took a deep breath as they all exchanged greetings. She managed a brief smile, mostly directed at Detective Rian. She hoped Cahill wouldn't be as rude as he'd been the last time. But he was the one who spoke first, a bit gruffly but without hostility.

"I'm glad you're here. We've got some news to run by all of you. First, the name of the deceased. Ever hear of a Vincent Milaeve? Sound familiar?" He studied each of their faces carefully.

Sarah shook her head as Mrs. Butler drifted in from the conference room.

Detective Cahill repeated the information for her

benefit. "It's spelled sort of weird." He enunciated each letter of the last name to be sure they caught it. "Older guy. Late fifties."

There was a momentary silence. Mr. Butler stared at the scuff marks on his shoes, deep in thought. "Tell you what," he said, looking up. "We'll check through our files and see if we ever had any clients by that name. We've come across a lot of people over the years."

"Appreciate it," said Cahill. "And we're not releasing his name to the general public at this point. Official procedure." He paused as Detective Rian took over.

"We're urging all of you to be careful. It looks as if Mr. Milaeve might have been shot while he was still on the sidewalk. He possibly grabbed the railing and pulled himself up the steps before he died. Maybe he hoped to get inside the church and find help." He looked at Sarah, a pained expression on his face.

Detective Cahill continued. "It appears as if he collapsed in the doorway and died of his wound. We're still reviewing all of the details."

A heavy silence fell over the room.

"It might have been a random street crime or something drug related. Victim's wallet was still on him, and no gun's been found yet. We're just telling everyone to be careful." Cahill looked at Sarah as he uttered these last words. Then his gaze swept the others. "If any of you can think of anything that could help, you know where to reach me or Detective Rian."

There was a low murmur of group assent before Sarah spoke. "Uh, excuse me. I do have something to tell you."

Everyone turned to look at her.

"I thought of something over the weekend and was wondering if I should call you. Maybe it's not important, but in all of the confusion the other morning I forgot about it completely. And now, after what you've just told us, it might mean something."

"That's okay," said Detective Rian. "What did you remember?" His tone was encouraging. Cahill had the good grace not to say anything.

She briefly told her story about the teen and how she'd shouted at him to stop taunting May. And then how he'd stalked off.

"It's probably nothing," she said. "I know this sort of thing isn't uncommon, but I thought you should know."

The detectives exchanged glances. Then Cahill spoke. "Would you be willing to come to the precinct and look at a few mugshots?"

Sarah nodded.

Cahill addressed his partner. "Gil, why don't you two set up a time for this?"

Sarah was relieved she wouldn't have to deal with Cahill. She and Detective Rian agreed to meet at the precinct on her lunch hour later that day. It was only a couple of blocks away.

Both men politely offered their thanks and left.

Now the small group lingered near Kelly's desk.

Edgar walked in from his office. "Sorry. I was on the phone. Is everything okay?"

Kelly eagerly retold the story, while everyone else pondered these recent developments.

"So, it's a random robbery." Edgar's voice was quiet.

"They said street crime, not robbery," Kelly said. "His wallet was still on him."

"So, whoever did it is still out there." Edgar readjusted his glasses as he spoke.

"Maybe it was that creepy teenager," suggested Kelly.

"Could've been," said Mr. Butler, watching his wife slip out at the sound of a ringing phone. "Just one more story in a wave of crimes." He tapped the folder in his hand against the bookcase. "Okay, we should probably get back to work now. Just be careful, everyone, okay?"

But Kelly found the discussions about crime more absorbing than the papers on her desk. "What about that guy who was rooting around in the garbage pails last week?"

"I told the cops about him the other day, but I never saw his face." Mr. Butler again consulted his scuffed shoes. "Haven't seen him since."

There was a brief silence.

"I wonder why the guy still had his wallet." Sarah was half thinking out loud now.

"Maybe he resisted giving it up," said Kelly. "They always say to just give over your money if you're being robbed. Maybe he didn't. That could be why he was shot."

Mr. Butler frowned. He was probably worried that Kelly might quit out of fright.

Kelly was right, though. If the shooting had been because the victim refused to give up his wallet, the criminal was especially dangerous. Was the teen capable of this? Or that vagrant looking through the garbage?

Kelly caught her breath and continued. "Now it seems like we're all sitting ducks. Maybe we'll never know what the story is, and that's worse."

Sarah's first thought was for May. She would have even more to fear, although most homeless people were in danger anyway, just by being out on the streets. Would she be safe? *But were any of them safe now?*

Chapter Seven

When Sarah pulled open the formidable door of the police precinct at lunchtime that day, it was to the sound of chaos. The squawk of an argument rang out in full force, and people ran and barked orders in every direction.

The desk officer looked up. "Sarah Quinlee, right?"

Obviously, her visit wasn't unexpected.

Before he could say more, Detective Rian appeared with a cheerful smile. He waved to the desk officer and led Sarah through a maze of desks and chairs that were even older and more worn than those at the Butler Agency and Father Haney's office combined, if that were possible. An assortment of people filled the place, from aggravated cops to angry or scared civilians. Some were sprawled in their seats with a practiced air of insolence. Others were on the verge of tears. As officers listened to their stories, their faces exhibited a range of emotions from compassion to frustration. Paper was scattered over every surface, and the air smelled like a combination of stale food and the subway at rush hour.

Detective Rian ushered Sarah into a small side room and invited her to sit.

"Are you doing okay after last week?"

"Thanks, yes," she said, appreciating his concern. "It almost seems like a terrible dream now. Like it couldn't have been real."

"I wish it hadn't been real."

There was a sudden commotion outside, which ended almost as abruptly as it began.

Detective Rian waited for the noise to subside. "Thanks so much for coming in. I'd like to find that teenager. He may or may not have any connection to the murder case, but he shouldn't be out there threatening people like he did to you and May." He inched the open book on the table closer to Sarah. "Here. Take a look. These are some people who've caused trouble in the neighborhood for a while. See if any of them look familiar."

Sarah relaxed, shutting out the remaining turmoil in the background as she turned her attention to the photos. A few minutes later, she pointed a tentative finger at one of them. "This *might* be him, but I couldn't swear to it. I mean it was starting to get dark and, well, this guy does have stringy hair and a similar shaped face, and he's around the right age. But I only got a good look at him when his face was so angry and contorted, not when he was calm like this…and… and…" Sarah stammered for a second as she looked up into the detective's earnest blue eyes. She quickly returned to the page in front of her. "And here's another thing. He had some sort of a tattoo on his right hand. The back of his hand. But this photo only shows his face."

"Could you see what kind of tattoo it was?"

Sarah sat back, staring into the space in front of her, trying to remember. "No, but it looked long and narrow. It didn't cover the whole back of his hand." She studied the photo once more. "It was his right hand. His cigarette was in the hand closest to May. And then a car drove by, and someone put lights on somewhere just as he raised his hand, like this." She mimicked the teen's dramatic gesture. "Then he took another puff and threw the cigarette into the gutter. That's when I saw the tattoo. At least it looked like a tattoo. And that's all I remember." She sighed. "I wish I could be more help."

"You *have* been a help," Detective Rian said.

There was a moment of silence before Sarah spoke.

"Detective Rian. You and your partner seem to know May. Look, I started working at the Butler Agency in September, and she's usually there most days for a little while. I mean, I feel bad for her, and I'm worried about her now. Before this, I didn't think anyone knew her or her name."

He nodded. "We all feel bad for her. We found out her first name by accident from a social worker in the neighborhood, but there's not much more of a background story. She hasn't broken any laws, and since she sits on the church steps and it's okay with them, we pretty much leave her alone. There're more cases out there like May, and some of them are a lot more complicated. There just aren't the resources to help as much as we'd like."

"I know. It's really a difficult time all around, isn't it?" Sarah drew her brows together. "But she goes away at night and some days, too. Where does she go?"

"At first, we thought she might go to a nearby shelter, but it doesn't seem like that's the case. She's not in trouble and isn't a victim of any crime." Detective Rian looked down at the mugshot book. "The story you've told us about the teenager harassing her is the first thing approaching a problem we've heard about."

"How long has she been there, um, on the steps?"

"Maybe since late summer. Not too long after the blackout in July," he said.

"Oh." Sarah pulled back a loose strand of her hair. Funny, but she'd assumed May had been there much longer.

There was another pause. Detective Rian seemed reluctant to bring their time to a close.

"I really appreciate your coming in," he finally said. "If there's anything else, or if you see the guy again, please let me know. And if it's okay, I'd like to keep in contact with you in case there's some other details that might come up."

"Oh, sure, that'd be fine," said Sarah. She offered her brightest smile as they both rose to leave the room.

Detective Rian led the way back through the labyrinth of chaos to the front area once more. "Thanks again for coming in. And, Sarah—Okay if I call you Sarah?"

"Of course." Sarah suppressed a blush.

"Please be careful." He then smiled. It was a truly nice smile.

"Thanks. I will."

Sarah turned toward the front door, feeling pleased about Detective Rian's wish to stay in touch with her. Of course, this was all just about police business.

As Sarah said goodbye to the desk officer, she spied Detective Cahill at a distance. He was leading a woman down a far hallway, perhaps to another small interview room. It was a familiar figure. Something she recognized about the way the woman walked.

Then Sarah stifled a gasp. The woman was Mrs.

Butler.

****

Lorna's call that night was no surprise. She'd caught Sarah's reaction at Captain Neptune's after Glen mentioned a killing in the news. Sarah wanted to confide in Lorna, a good friend with a sympathetic ear. But she worried that Lorna might tell the world, setting off calls from well-meaning Westervale people and on from there. The only other person Sarah could talk to was her childhood friend, Cookie, whom she'd finally be able to see this coming weekend.

"So, Sarah." Lorna got straight to the heart of things as usual. "What's this about someone being killed near where you work?"

Sarah gripped the phone receiver and closed her eyes. "Please don't tell this to anyone. Please promise. I need to work it through in my own mind. It's upsetting. Really upsetting."

"I promise." Lorna's voice was soft now.

Sarah took a deep breath and spoke. When her story was finished, Lorna's response was emphatic. "You *have* to leave that job! Apply to one of the larger places now. You don't belong in a small office like that, or in that neighborhood. Or go back to teaching. Just do something!"

"Look, I need to give the job a couple more months for a few reasons," Sarah said. "I mean, I signed an agreement with the employment agency." True, and there was some sort of penalty for leaving before the agreed-upon time. Plus, the agency guy was decent and found this job for her quickly, just when Sarah had a growing need to leave Westervale. He'd be a good ally for the future. "I'd feel guilty leaving the Butlers after only a short time there."

"Why? It's not as if insurance is the most exciting business in the world, or even what you wanted in the first place. After all, it's your life. You could start interviewing for other jobs now, and the moment that agency agreement is up, you can walk."

"Yeah, I know, I know," said Sarah. "But everyone there has been nice to me. And besides, if I leave the agency too soon, the cops might think I had some part in the crime."

"That's totally ridiculous," shot back Lorna.

"Okay, I know that, but do they?" Sarah had to admit to herself, though, that despite Detective Cahill's rude behavior, he probably didn't think she was guilty of anything more than stupidity for heading to a desolate church on a desolate street and then finding a dead guy outside. She also had to admit she was hoping the cops—okay, Detective Rian, at least—would find a reason to drop by again. But, of course, that was no reason to stay at the job. And she certainly wasn't planning on telling any of this to Lorna.

Lorna charged ahead. "Look, I know it's been a rough time for you all around. You had your aunt to worry about, and then your fiancé broke it off."

"Let's be honest. He unceremoniously dumped me, right before Aunt Addie died."

"Okay. I understand why you wanted some changes. Subletting Gen's apartment was a good deal. Then the new job came up, and I get why you wanted to leave Westervale. But it's time for more change. You need an exciting, youthful workplace in a safer area. Look at what just happened where you are now. And you need to get out more."

Lorna meant well. But, still.

"Look, Lorna, I need to think and then make a plan. Okay? A lot has happened really fast. And *please* don't say anything to anyone. If people start calling me, I'll only be able to tell this story so many times before going nuts."

Sarah felt a bit guilty. She hadn't told Lorna everything. Like how she'd been stunned to see Mrs. Butler at the police station. Like how she was worried about May and wished she could help her. Like about her chat with Detective Rian over a book of mugshots.

"I promise," Lorna agreed. "But please, think about what I said. And *please* be careful."

Sarah just hoped Lorna would keep her promise not to repeat the story. Maybe she shouldn't have gone to Captain Neptune's with the Westervale crowd so soon. Then the subject of the murder wouldn't have come up. And then she wouldn't have seen herself in that silly reflective wall covering and might have forgotten about the teenager. Then she wouldn't have told the cops and have seen Mrs. Butler at the precinct. Although there was nothing to worry about with that. *Was there?*

But looking at the mugshots wasn't bad. And it had been nice to spend a few minutes with Detective Rian.

Things were getting complicated.

Chapter Eight

Edgar dropped a sizeable stack of papers and forms on Sarah's desk, a loose thread from the sleeve of his brown jacket trailing along the top of the pile.

"Good morning, Edgar." Sarah felt awkward calling him by his first name, given his age and status with the firm. However, this seemed to be the way it was done. Edgar had been with the Butler Agency forever, or so Kelly confided, and he'd known Mr. and Mrs. Butler from their collective younger days. Where Kelly came by all of this random information was anyone's guess. Sarah suspected that eavesdropping was an enticing hobby for the young secretary in an otherwise boring workplace.

"This should keep me out of mischief for the morning." Sarah smiled, waving a hand in the direction of the new files on her desk.

Edgar adjusted the frames of his glasses, which seemed far too large for his longish, pleasant face. He was a man who basked in the various minute details of the insurance world and had grown to look the part.

"There's been a lot of action this week. You'll see," he said. "Calls, forms, letters. A little bit of everything."

"Anything left from July?" Sarah was still thinking about the city's massive blackout in mid-summer with millions in resulting damage. Only a very few claims were filed from this, but Edgar pointed out that many places hadn't been insured. Now a number of businesses who'd been lucky were looking to update their policies with a wary eye to the future.

"Not today," Edgar replied. "But there are a fair amount of attachments here for my special client reports. And you know how much I rely on you to check the numbers for me."

"Don't worry," said Sarah, a bit amused by this now familiar bit of conversation. Edgar thanked her and retreated to his office.

She picked up the first file on her desk. At least having been a business major was still paying off, along with having taught high school business courses and then working at Westervale. But she was grateful to have minored in art, a joy then as well as now when she pulled out her sketchpad. Combining it all would be great, but impossible during the current general financial crisis.

Mrs. Butler broke into her thoughts.

"Sarah, hello!"

"How are you, Mrs. Butler?"

"Just fine." Mrs. Butler patted her neat salt-and-pepper hair as she approached. "How did you do at the police station yesterday? Were you able to pick out that horrible teenager from the pictures?"

How interesting that this was the first thing on the woman's mind this morning.

"Not really. There was someone who might have been him, but I wasn't really sure. I wish I could have been more help."

Mrs. Butler inched closer until Sarah could clearly see the light catching the stone in her topaz pendant.

She leaned her fair-sized bulk in conspiratorially.

"Do you think it might have been him? That teenager? Do you think he might have come back later and killed that poor man?"

"I have no idea. The police certainly must have a lot of theories."

There was a pause. Mrs. Butler didn't utter a word as to why she was at the police station herself yesterday. Everyone knew Sarah had gone there on her lunch hour. They heard her tell the detectives about the teenager and make the appointment to look at mugshots. But Mrs. Butler was another matter. And Sarah had only seen her by chance walking down the hall with Detective Cahill and in the distance, at that.

"Well, let's hope they find out what's going on. Please be careful outside." With that, she patted Sarah on the arm and walked away.

Sarah stared down at the paperwork in front of her. But really, why hadn't Mrs. Butler said anything about being at the precinct? Maybe she was just frightened after the murder and wanted reassurance. Or it could have been about something else entirely. Instinct told Sarah not to mention it unless Mrs. Butler did. She was the boss's wife, and Sarah was fairly new at the agency. It might appear as if she was prying into something that was none of her business.

It was a long day buried in the files from Edgar, and Sarah planned on stopping at the little market on the way home. Groceries were one thing, but she had run out of ice cream. Even in the cold winter months, there was something relaxing, even comforting about it.

The door to the tiny market squealed as she pushed it open. Grabbing a basket, Sarah tossed in a can of coffee and some bread and milk. But the frozen food aisle was her primary destination. Chocolate ice cream seemed appealing today. On a whim, she picked up a small container of brightly colored sprinkles to go with it. Why not?

Hilda was on duty tonight as usual.

"Cold out there," said Sarah.

"And you'll be even colder after you eat that ice cream." Hilda laughed.

"It's my weakness," confessed Sarah. "Summer or winter."

Hilda chatted while ringing up Sarah's items. "How goes your Christmas shopping?"

"Haven't even started. There aren't too many people on my list, so I usually wait till after Thanksgiving."

"Well, considering that's in two weeks, you'd better start soon." Hilda looked up and smiled. "A week from Saturday, my women's crafts collective is having a holiday sale at the community house near the library. There'll be lots of wonderful gift-y things there. You should come. It's a *huge* collective—fifteen group chapters. And it's our twenty-fifth anniversary." Hilda proudly pulled a flyer from under the counter and stuffed it in Sarah's bag.

"Okay," said Sarah. She really liked this woman who'd been so friendly to her. "I'll plan on coming over for a little while."

Sarah thanked her, hugged her bag of groceries close, and walked out into the cool night air. Her thoughts turned back to yesterday and how nice Detective Rian was and how he had mentioned wanting to stay in touch with her. Of course, this was about police business, from the murder to the surly teen. But could there be a little more to it? Sarah was warmed by the possibility, even if it was a remote one.

The stores along the way home were starting to close now. The dress shop just shut its lights off as she passed. And the bookstore owner now reached up to lock the front door next to his display of the latest best sellers. Moving shadows of passersby were visible in all of the windows. Then for a brief second, Sarah was taken back by the shadow of a young man skulking by. He swaggered when he walked, and the silhouette of his hair seemed familiar. Then he was gone. Could it have been the copper-haired teen? Impossible.

Sarah wasn't near the office and church neighborhood, but not that terribly far away either. What if he'd followed her on the train tonight? What if he somehow found out she'd looked at the mugshots? Did he know something about the dead man on the church steps? The guy with the weird name. Something like Milvae or Millay or, what was it—Milaeve? Yes, that was it. Could he have even killed that poor man?

Sarah's eyes shot in all directions. *Silly!* There was no one nearby who looked like the copper-haired teen or like a teenager at all, for that matter. Her imagination had run wild with the sight of shadows distorted in the store windows.

But she shuddered and picked up her pace, hurrying home.

Chapter Nine

"These are top notch."

Mrs. Butler held out an enormous box of gorgeous chocolates, urging everyone to help themselves. From the look of it, there was more than one layer of candy inside.

"C'mon girls. Give these a try."

Sarah and Kelly gladly obliged.

Mr. Butler and Edgar both walked by, interest and amusement on their faces.

"From Rinaldi's Glass, I presume," said Mr. Butler, selecting a chocolate-covered truffle. "Nothing like a grateful client who says thank you like this." Edgar enthusiastically grabbed two pieces as he headed to his office.

"What's the occasion?" asked Kelly.

"They were extremely happy with a detailed analysis report and updated policy package we—well, mostly Edgar—put together for them." Mr. Butler grinned. "Now to *keep* them happy, since they're moving everything to their branch location. Hope this isn't a farewell gesture."

"They seemed totally pleased, given the size of that box," Sarah said.

"Just help yourselves. I think there's three layers," said Mrs. Butler, putting the box on Kelly's desk. "I'll leave it here for everyone, or else I'll eat too much myself."

A thought struck Sarah. "Okay if I bring a piece or two out to May?"

They looked at her, puzzled. Sarah realized that she might be the only one who actually knew the woman's name.

"The woman on the church steps."

"Oh, sure. Go ahead. There's plenty here," said Mrs. Butler.

Kelly handed Sarah a paper cup from the supply cabinet, and Sarah selected a few pieces to put inside. "I'll just be a minute. I won't even put on my coat. This sweater is warm."

"Careful. Don't freeze," Kelly said.

Sarah ran next door to the church steps. May's face was upturned as she enjoyed the warmth of the brilliant sun. Again, it occurred to Sarah how different May was from other street people. She only carried a small tote bag, not the usual burdensome cache of possessions that was the hallmark of so many others.

The woman looked up in surprise and pleasure as Sarah approached.

"May, I brought something for you."

She sat down and placed the cup in May's hands. "We have a big box of chocolates at the office. I thought you might like some."

May's face brightened even more.

"Enjoy them, May." She patted the woman's arm. "I have to get back to work now."

As Sarah rose, two familiar figures walked up the street. Detectives Cahill and Rian. Both greeted her at once, the older man with a respectful nod and his younger partner with that warm smile, which Sarah returned in equal measure.

"You're certainly a rugged individual," said Detective Cahill. "Out here with no coat."

Sarah quickly explained about sharing some candy with May.

"That was really nice of you to bring some to her."

Sarah tried not to blush at Detective Rian's comment. "If you'd both like some chocolate, please come inside. There's plenty there."

"We wish we could." Detective Rian looked eager at the suggestion.

"But we need to talk to Father Haney." Detective Cahill then thanked her for the offer.

"Great to see you again, Sarah," said Detective Rian.

They said their goodbyes as Sarah ran back into the office.

Mrs. Butler still lingered by Kelly's desk and plucked another chocolate-covered almond from the box. She continued to insist that she needed to avoid temptation and, therefore, the box should remain where it was.

"Did she like the chocolate?" asked Kelly as Sarah joined them.

"She certainly looked pleased. And I ran into our two detectives and asked if they wanted to come in for some chocolate, but they were going to see Father Haney."

Mrs. Butler's eyebrows raised. "They were here?"

"Well, they were just heading to the church."

"Did they say why?" Mrs. Butler persisted.

"No, they just said hello and sorry they couldn't stop inside for candy right now."

Suddenly quiet, Mrs. Butler took one last chocolate cream and walked toward her office.

When she was gone, Kelly twirled a strand of her long black hair and glanced around to see if anyone else was in earshot.

"Sarah?" She lowered her voice. "Would you have time for a cup of coffee after work today? Maybe we could talk or something?"

"Uh, sure. That'd be great. The place around the corner?" There was only one coffee shop nearby, and Sarah grimaced at the thought of its sticky tables and cracked cups and saucers.

"No way." Kelly made a face. "There's this other place. Dexter's. It's closer to the subway. Then we can grab our trains after."

"Sounds good." Sarah smiled.

Kelly's face lit up with relief as Sarah headed back to her desk.

What could this be about?

Could Kelly be having second thoughts about staying at her job after the murder? It wasn't a bad commute for her, but she could surely find work that was more exciting for such a really young person, probably not long out of high school.

Sarah now turned to the usual paperwork on her desk, including more of Edgar's pages of financial figures to be checked before he attached them to his private client reports. And Mrs. Butler had added more for both Sarah and Kelly to begin working on—completely organizing all client files and information, past and present. This was something to which they would be dedicating an increasing amount of time starting soon.

Lunchtime rolled around quickly, and Sarah had a specific errand in mind. The heel of her shoe, the one that had gotten caught on the jagged church step the day of the murder, needed to be fixed. She decided to try the shoe repair place on the street. It was convenient, and its old-fashioned appearance intrigued her. Edgar mentioned that the owner had an excellent reputation and, given Edgar's obvious dedication to his own job, Sarah figured he would be a good judge of someone with similar pride in his work. Funny, though, but Sarah rarely saw anyone go inside the shop, possibly because it wasn't open every day.

A twinkling chime announced her arrival as she pushed open the door. Vintage wooden shelves, displaying a random collection of shoes and boots, lined the walls of the room. A faint smell of shoe polish lingered in the air, although not unpleasantly.

An elderly man with a healthy crop of thick white hair sat behind the counter, the day's newspaper spread out in front of him. He looked up at the sound of the chimes. Pushing his glasses squarely up on his nose, he set the paper aside, rose with exceptional agility for his age, and moved from behind the worn countertop.

"What can I do for you, young lady?"

Sarah explained how the heel of her shoe had gotten caught on the jagged step.

"Here, let's have a look." He reached for the shoe in Sarah's outstretched hand and carefully examined it. "Would you like to wait? This won't take long."

"Sure. That'd be great," said Sarah.

The man indicated an aging wooden chair in a corner between shelves crammed with shoes, the likes of which Sarah had only seen in old photographs—two-toned women's pumps and old-style men's oxfords. She eased into the chair as the man began working. It was obvious, though, that he was also interested in chatting with his newest customer.

"I've seen you across the street. You work for the Butlers."

Sarah explained to the man, who by now had introduced himself as Gianni, about her new job. Not so new anymore, though. Going on three months there. "By the way," she added. "Edgar Frainie at work highly recommended you."

"Tell him thanks and hi for me." Gianni grabbed a couple of implements from a nearby shelf and continued chatting. "Bad what happened to that guy by the church."

"Yeah. It was awful." What else could she say?

He peered at Sarah over the rims of his glasses. Had he seen her sitting on the church steps with May and Father Haney after the police arrived? If so, he didn't say. He just continued to expertly use little tools and tubes of substances to set the heel of her shoe to rights.

"Getting to be a bit of a rough neighborhood." Gianni lowered his gaze to the heel of the shoe once more. "My sons want me to close up shop. Problem is," he continued, "I've lived and worked around here a long time. I'm used to it. Watched lots of people come and go." He stopped again to look up at Sarah. "My sons went to the church's grammar school, same as both of the Butlers. My boys were younger than them, though. Afterwards, everybody headed to city high schools or off to work and then went their separate ways. That was a long time ago."

This was a surprise.

"See that small building on the far side of the church?" He indicated the direction with his head, a snowy lock of hair falling across his face. "It used to be the school."

Sarah wondered about the building whenever she walked by. It seemed empty now, but it was still kept neatly and exuded a certain charm.

"Did you know that's where Lou and Mary Butler met?" asked Gianni. "They've known each other since they were kids back in the 1930s."

"Wow," said Sarah. "And their business is still here, too."

"It was Lou's father's business first. Back when this was a real neighborhood. Everybody stuck together and helped each other, right through the war." He smiled, adding, "World War II that is." He sighed. "But later on, a lot of people started to move. Lou Butler stayed to work with his dad and finally took over the place. It's smaller now, though."

Smaller? Were the Butlers losing business? Everyone seemed so busy, especially Edgar, who also did those planning and special reports. But Sarah didn't have a totally complete picture of things. Maybe the business really was shrinking.

Gianni added something from one more tube to the shoe. "We used to have a bigger place, but then my sons grew up and moved. Better for their families. After my wife was gone, I took a little apartment upstairs here. I do this more for a hobby now, to keep me going. And my boys are constantly telling me to move near them."

All Sarah could do was nod. She felt sorry that

Gianni was alone.

"I don't keep the shop open a lot. Usually two or three days a week. Other days, I visit some old friends uptown where I was raised. Those who're left, anyway." He looked up wistfully. "Of course, I visit my sons a lot, too. I'll probably end up moving, but change is hard."

Gianni gave a last look at Sarah's shoe. "Here you go. Let it set for a day. It'll be fine."

Sarah thanked him and settled the bill. Then she adjusted her scarf.

"That's fine embroidery on your scarf. My wife used to do that kind of work. She was an excellent seamstress and did embroidery, too. Like everything else, it's all become a lost art."

Gianni smiled. "Good to meet you, Sarah. Come in and visit any time. As you can see, things are a bit slow. Nice to have someone to talk to."

"Thanks. I will. And thanks for doing such a nice job on my shoe."

Sarah opened the door to leave, the twinkling melody of the chimes signaling her exit.

****

The back booth at Dexter's Coffee Shop was a fair distance from the office. It was as good a place as any for an after-work conversation without too much worry about eavesdroppers.

Kelly and Sarah faced each other, their coats stuffed into the respective corners of their red-plastic seats. The waitress left them alone with substantial, cream-colored mugs of coffee after they'd declined menus. Kelly fidgeted, running her finger over the handle of the coffee mug.

Sarah spoke first. "Is everything all right, Kelly?"

Kelly eyes were wide and troubled.

"Look, Sarah… I'm afraid." She took a long sip of her coffee.

"You mean because they still haven't caught whoever killed that poor man?"

"That's part of it." Kelly took a deep breath, as if for courage. "Sure, I'm afraid that the guy who did it is still out there. But there's more and, Sarah, I'm not sure why it bothers me."

Kelly stared deep into the contents of her coffee mug and then looked up. "I trust you, and I could have this all wrong, so please don't let on to anyone at work."

Sarah placed her hand reassuringly on Kelly's outstretched arm. "I promise."

"You know that my desk is in a good position to hear things and…and when I deliver mail and files, conversations sort of carry, you know?"

Sarah nodded. *Sure, Kelly eavesdropped. But who didn't?*

"Well, I mean, it was bad enough when that guy was killed, but after that, things changed." Kelly hesitated. "I know everyone's on edge, but it felt like there was more to it."

Sarah's eyes widened.

Kelly continued. "A couple of times when I went upstairs to bring files, I heard Mr. and Mrs. Butler arguing. That's not like them, is it?"

Sarah had to admit that it wasn't. On the other hand, everyone had their differences from time to time, and the Butlers were just like anyone else, she supposed.

"What was it about?" Even though a disagreement or two wasn't really surprising in any setting, the fact that Kelly was so troubled made it important.

"Nothing made sense, and I didn't quite catch everything. But Mr. Butler said if *that* happens—whatever *that* meant—they'd have to close the business. Then he said about something being torn down. And Mrs. Butler kept telling him he was being foolish."

Kelly paused to sip her coffee while Sarah speculated. "Maybe *that* meant if there was another crime like the murder, they'd need to close the business? Mr. Butler's always talking about the state of the neighborhood. But I wonder what the *torn down* part means."

"I don't know. I couldn't hear all of it. And Mrs. Butler kept saying that it didn't matter."

"Could it have been a serious issue with an insurance claim?" Sarah spoke in the most soothing voice she could muster, as much for her own benefit as for Kelly's.

"Listen, Sarah. I've worked for the Butlers for eight months now. This is different."

Sarah gulped some coffee, trying to make logical sense of it. But logic seemed to be taking a back seat these days.

"Mr. Butler said about closing the business? I wonder if it has anything to do with Mrs. Butler's sudden obsession with organizing all of the files to perfection," said Sarah.

"I wondered about that, too." Kelly absently ran her finger over the rim of her coffee mug now. "And whatever it is must have happened recently. Otherwise, why would they have hired both of us not that long ago? It feels like more's going on than there seems to be on the surface."

"Yeah, it does," Sarah said with a nod.

Was this why Mrs. Butler had gone to the police precinct? But that didn't make sense.

"Between that killer on the loose and this crazy business with the Butlers, I'm thinking of quitting my job. It's my first real job, too. I'd feel bad about leaving so soon, but I think I'm going to start looking now and hope that something comes up after the first of the year."

"I get it," said Sarah.

"Would you help me with my résumé, Sarah?"

"Of course. And in the meantime, we'll both be on the lookout at work. Maybe it'll just turn out to be a bad case of frayed nerves because of the murder."

"Maybe. But I'm still uncomfortable." Kelly shifted uneasily in her seat.

"I understand," said Sarah, "And I promise to help with your résumé."

"Thanks, Sarah." Kelly smiled with relief. "I feel so much better talking to you."

Although she might have reassured Kelly, Sarah was now feeling more on edge herself. As if a killer on the loose wasn't enough, here was a new worry. Something was wrong at work, something important enough to cause dissention between the Butlers, making them talk about closing their business. And Kelly's distress was real.

Sarah and Kelly finished their coffee in silence. When they ventured outside again, the shadows lengthening in the smoky autumn dusk seemed to add more of a bitter chill to the evening air.

Chapter Ten

Sunshine danced off the stately townhouse windows as Sarah strolled toward Fifth Avenue. She loved living only a brisk, fifteen-minute walk from the Metropolitan Museum of Art. Visiting there was always a treat, but today would be even more special. She'd spend the afternoon with her childhood friend Connie, better known as Cookie.

Sarah hurried up the sweeping stairway to the museum. Cookie was already waiting inside the expansive lobby by the information desk. She ran to hug Sarah with enthusiasm, her red curls dancing with abandon.

"How long has it been?" Cookie didn't even wait for an answer. "Forever! Forever since we've seen each other."

"And forever since we've had a marathon phone call," said Sarah.

They'd gone all through school together back in Queens, staying close friends, although their lives took different paths. Sarah commuted to Manhattan for college and work. Cookie stayed local for secretarial school and job, eventually marrying her high-school boyfriend.

"You're sure busy," said Sarah as they entered the coat check room. "Every time I've called, you've been on your way to someplace."

"I'll tell you everything." Cookie was beaming. "Let's eat and catch up and then we can hit the galleries. The cafeteria might get mobbed fast. There's some sort of special kids' event today. I saw the notice at the information desk. Something with the arms and armor exhibit."

"Remember how we loved that when we were kids?" Sarah smiled at the memory.

"I still love it," said Cookie.

The woman behind them at the coat check chimed in. "Me, too. All those gigantic knights in shining armor on horseback. I think I'll stop by later and join those kids."

They all laughed with collective enthusiasm.

"Makes you wish you were young again," the woman said.

"It's great to be a kid, right?" Cookie grinned.

By the time Sarah and Cookie got to the cafeteria, a fair-sized number of people already balanced lunch trays while in search of an empty table.

"Good thing we got here when we did," said Cookie as they got in line for their food. "We'll need to hurry up and grab seats as soon as we can."

When they had their sandwiches, they were lucky to score a table in a reasonably remote place where they could talk. "Okay, you have to fill me in on everything," said Cookie immediately. "I'm sorry I had to run the other night when you called, and the week before, too. You said a lot's been happening. Does it have to do with that homeless woman you mentioned?"

Sarah already told Cookie about May and a few general job details. But they hadn't been able to settle into a longer phone conversation since before the teenager incident—and the murder.

"Some of it does. Where did we leave off anyway? I've sort of lost track."

Sarah sipped some coffee, washing down a mouthful of tuna fish sandwich before launching into her story. Cookie was a good listener and always interested in what was happening with Sarah. But she stopped. Something was different today. Cookie almost seemed to be bouncing in her seat.

"Wait a minute," said Sarah. "How come you have a free afternoon? I'm thrilled you suggested meeting here today, but don't you and Jim usually go house hunting on Saturdays?"

"Normally," Cookie said. "But my brother-in-law needed help putting up some sort of paneling in his basement. All the guys are in on it."

"Three cheers for home renovation." Sarah saluted with her coffee cup. "Maybe they'll come up with other projects, and then you'll have a few more free weekend afternoons."

"We'll see," said Cookie with a mysterious grin.

Suddenly, Sarah forgot about her own recent events. "Out with it. I can see something's up with you. And it's got to be huge. And you've been ultra-busy for the past few weeks…"

Cookie's words flew out in a rush of excitement. "Sarah, I *had* to tell you everything in person. So many good things are happening."

The low hum of the growing cafeteria crowd faded into the background. They both put down their coffee cups and sandwiches.

"We put a deposit on a house!"

"That's fantastic!" Sarah was thrilled for Cookie

and Jim. They'd been looking every weekend for what seemed forever. "Where? What kind of house? When will you move?"

"Soon," said Cookie. "I'll tell you everything. But first, there's more news."

Sarah's eyes grew wide. "More news?"

"I'm going to have a baby."

A squeal erupted from both of them. Sarah leaned over and gave her friend a long hug. "That's the best news ever. And now you're going to have a grand new home for the baby." Sarah grinned. "Okay, now you've got to tell me everything."

"But you were going to tell me about you," said Cookie, still flushed with happiness.

"Boring stuff. That'll wait." Sarah couldn't talk about crime and murder now. Nothing should put a damper on Cookie's joy. "I want to hear everything about the baby and the house."

For the next half hour, Cookie filled Sarah in on their glowing future plans. And for just that while, Sarah forgot everything else, genuinely swept up in Cookie's news.

Eventually, they paused to finish their coffee. Cookie looked around. "It's sure insane here today. It'll be quieter when we get to the European paintings. By then, the kids and their parents will be safely at the arms and armor event."

"Well, that's what you'll be doing in a couple of years," said Sarah. "Bringing your kids here and introducing them to those knights on their horses all decked out in their armor."

"And the paintings and sculpture and mummies, too." Cookie laughed.

The usual Saturday crowds were piling into the cafeteria now while families with children were leaving for the special event. Sarah and Cookie needed to get to their favorite galleries soon if they wanted to have enough time to study the paintings and chat a bit more. Sarah would not tell any of her stories to Cookie today. This was a day for happy talk.

As they were tidying up their lunch trays and getting ready to leave, Sarah caught sight of a small family far across the vast room.

"Sarah? You okay? You look as if you've seen a ghost."

Sarah sat up straight. "Just thought I recognized someone on the other side of the room." She struggled to offer a half-smile. "I'll have to use my distance glasses more often these days."

But that wasn't the case at all. A man, a woman, and a little boy had just finished their lunch and got up from their table. It was Gil Rian. There was a pretty woman at his side along with a little boy with gently waving hair, just like his. The little boy hugged him.

Sarah watched as the trio walked to the exit— probably toward the room with the knights in shining armor.

****

Sarah did her best to put the cafeteria scene out of her mind. The two friends wandered for a few hours studying gold-framed paintings, serene statuary, and ancient relics. They were lost in history and its artistic creations. Thankfully, they ventured nowhere near arms and armor.

Sarah commented on the delicate lines of a marble sculpture. And Cookie spoke perceptively of the facial expressions captured in several century-old portraits. They reminisced about their after-school sketching classes and how unique these had been.

"Sarah, you really should take more art courses. I can see how much you still love it."

"I do love it. I've even taken out my sketchpad again." She thought back to a couple of pages she'd added the other night—the inside of Gianni's intriguing shop as well as a humorous drawing of Edgar with a huge batch of files about to topple off his desk. It had been fun.

"You're going to tell me everything about the job soon, right?" asked Cookie before they parted. "The stuff you didn't tell me today?"

"Absolutely," said Sarah with a smile. "The job stories will keep. Insurance isn't the most exciting game in town." *Unless it's peppered with behind-the-scenes intrigue and murder.*

"And you'll be at my mom's on Thanksgiving? Promise?"

"Of course. I wouldn't miss it."

"I'm so glad I had the chance to tell you everything in person before the whole extended batch of aunts and uncles and neighbors finds out on Thanksgiving. You're close family, Sarah." Cookie grinned. "This was such a wonderful afternoon."

Sarah tossed restlessly that night. Any other time she could have told Cookie the full details about the job, May, Kelly's strange tales, and the murder. And, yes, she could have told her about Gil Rian and of her dismay when she spied him at the museum, crushing the glimmer of a lovely fantasy that had begun to linger on the edges of her mind.

Chapter Eleven

Two Guys from Grenleah ~ Small moves for home and business ~ Serving the tristate

Sarah stopped to read the neat lettering on the side of the small truck double-parked outside the old church school. A worker was just locking the door to the building. She slowed down to let him pass as he rolled a small pile of old boxes across the sidewalk and toward the back of the truck.

"Thanks, lady," the guy called out.

She nodded.

"Just a batch of moldy old books and boxes," the workman said, noticing her interest and pointing at the school building. "Maybe they'll tear this down and build something new."

"Really?" Sarah was surprised.

His fellow worker began helping load the boxes onto the truck while weighing in with his own thoughts. "Economy stinks these days. Who'd put money into anything?"

"Who knows?" said the first guy. "That's real estate for you."

They wished Sarah a nice day, and she gave them a cheerful wave as they drove off.

A torn scrap of paper escaped from one of the boxes and lodged in the doorway for a moment before a breeze whisked it away. It drew her attention to the whole building, jutting out with an artful style all its own. The tall windows with sturdy, yet gracefully curved security bars were appealing. Several side basement-level windows were bricked over carefully, although blending into the lower border. Sarah admired its composition and weather-beaten charm. She vowed to draw a sketch of it soon while it was still standing. *Who owned this and why was it being emptied now?*

If Sarah had been uneasy after hearing Kelly's story on Friday, talking with the workmen this morning made her more so. Could the church school be at the heart of Mr. and Mrs. Butler's disagreement over something being torn down? *But why?*

"Happy Monday." Sarah tried for an upbeat greeting when she arrived at work. She'd caught Kelly's serious expression the moment she walked in the door.

Kelly motioned her over. "Did you see down the street? The movers?" she asked, worry in her voice.

Sarah nodded.

Kelly continued. "Can we meet again soon? I want to show you...you know. What I'm working on."

Ah, the résumé.

"Sure. Just let me know when you're ready."

Sarah gave Kelly a smile of reassurance and headed for her desk.

She had barely removed her coat when Edgar appeared. "Sarah, you have no idea how happy I am to see you." He'd obviously been hard at work for a while. *What time did Edgar get here anyway?*

"Uh-oh," joked Sarah, pointing to the impressive stack of files in Edgar's arms. The same brown thread as last week was still hanging from his jacket sleeve.

"Edgar, here, let me have those." Sarah reached for the files before Edgar could drop them, something he'd done in the past. She tried to sound as enthused about their contents as he was. But no one was as passionate about insurance as Edgar, not even the Butlers.

"I put notes on everything," he said. "It would be wonderful if you could give an extra close look at those attachment pages with the columns of figures. I so rely on you."

"Sure, don't worry." Sarah paused. "Oh, and by the way, I want to thank you for suggesting Gianni to fix my shoe. He did a marvelous job. He said to say hi to you."

"Thank you. That's so nice." Edgar's response was reserved.

Head down and offering more thanks, Edgar scurried off to the next file on his desk.

Moments later, Mr. Butler's voice came from the direction of the front door. From the sound of it, he was alone. Usually, he came to work together with his wife.

"Morning, Sarah."

"Good morning, Mr. Butler…" Sarah was about to exchange some pleasantry with him, but he seemed in a hurry.

"My wife is at a meeting this morning," he said. "If anyone calls with a question for her specifically, please send them to me. Thanks."

With that, he headed upstairs to his office. This was odd. Most times, it was Mr. Butler or Edgar, not Mrs. Butler, who visited clients and companies on their own turf. This was a lovely accommodation on the part of the agency, perhaps part of it growing from Mr. Butler's worries about crime in the area. Still, it wasn't as if criminals were running up and down the street all hours of the day, mugging and pillaging. As a matter of fact, it had been extremely quiet lately. And what had become of such disreputable figures as the garbage rummager and the surly teenager? They seemed to have vanished.

****

Lunchtime was welcome. It wasn't that Sarah was hungry, but she wanted some fresh air and a break from paperwork.

Out in the brilliant November sun, she felt better. May was there, and Sarah walked over.

"It's good to see you, May."

There was a nice smile on May's face. She pointed to Sarah's scarf, as usual, always focusing on the embroidered flowers. She reached out tentatively to touch a pink flower, lingering gently for a few seconds on its outline and nodding as she withdrew her hand.

"This belonged to my Aunt Addie," said Sarah. It seemed as if May comprehended this. And she also seemed to be enjoying Sarah's attention.

Across the street, Gianni stepped outside his shop, presumably also for a breath of fresh air. May looked over at him with interest. Sarah waved, and Gianni waved heartily in return. She vowed to stop in and visit him again soon, even if she didn't have any more shoes to be repaired. After all, the man invited her to chat anytime. He seemed so lonely.

May began humming her little notes as she looked down the street.

"Song?" asked Sarah. But just then the church bells started to ring. Perhaps May was trying to replicate their sound?

May turned again to look at Sarah, who smiled and headed up the stairs into the church. Inside it was quiet and empty. She was glad it was still open.

Sliding into a pew, she sat for a few minutes. Her thoughts bounced from the murdered man to the teen, from Kelly to the Butlers, and back to the weekend. But she kept returning to May. Sarah decided then and there that she would find help for her.

She sat for a little while, until it was time to get back to her desk, gobble up her sandwich, and continue tackling Edgar's files with their requisite notes and calls and questions. As Sarah approached the door, she saw Father Haney in the vestibule. He was straightening little pamphlets, booklets, and flyers into neat piles on a long table just inside the entrance.

"Father, how are you?"

"Just fine, Sarah. And you? I didn't want to disturb you inside."

"I'm doing pretty well," she said. "Close to Thanksgiving. Can't believe it."

And so went the conversational dance. But the priest saw that Sarah had more on her mind than just passing the time with general pleasantries.

"I need to get back to work soon. But can I ask you something?"

"Of course." He adjusted his glasses and gave her his full attention.

"I just wondered if there are going to be any changes on the street. Some workmen were clearing out boxes from the old school this morning."

He nodded. "There's always been talk about the building being torn down. Like a lot of other places. But I really don't know." Father Haney looked at her curiously. "Actually, I've only been here for three years. My predecessor would have known more. He was here for a long time before he passed away."

"Oh, I'm sorry."

There was a pause.

"I was told that books and files from some old businesses are stored there. The church hasn't had access to the building for a long time. Now it's just a quiet place."

Father Haney seemed willing to talk, and Sarah was curious. Was the empty building tied to the current neighborhood, the Butler Insurance Agency, the inexplicable issues making Kelly anxious? *The murdered man?* No, it was all too far-fetched.

"If you're interested in the history of the school and the church itself," he continued, "our library has some old pamphlets and photos you might enjoy. Come over anytime and take a look. We also have a nice selection of books on spiritual topics."

Sarah was touched by this gesture. "Thanks so much, Father. I'll definitely do that. Could I come on Thursday? On my lunch hour?" Perhaps then, she could sit down with him and talk about May. "Right now, though, I have to get back to work."

****

If Sarah hoped to return to her desk without interruption, she was sorely mistaken. As soon as she walked in the door, Kelly subtly inclined her head toward the men who were casually chatting together, passing a few random moments while waiting for Sarah.

Once again, Detectives Cahill and Rian had invaded the premises.

"You're just the person we'd like to see," said Cahill.

Detective Rian offered his warm, friendly smile.

Sarah had an overwhelming urge to run back out the door. Instead, she tried for a friendly, yet professional tone. "What can I do for you, gentlemen?" Her words sounded stiff, especially to her own ears.

Cahill took the lead. Just as well. Sarah felt awkward looking at Detective Rian. She realized she'd misread his previous friendliness toward her as possibly something more. He was probably friendly with everyone. It was his natural personality. Like Cahill's personality was abrupt. *What a team.* And now, she felt enormously self-conscious.

"Miss Quinlee." Cahill was quite civil as he spoke. "We need you to look at a sketch. It might be the person you confronted." He handed her a piece of paper.

"We were hoping you could identify him." Gil Rian looked at Sarah with confusion.

She was afraid to meet the direct gaze of his blue eyes. Instead, she studied the sketch closely, as if it was the most important thing in the world. Perhaps, at the moment, it was.

"Not really." She turned to Kelly. "Do you have a blank piece of paper?"

Kelly fished a sheet out of the drawer and handed it to Sarah, who had already grabbed a pencil. She leaned against the desktop and sketched a few strokes on the blank page, still studying the police drawing she had placed down next to it. Both officers and Kelly were quiet, absorbed in Sarah's quickly emerging alternative to the police-drawn likeness.

"See?" She kept her eyes trained on her sketch. "His face was a bit longer and the eyes set a little closer. The eyebrows are more defined. Like this. And he was younger than the guy in your sketch. Then, of course, there was the stringy hair. But the look on his face really stuck with me." She added a couple more strokes to emphasize the teen's scowling expression.

"Oh, and there was that tattoo," she continued, quickly drawing what she remembered. Finally, she used the pencil to point to her picture. "I don't know if this is any help. It all happened so fast. It's just that your sketch doesn't seem like the same guy."

She looked up. Everyone was speechless.

Cahill was the first to speak. "You ever want a new job, come and see us."

"Sarah, this is amazing." Detective Rian couldn't stop looking at the sketch.

Cahill tossed him an amused look.

"Thanks. Um, I used to study drawing... Could you tell me why you're asking about the sketch you brought in?"

"We thought the guy you confronted taunting May might have been the same one who mugged a woman coming out of the coffee shop around the corner the other day," said Gil Rian.

Kelly and Sarah exchanged a knowing look, glad they hadn't met there last Friday.

"Is she all right?" asked Sarah.

"Badly shaken, but okay," said Cahill. "But now it looks as if we might have two guys to be on the lookout for."

Kelly jumped in. "Could they have anything to do with the man who was murdered?"

"We're looking into everything." Cahill seemed evasive.

"Could we take your sketch?" Detective Rian asked Sarah.

"Of course." Sarah really hoped it would help. She also hoped they would leave.

Sarah thought Gil Rian looked a bit sad but, once more, she knew she was probably projecting her own feelings. She offered a tiny, wan smile as they said thanks and left.

****

That night, it was Sarah who called Lorna.

"Hey, lady," answered Lorna, clearly delighted to hear from Sarah. "What's happening?"

Sarah had to admit that Lorna's upbeat voice was always welcome.

"Do you have an hour or so for drinks or coffee soon? I know you're planning your wedding and all, but if you're free that'd be great. I'd like to run something by you."

"First of all, no coffee. We'll have to make it drinks, precisely *because* I'm planning a wedding. And trust me, it would be easier to elope."

Sarah laughed. "Definitely drinks then. Dinner, too, if you'd like."

"Even better. And if you're free tomorrow night, even better than that. I'm taking the week off from nuptial madness. But you're going to have to suffer through rants about my mom wanting the same solo that was sung at her wedding, and my sister Keesha complaining that the maid-of-honor dress makes her look ugly. And it all grows from there."

"It's a deal," agreed Sarah. "Feel free to cry on my

shoulder all you want."

"And I want to hear everything—and I do mean *everything*—going on with you," said Lorna. "By the way, scout's honor, I have not breathed a word to anyone about that dead guy."

"And I thank you for that," said Sarah, letting out a silent sigh of relief.

Chapter Twelve

Sarah was lost in thought on her way to work the next morning. Was another unscrupulous character trolling the neighborhood in addition to the obnoxious teenager? The official police sketch appeared to be someone older than the teen. Could it have been Mr. Butler's trash rummager? The murderer?

May was already on her step. Sarah walked over.

"Hi, May. I brought you some breakfast." Sarah placed a coffee cup on the step and a small paper bag next to it that contained a chocolate donut. May seemed pleased with the chocolate candy last week, so Sarah thought she might enjoy this now.

May's face brightened. She extended a gloved hand in Sarah's direction, the same worn suede gloves that Sarah had noticed before. Sarah grasped May's outstretched hand.

"Your gloves are beautiful, May."

The woman faintly whispered something in return. Perhaps "glove"?

"Have a lovely morning, May," Sarah said, giving May's hand a little squeeze before heading for work. As she walked away, she heard May humming.

****

Mr. and Mrs. Butler had become increasingly quiet around the office. It was business as usual, but the atmosphere was indefinably tense. Kelly was right.

Something had changed. Mrs. Butler regularly gave Sarah additional files and placed more emphasis on the organizing project she'd asked Sarah and Kelly to work on. What did it all mean?

One thing was for certain. Edgar was still himself. Here was a man who was absolutely in love with the insurance industry.

Mid-morning, Sarah's phone rang. She assumed it was a company getting back to her with an answer to a simple request for information.

"Sarah Quinlee, please," said the vaguely familiar voice.

"Speaking."

"Okay, Sarah. This is Dave. Don't let on. I'm not supposed to be calling you at work."

Ah, Dave, the employment agent with the used car salesman wardrobe.

"What can I do for you?" Sarah played along, trying to make it sound like official work. This was no casual call. A hot job prospect? A bit premature, although this wasn't unusual in his business. Still, it wasn't exactly good form to begin stealing the sheep so early in the game.

"Sarah. I've got something that would be a great fit for you. Just listen." Dave began a rapid-fire description of a position in the benefits department of a major bank. They wanted someone with some experience in a medically related field. After all, he gushed, her time at Westervale would qualify. Plus, her most recent job in insurance would be the clincher.

"Ahem." Sarah cleared her throat and wondered how to begin speaking in code should anyone wander by. "Well, I certainly appreciate the information. Can you clarify that a bit?"

"Good girl," Dave continued as Sarah rolled her eyes. "Here's the deal. You freshen up your résumé and bring it to me. We'll get an interview in motion. Meanwhile, the holidays are coming up, so they won't be ready to act with an offer immediately. And pretty soon, your placement agreement with the Butlers will be up, and we're both free to take it from there."

He relayed all of this information in less than a record sixty seconds.

"That's all quite helpful." She felt like an idiot engaging in this cat-and-mouse dialogue.

"Can you drop off the résumé this week? Tomorrow?"

"Uh, perhaps a little additional time to complete the paperwork?"

"Okay," said Dave. "How about Thursday? I'm here till six o'clock. That work?"

"Yeah."

Dave signed off, and Sarah caught her breath. Probably nothing wrong in exploring another job, but she'd feel bad leaving the Butlers too soon. Although she was certain they'd understand and even encourage her to work in a safer area. But suppose Mrs. Butler was planning on retiring and needed Sarah? Then again, Sarah could suppose anything. But did she want to work in a bank benefits department? She inwardly groaned. There were no answers.

****

Lorna clutched her drink and began tracing a pattern on the side of the glass. They sat at a quiet table in a small pub that evening, not far from Sarah's apartment.

"Gin and tonic?" Sarah smiled. She watched Lorna take a deep swallow while she nursed a sip of her usual white wine spritzer. "Those wedding plans must really be getting stressful."

"Believe it." Lorna picked up her menu. "Don't ever plan a large wedding. Just elope."

Sarah burst out laughing. "That's not a big worry now. So, tell me, what's happening?"

They each ordered shepherd's pies and salads, and then Lorna spoke of her long list of pre-wedding woes, from clothing and photos to seating charts and wedding cake.

"Can you believe they're insisting I pick a wedding cake with this little fountain in the middle? Suppose it collapses?"

Lorna was certainly entertaining as she told of her pre-wedding misadventures and for a while, Sarah forgot some of her anxiety. Eventually, though, Lorna sat back and looked at Sarah. They were more than midway through their dinners. "So, it's your turn now. What's going on?"

Sarah took another forkful of food and launched into her story. She filled Lorna in on the increasing worries about crime near her workplace and how they were probably going to tear down the building that had once been the local church school. When she saw the frown on Lorna's face, she quickly mentioned her phone call from Dave, the employment agent.

"Yes!" Lorna exclaimed. "That's exactly the thing. Do this as soon as you can. You've got to get out of where you are now."

"I guess," said Sarah. "But I'm not sure the benefits department of a bank would be any more thrilling than insurance."

"Who cares? You don't have to do it forever."

"I know," said Sarah. "And don't worry. I'm going to drop off my résumé with Dave after work on Thursday. Believe me, he doesn't waste any time. I'm sure he'll have an interview set up before I can wonder if I have an appropriate outfit to wear."

"Just do it." Lorna was emphatic. "It sounds good."

"Yeah, I'll definitely follow it up. Dave is certainly on the ball. It's just that I don't want to be railroaded into too many changes and look like a job hopper."

"Quit worrying. If you get the job and it doesn't work out, there's lots of creative ways of dealing with it on your résumé." Lorna raised an eyebrow and gave a mischievous smile.

They ordered some coffee, and then Sarah changed the subject.

"So, I need to ask you something. And it's going to sound weird. You know the homeless woman, May? The one I told you about? I'm worried about her."

Lorna nodded. "Figures. Sounds like you."

"I was thinking. And I don't know if this is even remotely possible, but could there be some sort of special program at Westervale for someone like her?"

Lorna's eyes grew wide. "You want to get May into Westervale? Sarah, she's homeless!"

"Yeah, I know. But it seems like there's more to her story. She's only been around for a few months, and if she's out on the street much longer, someone's going to hurt her."

"Look, these people move on. And the system can't take care of them, and…" Lorna stopped and carefully studied Sarah's face. "You really care about this woman, don't you?" Lorna spoke gently now. "Could it be that you're in a way thinking of her like…"

"A substitute for Aunt Addie?" finished Sarah. "Yeah, you're probably right about that. But that's neither here nor there. I'm just worried about what's going to happen to her."

Lorna drew a long breath as she stirred some sugar into her coffee. "Look, I have some contacts with social workers and a few other helpful souls who might point you in the right direction, although it won't be at Westervale. And what about that priest? Can't he do something?"

"I'm going to sit down with him this week and see what he can suggest. It's time to figure things out for May, especially since there was another recent mugging."

"Jeez, Sarah!" Lorna's spoon clattered onto the table. "Okay, I hear you. But you gotta take care of yourself, too."

They sipped their coffees and glanced around the dark, cozy pub. People were huddled deep in conversation at the tables, while those at the bar were cheering the end of the day.

"Thanks, Lorna. I really appreciate your help."

Lorna grinned. "Remember, you're gonna have to listen to every last story of wedding planning terror between now and June."

"I wouldn't have it any other way."

Chapter Thirteen

Aside from natural curiosity, Sarah was interested in the old church school because Kelly had overheard Mr. Butler talking about something going to be torn down. The empty school seemed like a good possibility. What this had to do with the Butlers was anyone's guess. But it had made Kelly uneasy, and that was enough.

Sarah and Kelly met again briefly to discuss Kelly's résumé. When Sarah dropped off her own freshly minted résumé with Dave, she'd bring Kelly's, too, as the young woman had requested. But Sarah felt repetitive twinges of guilt and remorse in the pit of her stomach. *What would Mr. and Mrs. Butler do if they both left?*

Something else bothered Sarah now as she entered the church for her lunchtime appointment with Father Haney. She felt she couldn't leave the Butler Agency yet because of unfinished business—specifically, needing to find help for May.

"Sarah, it's good to see you." The priest was kind and Sarah felt sorry for him. He was struggling to keep his dwindling congregation afloat. The murder hadn't helped matters.

He led her into the library with its old wooden table and chairs. Bookshelves lined two of the walls and contained a selection of religious and spiritual volumes.

But she was here to check out the photos and stories about the old school and, mostly, to speak to the priest about May.

True to his promise, Father Haney pointed to several pamphlets on the table. "You're the first person in what appears to be many years who's asked about the school or the church history. I dug around and found a few pamphlets with some background details. It's not a lot, but you'll probably find them interesting. We have more copies, so you can keep these. And we can also take a look at those old photos on the wall over there." He looked at Sarah and waited, as if she might give a more substantial reason, beyond curiosity, for her request.

"I guess I'm just interested in what the neighborhood was like a while ago. People keep saying how it's changed, and I wanted to get a feel for it."

"Since you work here, that makes sense." He paused. "Sarah, you also mentioned you wanted to talk to me?"

Now to the real reason for her visit.

"Yes. Look, I know this might really be none of my business, and maybe I can't do anything about it, but I'm worried about May. About her safety. I mean, I know she's supposed to be homeless, but she seems different, and I can't really explain it."

Father Haney motioned for Sarah to sit before continuing.

"And after that man was killed, and then the mugging near the coffee shop…and then that teenager taunting her…"

"A teenager was taunting her?" Father Haney interrupted in surprise.

"Yeah, the night before the murder. There was a teenager taunting May. I yelled at him to stop and he stormed off, but it was scary. I told the cops, but I guess no one's seen him again. He wasn't the mugger at the coffee shop. But I guess you knew about that one."

Father Haney shifted forward in his chair, elbows on the table, and a stricken expression on his face. "I needed to talk to the cops about the coffee shop incident since the victim was connected to the church. But I had no idea about anyone taunting May."

"Look, Father. Is there anything the church or any church agency can do that could help May? I'm worried. And the cops said that the city just doesn't have the resources."

The priest took a moment before he spoke. "Up until now, it seemed as if May chose where she wanted to be. She doesn't harm anyone sitting on the steps, and it's not always for that long or every day. But having someone harass her is another story. And there's the upcoming bad winter weather to think about. Wherever she goes at night, I wish they could persuade her to stay there during the day."

"Well, that's the thing," said Sarah. "According to the cops, no one really knows where she goes at night. Or where she was before this. And I guess she's only been here for a few months."

Father Haney looked into the distance. "If I remember correctly, we started seeing her a little while after the big blackout in July."

"Could it be connected to that? It's something to think about. That wasn't a good time for anyone. I wasn't working here yet, but it was scary all over."

"The city's still recuperating," he said. "And it

could have caused problems of some sort for people with issues like May's."

"I've tried to talk to her. All she can do is try to say part of a word. I can't understand it, though. And she points to the embroidery on the scarf I sometimes wear. And she hums, too."

Father Haney's face creased into a deep frown. He looked at the ceiling as if for guidance. "Let me talk to a few people. See what I can figure out."

"I've talked to my friend from the nursing home where I used to work. She has a lot of contacts, and I'm hoping she can also come up with some ideas." Sarah ran her finger over a worn spot on the table. "You know, May's just different than other homeless people."

"How so?"

"I mean, her clothes are old and worn, but they're not totally shabby or soiled. And her gloves and hat must have been stylish at one time. And have you ever noticed she only carries a small tote bag? Not the usual cart or huge bag of belongings that other people on the street have. She's different. I can't really explain it."

Father Haney's eyes swept the room. "Okay, Sarah. Let me see if there's anything I can do." Then he gestured to the pamphlets on the table. "In the meantime, please keep those. And, here," he said, pulling several little spiritual booklets from a nearby rack and handing them to her. "Maybe you'll also find these of some interest."

"That's awfully nice of you," said Sarah. She couldn't blame the priest for doing a little church outreach.

"Why don't we take a look at those pictures now?"

He led Sarah to some framed photos on one of the walls. "I checked these out earlier today. They're certainly historic." He first indicated a few faded images of the church before the turn of the century. Then he waved toward others with groups of students. "Here's the first graduating class from 1935." He pointed to a gathering of young people barely into their teens. "I don't recognize any of the names, though."

Sarah squinted at the photo. The students looked so young. From what Gianni had said, the students then went on to a city high school or to work after finishing at the church school.

Father Haney pointed to the next picture. "Over here. This is the class of 1936. I believe that's your boss, Mr. Butler."

Sarah squinted even harder. There was Mr. Butler at around age fourteen. Of course, many years had passed, but the serious expression on his face was one she recognized. She wondered if he ran his hand over his hair in frustration back then, the way he did now.

"Is Mrs. Butler in any of these photos? Gianni told me they'd met here."

Father Haney looked carefully at the names below the picture. "There's a 'Mary' here. Mary Vandert. Possibly Mrs. Butler, but I only know her married name."

"Seems reasonable it could be her, although she could have graduated in another class year," said Sarah. She tried to imagine the young girl in the photo aged more than four decades and with a totally different hairstyle.

"And look at this," said the priest. There was a little typewritten caption below each of those class photos, listing the names of students as well as achievement awards that some had received. Evidently Mr. Butler hadn't gotten anything. It was probably doubtful they gave awards for insurance studies at that age, thought Sarah with a smile.

She studied the captions. "If that *is* Mrs. Butler, looks like she got an award for spelling."

"Next time you come in," said Father Haney, "why don't you spend some more time with the photos? I'll find a magnifying glass to make them easier to see. They're quite interesting and they give a real sense of those early days. Too bad the school didn't stay open longer than it did."

They quickly checked another few photos on the wall, but Sarah had to leave.

"Thanks so much, Father. I'll definitely be back."

****

Later on after work, Sarah hurried to get to her appointment with Dave. Kelly had slipped a copy of her own revised résumé into Sarah's hands earlier while the two of them were in the conference room and working on what they'd begun referring to as "Mrs. B's Organizing Obsession." Now Sarah had two résumés in her purse. Dave would be thrilled.

Dashing through the subway door, she elbowed her way into a secure standing niche. The ride gave her a few moments to ponder recent events. It'd be fun to know a little of the old school building's history, but it didn't concern her. She reminded herself that her real purpose in meeting with Father Haney had been to find some help for May. But she couldn't stop thinking about Mr. Butler, and possibly Mrs. Butler, and their young faces in the aging photos. Could there be a connection between then and now? Something to do with Kelly's fears and the conversation she'd overheard? *Could it have anything to do with the dead guy?*

Sarah shook off this crazy thought as she pushed open the door to the employment agency. There was the unmistakable presence of Dave in one of his outrageous sports jackets.

"Sarah, Sarah. This is perfect timing." As usual, he waved a ballpoint pen in the air as if contemplating the deal of the century. "I just got off the phone. You're all set up with an interview for the Tuesday after Thanksgiving. I made it at the same time as this so you don't have to spin one of those dental appointment excuses to slip out of work during the day."

What?

"Look, Dave." Sarah slid into a nearby chair without taking off her coat. "You haven't even *seen* my updated résumé yet. Isn't this pushing things a bit too fast? And besides, you haven't told me much about the job at all. And what will happen to the Butlers if I leave?"

Sarah spoke rapidly before Dave had a chance to interrupt. With him, there was no other way. Then, she fished the neatly folded résumé from her purse and placed it on his desk.

"You worry too much," he said with a sly smile. "So it's a job writing up standard benefits summaries, outlining the basics for new staff, etc., etc., etc. They'll fill you in on the rest. Great company. Great location. A couple more dollars than you're getting now."

Sarah was exhausted from Dave's fast-talking hustle. "But what about the Butlers?"

"Okay, Sarah. By the time you go through the interviews and we get past the holidays, you wouldn't have to give notice until the end of December. Our three-month agreement with the Butlers will be long over by then, so everyone will have lived up to their part of the bargain."

"What will they do if I quit? Mrs. Butler is giving me more work. Maybe she wants to retire…" Sarah held up her hand. "Wait. I know. You're already working on my replacement."

Dave's smile said it all.

"So, what's the problem, Sarah?"

"For starters, I'll look like a job hopper. And I don't know if I want to work in the benefits department of a large company."

"You're overthinking this. Look." Dave leaned forward at his desk, twirling that ever-present cheap ballpoint pen. "What harm is it to go for a couple of interviews? It'll get you back in action. Scope things out. Nothing says they'll make you an offer or that you have to take it."

If Dave really had been the used-car salesman he looked like, he'd now be circling in to close the deal.

"Hey, Sarah." He stopped the fast talk for a moment. "If you don't want to work for a larger company like this, then what *do* you really want to do?"

They studied each other. "Truthfully, Dave, I'm still working on it. And this is going to sound crazy, but I'd really like to combine my business background and my interest in art."

Dave was quiet—a first, in Sarah's experience. "Look. Just go on the interview. Based on what you've just told me, I think you'll find it more than interesting.

Remember, nothing's a done deal till there's an offer or an acceptance. And you're keeping the energy going."

"Fair enough. Oh, and the Butlers' secretary is starting to look for another job."

Dave jumped right in before she could finish. "Send her along whenever she's ready."

"I'll do better than that." Sarah grinned as she handed him the envelope. "Here's her résumé, in case you might want to consider her as a client."

Chapter Fourteen

Saturday morning dawned overcast with rain in the air. Sarah made a pot of coffee and pondered the day ahead. There were a hundred things she should be doing—bills, phone calls. Heck, it was probably time to start writing out the Christmas cards she had yet to buy.

She pushed away some papers on the table to make room for her bagel and mug of coffee. A lone sheet drifted off the pile and landed on the floor, its red-and-green colors cheerful against the area rug. Sarah picked it up. It was the flyer advertising the huge crafts fair that Hilda put in her grocery bag last week.

Sarah studied the flyer. It was happening today. For two dollars' admission, you could browse scores of tables with fine handmade creations from numerous chapters of a local women's crafts collective. *Jewelry... Knitted Items... Leather Goods... Ceramics... Wood Carvings... Paper Goods... Metal Art...* The list seemed endless, not to mention the additional special features of the event. *Music... Raffle Prizes... Food...* All in honor of the twenty-fifth anniversary of the collective.

Sarah looked at the address. The large community center wasn't far. Why not? Wandering the crafts tables could be fun. Get her mind off things. Maybe find a small gift or two. It was certainly getting to be the season, and she was far from ready for it.

By the time Sarah finished washing her breakfast dishes and straightening up the apartment, she was beginning to really look forward to the event. Pulling on her warm jacket, she headed out the door for the brief walk to the crafts fair.

As gloomy as the outside world appeared, the inside of the community center was like a vibrant party in progress. The place was packed. Vibrant red-and-green lights made the spacious room glow. High levels of excited chatter rose above the strains of live musicians, their pre-holiday and light popular songs wafting through the room from the small stage at the front. The shuffling of dozens of feet on the wooden floor added a percussive layer of sound, filling the room with even more energy.

Sarah paid her admission fee, hung her coat on an already crammed clothes rack, and began drifting from table to table. Hilda had been right. It was, indeed, an astonishing array of crafts displayed for sale. And only minutes later, she heard her name called above the noise. It was Hilda. She was sitting nearby and helping a friend sell boxed Christmas cards displayed in several towering piles.

"Sarah, I'm so glad you came!"

"Me, too! I'm enjoying wandering. Trust me, I'll definitely be getting some gifts here."

Sarah studied their holiday cards and chose a box with a picture of cheerful ornaments dotting lush, snow-covered pine trees. "Exactly what I need," she said, paying Hilda's friend.

"Have fun," urged the women as Sarah continued on.

Absorbed in the displays, Sarah forgot about

everything else. She bought several unusual yarn ornaments, each snug in a little silver bag. Next was a handmade bracelet for Lorna and a cute beaded change purse for Kelly. She soon accumulated a number of small bags of purchases.

Then a shout rang through the air. "Raffle! Last chance." A woman held a thatched basket high over her head with one hand and brandished a row of tickets strung together like sausages in the other. Enthusiastic buyers crowded around.

"All proceeds go to charity. Prizes for twenty lucky winners."

Getting into the spirit, Sarah struggled with her bags, grabbed some change from her purse, and bought a ticket from the woman. A couple of minutes later, Hilda ran over holding out a shopping bag. "Looks like you could use this."

"You're a lifesaver, Hilda."

Hilda helped Sarah arrange her purchases in the bag, just as the next announcement came loud and clear. "Listen up. It's time to pick the raffle winners."

Sarah showed Hilda her ticket. "I usually don't win anything at raffles."

"You never know," Hilda said, guiding Sarah closer to the crowd near the raffle woman. The thatched basket, loaded with ticket stubs, sat on a small table next to her.

"For the lovely crocheted blanket." The woman sang out while her second in command pulled a stub from deep within the basket and waved it high. The women were definitely old pros at this.

"Number 53702."

There was a scream and a burst of applause as a

woman in a red holiday sweater, complete with reindeer appliqué and decorative bells, ran forward to claim her gift.

And so it went through numerous items—a set of festive serving utensils, a colorful knitted muffler, a box of carved wooden Christmas ornaments.

"Number 54708."

"Hilda, that's me!"

Hilda provided the soundtrack as Sarah rushed forward to claim her prize. It was a large basket made entirely of red-and-white striped peppermint candy and filled with matching, individually wrapped miniatures.

"Hilda, you were right! You never know, do you?"

After giving Sarah a warm hug, Hilda returned to her post at the Christmas card table, leaving Sarah to wonder what on earth she would do with her raffle prize. It would take a year to eat all of that peppermint. And as she thought back to everyone at work greedily devouring the box of chocolates, she couldn't imagine the same enthusiasm for peppermints.

A few raffle winners were gathered nearby and talking.

"That's a magnificent basket," said someone a few inches away. The woman brandished her newly won ceramic cake server emblazoned with a snow-encrusted holiday sleigh.

"Sure is," said her friend. "Wish I'd won that instead." She held up a small, yet attractive, cloth-bound book titled *Fifty Years of Food: Recipes & Recollections.* "I got the recipe book in honor of the crafts collective's anniversary, but I already have a copy."

Sarah spied a few people nearby exchanging their

winnings. Why not at least make an offer? "I'll trade if you'd like," she said to the woman with the recipe book. "It'd take me till next Christmas to eat all of this candy, and I have no idea who I'd give it to."

"Really?" The woman was genuinely thrilled. "That'd be great!"

They traded their items, thanking each other profusely, as more raffle numbers continued to be called. Sarah stepped aside to look for room inside her shopping bag.

"Good trade," commented a voice nearby.

She looked up into the amused hazel eyes of a young man with well-groomed dark hair. He placed a box on the table nearby. More copies of the recipe book peeked from its interior.

"You'll find a lot of great recipes in there if you like to cook," he said, "and stories to go with them. They're selling these all over the neighborhood during the holidays."

"I'm sure I'll enjoy it," replied Sarah. "Otherwise, I'd be eating peppermint for a year."

He laughed easily. "I'm Matt Andreuws. My company printed the recipe book for the crafts collective's anniversary."

"Sarah Quinlee. I'm a new fan of the crafts collective."

"Nice to meet you, Sarah Quinlee." He shook hands with her, holding on a few seconds extra. It suited his friendly, casual manner.

They chatted for another couple of minutes about the fair. Sarah repeated how happy she was to have exchanged the peppermint basket for the book. "People at work seem to prefer chocolate."

"So do I," Matt said. "Where do you work?"

When she told him, he seemed genuinely taken back, his eyebrows raised in surprise.

"That's a couple of blocks from my office. We're work neighbors. For now, at least."

"Small world."

"You've worked there for a while?"

"Not at all," said Sarah. "Just a few months. The people are lovely, but the area's kind of quiet." She paused. "By the way, what did you mean by we're neighbors for now, at least?"

"I'm relocating my office soon." Matt pulled an invitation-sized card from his jacket. "So it's a lucky coincidence we ran into each other before I move. I would have hated to miss meeting you, Sarah."

The recipe book was still in Sarah's hands. Matt leaned over and opened the cover, carefully tucking the card inside. "Here, for you, since you won a copy of the book."

He stepped back before continuing.

"A week from tomorrow I'm having an open-house party to kick off the holidays and because I'll be officially moving soon. We'll even have chocolate," he said with a grin. "The building owner insisted I throw this party upstairs from my office in an old café that closed a few years ago. There's more space there, and it's still sort of charming." Matt's eyes met Sarah's directly. "I hope you'll come. The invitation is for two, so you can bring a friend if you'd like. But if you come by yourself, I'll definitely make sure you won't feel alone."

"Thanks, Matt. So nice meeting you."

"The pleasure's all mine." He gave a brief wink. "I

really hope to see you next week."

The crafts fair was definitely having its surprises.

They said their goodbyes, and Sarah approached what she promised herself would be the last table she'd visit. It was time to go home before her shopping bag became too heavy to carry.

This table was a lavish one, filled with all manner of little ceramic figurines, pewter and silver pieces, carved wooden keepsake boxes, and other unusual items. Sarah studied all of them carefully. The elderly woman sitting at the table there studied Sarah carefully, in turn.

"These are unique," the woman said, adjusting several strands of beaded necklaces that decorated her sweater. Of course, Sarah had heard this phrase several times at other tables.

Sarah picked up an elegant, well-designed wooden box, generous enough for favorite pieces of jewelry. Perfect for Gen. And there was still plenty of time to pack and mail it to her overseas.

Sarah handed it to the woman. "I'll definitely take this," she said, still looking over other items at the table. She also decided on some stocking-stuffers, including several gleaming, silvery bookmarks. She'd include them in cards to some distant, out-of-state cousins.

Next, Sarah lingered over one eye-catching piece. "What a cute little mug." She ran her finger over its smooth, pewter-y surface, drawn to its stylish handle and the gracious lines of its ample, pot-bellied form. But there was no one to give it to. Except maybe herself.

"You can use it for coffee or cold drinks," said the

woman. "Or even fill it with flowers."

The idea of flowers struck Sarah as lovely. It would be fun to sketch the little mug with small petals flowing over the top.

"Flowers would be perfect," agreed Sarah.

"Deep purple or a mix of purple and yellow would look beautiful." The woman thought for a moment. "There's a place just north of here…it's Roses Blooming or A Dozen Roses…"

"A Dozen Roses," called out the other woman working at the table, not too busy with her current customer to tune into their conversation. "It used to be Roses Blooming."

The old woman didn't miss a beat. "They have the most wonderful flowers."

On impulse, Sarah realized she wanted this unusual piece. Nothing wrong with getting a gift for oneself, was there? "I'll take this, too."

The woman individually wrapped the items in tissue paper and put each in a separate box with her shop's logo. She also inserted the bookmarks into artfully designed cardboard sleeves and handed Sarah a whimsical business card that read *Crafty Crafts*. "Please come and visit us anytime. I'm Amelia, and this is Grace." She indicated the middle-aged woman, now wrapping a ceramic bowl for a customer with two shopping bags already filled to the brim. Grace smiled and nodded, a strand of straight brown hair falling over her eyes.

Amelia continued. "And let me write down the address of A Dozen Roses for you." She grabbed a second business card and scribbled on the back. "Their flowers are exceptional."

Sarah now needed to put her new purchases into her own well-stocked shopping bag.

"Here, let me help you." Amelia slowly rose from her chair and placed the shopping bag on a clear table space next to her. Obviously adept at packing, she was also well supplied with tissue paper, plastic bags, and scraps of fabric to aid in the process.

"You certainly seem prepared," said Sarah, admiring the woman's deft handiwork.

"Don't throw anything away." Amelia laughed. "You never know when it will come in handy. You should see what I keep at the shop."

"That's for sure." Grace rolled her eyes at Amelia's last statement as she brushed back another piece of rogue hair.

"I saw you won in the raffle." Amelia didn't miss much. "Good for you."

Sarah nodded. "Yes, well, I won the peppermint basket. To be truthful, I didn't know what I'd do with it." Then she described the exchange of her raffle item for the recipe book.

"You'll enjoy that a lot. Be sure to try some of those recipes. They're from way back when and they're good. And so are the local stories."

Again, a subtle eye roll from Grace, who added, "It's in of honor the crafts collective's anniversary. That's why this event is so big." She sighed. "And so busy."

Amelia handed the carefully re-packed shopping bag to Sarah. "Now please visit our shop. We have a lot more on display there. Christmas is coming, you know."

Sarah thanked them both and promised to visit.

Finally, she grabbed her coat from the overstuffed rack and headed home.

After her sandwich-and-salad dinner, Sarah relaxed on the blue couch and turned on the radio to an orchestral medley of songs from Noel Coward's operetta *Bitter Sweet*. She hummed along with its two most popular songs, "Zigeuner" and "I'll See You Again." They were particular favorites of Aunt Addie's. Sarah recalled a musical afternoon at Westervale when a dark-haired soprano in a green sparkly dress ended her program with those same two melodies.

As she hummed, Sarah drifted into a peaceful nap, enjoying the beautiful music and the lingering good feelings from her fun afternoon.

Chapter Fifteen

Sarah slept late on Sunday morning. With another free day ahead, there was no excuse to avoid tackling her to-do list. She could also sort her purchases from the crafts fair the previous day and check out those pamphlets from Father Haney.

Instead, though, she lingered with a second mug of coffee. Going out yesterday had been wonderful. Why not do it again today? Chores could wait. Weekends were a time for crafts fairs, local concerts, walks, and museums, although maybe not the Met.

Sarah picked up her sketchpad and flipped through a few pages of her most recent drawings. They were more elaborate than those she included in her letters to Gen, but she still only considered them to be the basis for more finished pieces she hoped to create soon, maybe even in preparation for taking another sketching class.

She turned to her profile of May. *Does she sit on her church step on weekends?* When this random thought popped into Sarah's head, she suddenly became curious. It seemed silly to go to her work area on a day off, but she'd been wanting to sketch the old school and, despite having created a basic drawing of it from memory, there was no substitute for studying the details in person. What better time than on a quiet Sunday? Energized, Sarah tossed sketchpad and pencils into her shoulder bag and was soon out the door.

It wasn't long before she strolled up the street toward the old church school. The whole area was peaceful and quiet, and Sarah settled into the corner of a brownstone step across the street from the school and pulled out her sketchpad. Despite the cold nip in the air, she'd be all right for a little while. She carefully took in the old building, focusing on a few distinctive details she hadn't noticed before—a subtle arch above the window here and a bit of gentle scrollwork there. Weather-beaten but appealing, it jutted out slightly beyond the footprint of the church itself as well as from its neighbors on the other side.

After adding soft pencil strokes to the page for a while, Sarah caught sight of May out of the corner of her eye. She was now on her church step. It was time to go over and say hello. Perhaps she could show the woman some of her sketches.

As she closed her sketchpad, Sarah noticed activity at the church. A very few individuals were leaving Mass. She stopped in surprise when she saw Edgar among them, wearing his best Sunday coat, a far cut above his everyday work outfits. It looked as if he had some lovely companionship, too, as he came down the steps together with a nice-looking woman. She took his arm and they walked off in the far direction. Good for him. She gave the pair one more glance—and, surely, she was mistaken—but it looked as if Edgar wasn't wearing his glasses. Perhaps a bit of vanity? Wanting to look more attractive for the woman? But could he see well enough without the glasses? Or did he possibly wear contact lenses for social occasions? Perhaps she had been mistaken.

Sarah waited until the street returned to its previous emptiness once more. Now she'd go over and say hello to May. But as she finished gathering her sketching things, May rose from the step and headed in the direction Edgar had gone. Sarah hurried to catch up.

Suddenly it occurred to her that perhaps she should just follow May. If she knew where May was sheltered when not on the church steps, then she'd have some more information that might be useful in getting help for the woman. Sarah quickened her pace while deciding if this was a good idea or an awful one. May had already rounded a corner out of sight.

As Sarah hurried on, footsteps abruptly grabbed her attention. Footsteps from behind, matching Sarah's increasing pace. Suddenly on alert, she wheeled around and gasped.

The copper-haired teen appeared out of nowhere.

"Hey, you!" he barked. "Why don't you follow your crazy friend and just beat it."

"Why don't you leave me alone?"

"Because I don't want to."

Church was over. Not a soul was on the street. Where had he come from? And why?

The teen took a menacing step closer. "I said beat it."

Sarah stood facing him, afraid to turn away. She yelled in her loudest voice. "*And I said leave me alone!*"

A nearby door suddenly swung open, and Gianni's snowy head appeared. He strode easily in their direction, wielding a pipe of some sort in his right hand.

"You heard the lady," he said evenly to the teen, closing the distance between them.

"What's it to you, old man?"

Gianni came closer. He raised the pipe a deliberate notch, his gaze leveled at the teen. "The question is: what's it to you?"

A flicker of anxiety registered in the teen's eyes.

Relief swept over Sarah at Gianni's approach, followed by a wave of anger at the teen. "The cops are looking for you. They probably think you killed that man on the church steps."

In a heartbeat, the teen's scowl transformed into unmistakable fear. When he held up his hands as if to ward off some demon, Sarah caught a split-second glimpse of that slender tattoo once again.

"Killed? No! I didn't kill nobody. I never killed nobody."

"Why are you harassing this young woman?" Gianni raised the pipe a little more.

"For a few bucks…to scare…" He choked on his words. Then he turned and ran. It would have been pointless to chase him. He was too young, too fast— and too frightened.

Sarah let out a heavy sigh of relief. "Gianni, thank you."

He nodded. "Are you okay?'

"Yeah. I'm fine."

"Good. Why don't you come in the store and sit down for a few minutes. We should report this to the cops."

"Thanks… The cops?" This hadn't occurred to her. "I guess so. I mean they were looking for him, but I don't really think he killed that man. I was just angry."

When they got inside, Gianni picked up the phone as Sarah sat down in the corner wooden chair. She would have preferred not to have called the cops at all, but Gianni said it was a good idea in case of any further troubles. When he was done, he pulled out his own chair from behind the counter and joined her.

"Working on a Sunday?"

She shook her head. "No. You'll think I'm crazy, but here's what I was going to do." Then she told him about her sketches and wanting to check on May. Maybe even figuring out where she went to see if it was a safe place.

He listened and didn't take her to task for such a foolish plan.

"Once in a while I see her on weekends. Not always. As for following to see where she goes…" His voice trailed off. "Sometimes there's things we can't fix, Sarah. You have a good heart. But I don't want to see you get hurt."

"Thanks, Gianni. Me neither. But I feel so bad for May."

"What I want to know is what that kid's story is. He was getting a few bucks to scare who? You? People around here?"

"What about the tattoo on his hand?" asked Sarah.

"Yeah, I noticed that, too. Might be something just for show. Not from any gang I've seen. And even gang wannabes don't bother with this kind of harassment, no matter how young they are." He shook his head. "There's got to be more to his story, though. That kid's scared."

"It's not the first time I've seen him." Sarah then told Gianni about her earlier encounter with the teen.

"Sarah. You really have to be careful. Something's going on here."

They were interrupted by a knock on the door. Gianni waved in a young cop. "Thanks for coming over, Officer. No real trouble, but we wanted to go on record."

They both gave brief renditions of the episode, omitting the fact that Gianni had brought out a pipe as extra insurance against any real difficulties.

The cop offered to have them look at mugshots, but Sarah told him she'd already done that. "Detectives Cahill and Rian know about the guy. He's just a kid. But we wanted you to be aware that he's still around. Everything's okay. Really."

After the cop left, Sarah looked at her friend. "I can't begin to thank you enough."

"Glad I was here, Sarah. I usually visit a friend on Sunday, but he didn't feel well today."

Sarah nodded. "I hope he gets better soon."

Now she wanted to assure Gianni that she wasn't completely crazy. "Would you like to see some of the things I've been sketching?"

"Of course."

Sarah pulled out her sketchpad. "These are just preliminary sketches."

As they paged through, Gianni studied them with interest. "There's one of me and my shop." There was pride in his voice.

"If you like, I'll make a really nice copy for you."

"I would be honored, Sarah. You're very talented."

Sarah thanked him and soon rose to leave.

"I'm walking you to your train," he said. "Just to be on the safe side."

****

The next morning as Sarah headed down the street

toward work, she spied a figure lingering outside the entrance to the Butler Agency. One quick glance and she knew it was Detective Rian. As she came closer, she saw worry etched into his handsome face.

"Are you okay, Sarah? I saw the report when I came in this morning."

Sarah swallowed hard. "Absolutely fine. Thanks. Umm, maybe a report wasn't really necessary, but Gianni said that we should probably go on record."

"He was right. It was the same teenager?"

"Yeah." Then Sarah described the incident. "I yelled at the kid and said that the police were looking for him and maybe thought he had killed that man on the church steps. I was just angry, but he got really frightened and swore he didn't kill anyone. He also started to say he'd only gotten a few bucks to scare someone or something or other, but then he stopped talking and just ran. Fast." Sarah looked away. "He didn't say who he was supposed to scare or why."

Detective Rian hesitated. "Okay. So you were working yesterday?"

"No, I…"

She looked at him and then told him everything. At least the part about wanting to do some sketches didn't sound too lunatic. But wanting to follow May was something else.

When she finished, Detective Rian nodded and, like Gianni, he didn't tell her what a bad idea this had been. "I know you want to help, Sarah. It's a tough situation. But I'm worried you'll put yourself in danger. And sometimes there's not a lot that any of us can do for someone like May. In the meantime, we have no idea what the story is with that teenager. Please, Sarah.

I want you to be safe."

"Thanks. And, umm, thanks for following up with me now." She had to look away. It might have been easier to deal with Detective Cahill's rudeness instead of these kind eyes and look of concern.

"Is there anything I can do?" It seemed as if there was more he wanted to say.

"Sarah? Detective Rian?" Mr. Butler stuck his head out the front door.

"Just following up on a report, Mr. Butler," said the detective. "Everything's okay."

"Thanks, Detective Rian." Sarah was grateful for Mr. Butler's interruption. "I have to get to work now." It was impossible to meet his gaze.

"Okay." There was a pause. "Sarah, please take care."

Chapter Sixteen

Sarah needed to think about Thanksgiving. Cookie's parents were hosting, and Sarah would again join their relatives, friends, and neighbors, all happily cramming into their small Queens apartment for the holiday. Everyone was welcome, and Sarah already dreamed of the wonderful main meal to come with lots of unusual sides—herbed muffins, sautéed chestnuts, cranberry relish studded with rum-soaked fruits.

She stopped on the way home from work now to buy some wine to bring with her. Cookie's mom, Lil, turned down Sarah's offer of another side dish. "There'll be way too much food already. Just bring yourself. We're thrilled to be seeing you."

Lil and her husband also urged Sarah to stay overnight with them on Thanksgiving. Cookie and Jim's apartment was far too small for this, but no one wanted Sarah going back home from Queens really late on the subway.

"Besides," Cookie said, "I'll come over on Friday morning. Mom will make breakfast, and the three of us can sit and catch up on all the stuff you haven't been telling me. We'll leave Dad and Jim the luxury of sleeping late." Sarah readily agreed. Only two days away, and Sarah looked forward to it. They were like family.

Tonight, though, Sarah planned to relax a bit. She

glanced at the bag of holiday gifts from the crafts fair and decided to wrap Gen's gift and send it out to her over the weekend. At the same time, it seemed like a good idea to take a look at everything she'd bought and figure out what other Christmas gifts she'd need to get. Shopping days were beginning to dwindle.

As always, Sarah turned on the radio while making her quick dinner of grilled cheese and tomato soup. The background music was soothing. First up were two old Jerome Kern songs, "Look for the Silver Lining" and "Make Believe." Aunt Addie had loved these melodies, too.

Sarah laughed when she heard "Make Believe" and hummed along for a few bars. This was also the name of a little children's toy and clothing store nearby. Were the owners inspired by the song title, or had it just been coincidental? She made a mental note to visit the place soon to check out future gift possibilities for Cookie and Jim's baby.

When she'd finished the last spoonful of soup, Sarah cleared the table and unpacked her crafts fair purchases on its small surface. First, there was Gen's gift. She selected some nice wrapping she'd recently bought and carefully placed it around the gift, taking time to write a thoughtful card. She'd also purchased a sturdy mailing box, and cushioned the wrapped gift inside this box with some of the tissue and fabric scraps that Amelia had used to re-pack her shopping bag. Amelia was certainly a practical woman, even though her helper, Grace, had rolled her eyes at the mention of saving everything. In this case, it turned out to be quite useful.

Then Sarah took out the little pot-bellied pewter

mug that she bought for herself. She stood back to admire its appealing lines and how the smooth surface glowed warmly in the light. Amelia said that Blooming Roses or A Dozen Roses—whatever its name was—had some exquisite flowers, and Sarah decided to visit them soon. Once the little mug was full of lovely petals, she would enjoy sketching it.

Next was her raffle gift, *Fifty Years of Food: Recipes and Recollections*, the book she'd gotten in exchange for that enormous peppermint basket. Sarah couldn't resist settling in on the sofa and spending a few minutes with it now. The party invitation from Matt was still tucked firmly inside the cover. It was nice of him to invite her. He'd been right. Rapid Printing really wasn't far from the Butler Agency at all. Matt was a pleasant guy and seemed genuinely interested in making a connection with her. According to the invitation, the party was being held in the old café upstairs in his building, a onetime landmark now closed. It could be fun to see the old café. Although the invitation was for two, Matt had made it clear that coming alone would be quite all right, perhaps even more welcome.

Setting aside the invitation, Sarah started browsing through the book. There were lots of old-fashioned recipes, each one including a few lines or paragraphs of intriguing historical and current anecdotal asides about people and places. Even Hilda from the supermarket, who'd given her the flyer for the crafts fair in the first place, had contributed one of her old family favorites, scalloped potatoes with cheese and bacon. And Sarah spied recipes from other familiar names, including Amelia and Grace.

There were separate sections for favorite dishes from restaurants, local businesses, and social groups, many long gone. Their capsule histories helped bring them to life again. They included a huge ethnic variety and offered a vivid sense of what the neighborhood area was like in the past. It had seemed to be much more cohesive then than now.

A tasty holiday fruit and nut bread from the Hoefflers, an old tailor and his wife, looked reasonably simple. Sarah thought she might give it a try at Christmastime. The recipe was followed by a brief story of how the couple enjoyed making small individual loaves for their customers during the holiday season.

Sarah laughed at a wild punch concoction, popular at gatherings of a local singing society. It was said to have been mixed to perfection by one of their more gregarious tenors, Karl Brulner. This page even included a reproduction of a program from one of their songfests. Then the group dwindled out, their building now gone as were most of its members.

Next, Sarah turned to the pages about Two Violins, a popular and well-known restaurant. There were stories and recipes interspersed with humorous quotes from the Gaspar family, who'd owned the place, as well as from their popular headwaiter, Lel Vandert. Decades ago, before closing their doors, the Gaspars finally shared the secret recipe for their famous goulash. It was a special favorite of a local engraver and his wife every time they dined there. They were such frequent customers that it became a good-natured joke at the restaurant. They loved Two Violins, and it was just a few short blocks from where the couple lived and operated their business. There was even a replica of the engraver's business advertisement included, dating from before World War II. Sarah was surprised to recognize the address. It appeared to have been in the same building as Matt's Rapid Printing where the party would be held next weekend.

But then Sarah stared dumbfounded at the old advertisement.

High-Quality Engraving
By Milaeve
Rhymes with "Engrave"

Chapter Seventeen

Milaeve was the last name of the dead man on the church steps. But the details in the recipe book were from long ago, and the brief text said that the business had been a neighborhood fixture only through the 1940s. The dead man might not have been related closely or at all. And the engraver's ad was at the same address then as Rapid Printing's was now. But what of it? There were probably dozens of tenants in the same building then and dozens more in the intervening years. Would Matt know anything about the old engravers? He was young, most likely no more than a couple of years older than Sarah. The Milaeves had lived there long ago.

But the police asked if the name sounded familiar to anyone. Could this old page provide some help? It was pretty far-fetched, but maybe she really should say something.

Sarah tossed and turned that night, waking early to the day before Thanksgiving and her same dilemma. Should she tell the police? Copy the page and go to the precinct on her lunch hour? And what were the chances that either of the detectives would even be on duty?

She closed her eyes and told herself to think. It was just a name. In a recipe book, for heaven sakes. Just a copy of an old advertisement with a line or two about people and places from decades ago. Then she laughed out loud. *But it's not as if the name were Smith or Jones. Milaeve was not a common name.* And the detectives did ask if anyone had heard the name.

The detectives might laugh or think she was wasting their time. The NYC police were an efficient bunch. They probably didn't need this small detail. And what would a name from over three decades ago have to do with a current crime?

But there was a lot of crime these days, and the city had had a rotten go of it, especially this past summer in the aftermath of the blackout and other events. The police were short-staffed and facing tremendous cuts. Maybe even a little detail could help with something.

Sarah paced a trail back and forth in her apartment, listening to a random door slam out in the hall and the impatient horn of a cab down on the street. Yes, telling the cops was the right thing to do.

When she got to work, Sarah managed to get to the copy machine mid-morning, subtly duplicating the two pages. Breathing a sigh of relief, she slid both the book and copies back into her shoulder bag. Everyone was where they should be—the Butlers, Edgar, Kelly. Everything seemed normal. *But normal now seemed a notch off center everywhere.*

Closer to lunchtime, Sarah looked around. No one was nearby. She dialed the precinct. The voice on the other end sounded like the guy who'd been manning the desk the day she'd looked at the mugshots. Cupping her hand over the receiver, she launched into her story.

"Hi, this is Sarah Quinlee. I was at the precinct a couple of weeks ago. I'd like to speak with Detective Cahill or Detective Rian. Or maybe I could just stop in now and leave something for them. If that would be okay." Sarah almost managed to get this out in one breath. Yes, leaving the pages, maybe with a brief note, would be easiest.

"Hang on a second." The officer was back on in record time. "You can drop by now if you want. Looks like at least one of them is here."

"Thanks. I'm on my way."

Of course, he hadn't said which one. It didn't matter. She could handle Detective Cahill's gruffness. As for Detective Rian, she'd misread his friendliness, although her face now flushed at the thought. But she'd be very professional and, with luck, maybe they'd be too busy to see her.

Sarah grabbed her coat and ran. Breathless when she reached the heavy outer door of the precinct, she pulled hard and entered. Today the place was quiet. Well, it was the day before Thanksgiving. Maybe even criminals were home preparing their turkeys just like everyone else.

Sarah had been right. It was the same guy at the desk. They smiled at each other.

"Miss Quinlee. Good to see you again." He tilted his head toward the main room with a look of amusement. "Your lucky day. They're both in. Said to just send you back as soon as you got here."

Sarah thanked him and headed for the main room. Both detectives sat at ancient desks near each other. Detective Cahill saw her first and waved her over. Detective Rian was on the phone, but when he realized Sarah was there, he looked up with that warm smile. Sarah swallowed a lump in her throat. Both men stood as she approached.

But just at that moment, there was the shrill peal of

a phone. Somewhere. An abrupt shout followed a split-second later. In a flash, there was pandemonium.

If anyone were to have asked Sarah later to describe the next sequence of events, she was sure she'd have had no idea. She only remembered a flurry of shouts, ringing phones, and a rush of officers grabbing coats and running, Detectives Cahill and Rian among them. Sarah backed herself against a file cabinet to avoid a collision in the blaze of activity. It burst like a rocket out of the previous quiet.

In the midst of it all, someone lightly touched her arm, bringing her gaze into focus. She turned to look directly into serious blue eyes and a face filled with concern. Detective Rian.

"Sarah, I'm so sorry. We have an emergency." With that he ran, catching up with Cahill, whose coat had just swept through the door.

And then it was over, just as suddenly as it all began.

Whatever caused half the police precinct to run on a moment's notice couldn't have been good. On her way out, Sarah approached the desk officer, her face scrunched in confusion.

"Happens." The man shrugged, a grimace under his dark moustache.

"Sergeant Brus…" Sarah hesitated while deciphering the letters on the nameplate.

This brought the hint of a smile to the man's somber face. "Everyone calls me Brushie." He waved a hand toward his nameplate. "That's far too complicated."

"Oh, um, thanks… Sergeant Brushie."

"So is there anything I can do for you?"

"No, thanks. I just wanted to show the detectives an old name and address I thought might be of help, but after seeing everyone run like this for an emergency, I realized that it's not important at all. I feel sort of foolish."

"I'm sure it's not foolish. Even if it's something small, you're trying to help. And not a lot of people want to help us these days." His face was kind. "Tell you what. I'll remind them you wanted to speak to them, although I'm sure they'll remember. Today looks like it's going to be crazy, and then tomorrow's Thanksgiving and all. Paperwork will be flying."

"Please don't worry," Sarah said. "This can certainly wait until next week."

After thanking him again, Sarah left. She was probably wasting the detectives' time.

****

The twinkling chimes announcing Sarah's entrance to the shoe repair shop were soothing. With a little extra time left on her lunch hour, she decided to stop in and wish Gianni a happy Thanksgiving. She also welcomed a bit of calm after the chaos at the police precinct.

Gianni's snowy head raised from the newspaper at the sound of the chimes. Breaking into a broad smile, he rose to greet her.

"Sarah, it's good to see you. No shoes for me today, I see."

He indicated the corner chair, which was now a comfortably welcoming place for her.

"Sit, please." He pulled his own wooden chair from behind the counter to join her. "Doing okay after Sunday?"

"Yeah." Sarah smiled. "Thanks again for rescuing

me. I really appreciate it."

"Glad I could help. Just wish we knew who that kid is and who he's supposed to scare."

"He sure scared me. But once he got rid of that scowl, he didn't look as threatening."

"He was definitely terrified when you mentioned the dead guy and that maybe the cops thought he had something to do with it."

"Truthfully, Gianni, I doubt he had anything to do with it. I was just mad. And I'd sure like to know how that dead man fits into things. There's something strange about all of it. A rise in crime is one thing, but it feels like there's more going on."

Gianni looked up, waiting for her to continue.

Then Sarah told Gianni everything—from the day she discovered the murdered man to how she coincidentally found the same last name in the recipe book. She handed him the page.

"Milaeve?" Gianni's surprise was obvious. "You knew the name?"

"From the cops." Sarah was also startled. "Didn't they ask if you recognized it? They came to our office a few days afterward."

"I was away visiting one of my sons for a few days. They might've come then."

"Oh." Sarah hadn't considered the possibility that Gianni wasn't told the dead man's name or any of the other brief details the cops shared at her office.

"Sarah, I had no idea." He paused. "Milaeve was an old name around here. It was a fine engraving business, just like it says here." He pointed to the page from the recipe book. "Mr. Milaeve did work for a lot of rich people back in the day. People in those big town houses. Yeah, he was the one who used to eat with his wife at Two Violins. They briefly brought their young son into the business, but there was some sort of a falling out. According to gossip back then, the son went in the army and never came back here after."

"Could that son have been Vincent Milaeve?" asked Sarah. "The cops said the dead man was in his late fifties."

"I guess that'd be about right. The couple who ate at Two Violins would have been his parents. They moved a little ways upstate near their married daughter, I think, sometime after the war. They were a bit young to retire, but the business had done really well. At least that's the last I heard, and that was a long time ago." Gianni looked out the window now. "The cops are sure the dead guy was Vincent Milaeve?"

"That's what they said. Wonder what he was doing here after all these years."

"Good question." Gianni turned to Sarah. "Did anyone at work remember him? The Butlers or Edgar?"

"Not that I heard." Suddenly the image of Mrs. Butler walking down the hall with Detective Cahill at the police precinct popped into her head.

Gianni continued. "I guess my sons might have been a year or two younger than Vincent. I don't think he went to the church school, though, and I didn't know the family. Just heard this much because a few of my old customers liked to fill me in on all the neighborhood gossip while they waited." He looked at Sarah. "Even those guys are dead now… I should probably tell the cops, but I don't know what good it would do. It was all so long ago."

"You'd sure make me feel better if you spoke to

them," Sarah said. "I was starting to think it was totally foolish walking in with a page from a recipe book, even though they asked if we'd ever heard the name. And they said something about not releasing the name in general yet. Maybe they had to notify his close relatives or something. Anyway, you probably won't get anywhere trying to talk to them today."

Then Sarah told Gianni about her experience at the precinct just a little while ago.

"Not surprised. The whole city's on edge, especially after everything that happened this summer. It doesn't take much to trigger an emergency these days." Gianni handed the recipe pages back to Sarah. "Anything I can tell them is second-hand and from decades ago. It'll have to wait till next week. I'll be at my son's house for a few days."

"My story will have to wait, too. And speaking of the holiday, that's why I wanted to stop in. To wish you a happy Thanksgiving."

Gianni's face lit up. "Thanks! You, too. I'm looking forward to it. Always good to be with family on the holidays. How about you?"

Sarah filled him in on her plans to spend the day with Cookie's family. But then she again brought up the subject of the church school. "So, I was wondering," she said, running her fingers over the embroidered flowers on Aunt Addie's scarf. "The other morning when I was going to work, there were people moving things out of the old school building. Just some boxes. Do you really think they'll tear it down?"

"That's the rumor been going around for a long while." He looked absently toward the front window. "Who knows? Maybe they'll renovate instead."

Sarah couldn't help probing more. "Who owns it anyway?"

"I don't know. Some offices were in there for a while. Then a couple of community groups. Now it's empty. I'm guessing some sort of management company owns or runs it."

"Oh," said Sarah.

Gianni continued. "My sons have fond memories of the school. They were really young then. But it was a different time. More of a neighborhood. Most people talked to each other—or *about* each other." He laughed. "But then, nothing stays the same forever."

"I guess Mr. and Mrs. Butler have good memories, too," Sarah said. "We've never talked about it, but it must be special to them. I suppose everyone will be sad if it's torn down."

"That's progress for you, Sarah. I haven't talked to the Butlers in a while. Edgar either. He and his twin brother went there, too. My boys were younger than all of them."

Sarah looked up in surprise. "Edgar was a twin?"

Gianni shifted in his chair to a more comfortable position and went on. "Identical—but different. Edgar was so shy. He wore those glasses early on and always had some childhood cold or other and couldn't eat this or that."

He looked up at a shelf lined with a neat row of worn oxfords, their laces carefully tied. "But Elwyn. Now there was a real outgoing guy. Knew how to take care of himself on the street, too. He was a fine actor, even as a kid. Then the war came and a whole lot of them enlisted. They were so young, too." Gianni shook his head, his face now serious. "A real shame. Elwyn

119

was injured in the war, and I heard much later that he died a few years after as a result."

"That's awful," said Sarah. "Poor Edgar. It must have been so hard for him." She felt a rush of sympathy for the poor man who was so passionate about insurance.

"It was. He was one of the ones who came back, too." Gianni sighed deeply as if still trying to assimilate these past events. "Didn't see him after the war. His mother had moved by then, and he stayed away for years. Funny, but when he was really young, he worked for old Mr. Butler, just before the war. Couldn't have been too long. Then I guess he signed on again with Lou and Mary years later when he came back to the old neighborhood. Don't see him much."

"He seems to love his job." Sarah didn't know what else to say. She felt sad at how the war had damaged so many lives like Edgar's, left behind to mourn his twin brother. She was happy he had some companionship with that woman who took his arm on Sunday after Mass. Church was probably a comfort to him, too.

"Yeah. It was nice that things worked out for him. The Butlers are decent people."

They chatted for a few more minutes before Sarah needed to get back to work.

They wished each other happy Thanksgiving before the twinkling chimes announced Sarah's exit.

****

When Sarah came back after lunch, Kelly waved her over. She lowered her voice as Sarah came closer. "Got a call from your friend."

Ah, Dave, the employment agent. He certainly

didn't waste any time. Although to Sarah's knowledge, he never did.

Kelly lowered her voice even further. "Tuesday, after work."

Sarah gave her a thumbs-up just as a creaking sound on the stairs announced Edgar's descent from Mr. and Mrs. Butler's offices. His arms were laden with dog-eared files, and with each step he took, several threatened to completely escape from his grasp.

"Edgar." Sarah held out her arms, feeling even more empathy for the man after just learning about the tragedy in his past. She now understood why Edgar immersed himself in his job. Being busy probably helped. "Here, let me help you with some of those."

Kelly got up as well, both hoping to avoid the possibility of retrieving and reassembling several dozen files from a scattered heap on the floor. Like the Butlers, Edgar wasn't a young man, and he gratefully accepted their help. The two young women placed the files safely on a nearby table. Kelly returned to her desk as Edgar thanked them profusely. "You're both very kind."

"I set these aside for you," he said to Sarah with a tiny smile, pointing to the blue-colored folders at the top of the batch. She picked up the substantial collection from the pile.

"Oh, and just let me check that any others didn't get mixed in." Edgar leaned over the remaining folders on the table, his glasses slipping down his nose, a now familiar sight. But as he did so, the glasses slid completely off and skittered into a corner cobweb.

"Here. Let me get those for you." Sarah ran to retrieve the glasses. "Oh, Edgar. Looks like some dust got on your lenses. And I hope I didn't smudge anything when I picked them up." Sarah held the glasses up quickly, checking the lenses for smudges.

Strange. They looked like plain glass, without the usual distortion that indicated serious prescription lenses. The kind that Aunt Addie and other Westervale residents had worn.

"Let me get a tissue and clean them," said Sarah.

But Edgar immediately held out his hand for the glasses as he fumbled in his pocket. "Thanks, but I have a handkerchief."

Edgar accepted the glasses and carefully wiped the lenses before putting them back on. "Good as new. Thanks, Sarah. I don't know what I'd do without you."

Sarah smiled at him, gathered the blue folders, and walked to her desk.

But they really did seem to be plain glass lenses.

Chapter Eighteen

Remnants of a humongous turkey, stray morsels of stuffing tumbling out of its interior, still commanded a place of honor at the main table. It sat in the midst of platters recently piled high with sweet potatoes, casseroles, corn, root vegetables, and more. Cardboard replicas of pilgrims vied for choice positions on tablecloths splayed with patterns of autumn leaves.

It was Thanksgiving, and Cookie's mom Lil had outdone herself, as always, with a spectacular celebration. More than two dozen relatives and friends of Cookie's and Jim's families were squeezed side-by-side at tables stretching continuously from dining room to living room. Dinner was over, but dessert was yet to come. A short intermission, however, was necessary for everyone to breathe deeply and loosen a belt notch or two.

This was the moment. Cookie and Jim stood, asking everyone to raise their wine glasses.

"We want to share something wonderful with all of you," began Jim. Then together, he and Cookie announced their double-header good news—both baby and house were on the way.

Cheers burst throughout the small apartment, echoing into the outside hallway and to the street three floors below. Within minutes of the shouts and hugs and congratulations, the inevitable questions came fast and furious. "When's the baby due?" "Where's the house?"

All afternoon, Sarah was swept up in the events of this lively day, jumping through rounds of continuous conversations with batches of her hosts' assorted relatives and friends, all eager to catch up on the couple of years since she'd last been at this most favorite of large gatherings. Joyous chatter was nonstop right through dessert, and by the time people were groaning from "just-one-more-sliver" of that pie, it was getting late. Sarah made several dozen trips to the kitchen to help clear the table and assemble the obligatory take-home leftover packages. Little by little, aunts, uncles, cousins, and close friends started to drift out the door in a flurry of more hugs and congratulations. Although Thanksgiving had always been a huge event for Cookie's family, this year it was even more so.

Sarah was happy but exhausted, glad that Lil insisted she stay overnight. Cookie was ecstatic about their "girls only" brunch the next morning, a day off work for all. But now, Sarah was glad to collapse into bed. It was sometime after midnight, and she craved sleep.

Tired as her body was, Sarah's mind was working overtime when her head hit the pillow. There was her job, May, Gianni, the Butlers. And she kept returning again to the frantic events at the police precinct. It was the last thing she remembered as she finally drifted off to sleep.

****

The smell of strong coffee brewing filled the air the next morning. Lil was already in action, still the same energetic woman Sarah remembered from her childhood. And considering she had prepared for and hosted her traditional Thanksgiving spectacular the previous day, maintaining such energy this morning was quite an accomplishment.

Somewhere, there was the sound of a ringing phone. Sarah checked the clock. It was already 9:08. She dressed and headed for the kitchen, the aroma of coffee leading the way.

"Smells wonderful, Lil," said Sarah. "All those people here yesterday, and you're still the first one up and running."

Lil laughed. "Morning's the best part of the day." She poured coffee into a sturdy brown mug and handed it to Sarah. "Here. This will make the morning even better."

"Thanks. I think I overslept." Sarah took a welcome sip of coffee. "Can I help you?"

"Just keep me company," Lil said, as she mixed up some pancake batter. "You're an early riser compared to some. Tom's still sawing wood." She indicated the room where Cookie's dad could be heard gently snoring.

Lil poured pancake batter as Sarah watched. Sausages already simmered nearby.

"Is Cookie coming over soon?" Sarah was worried that the first batch of pancakes might get cold before Cookie could join them.

Lil poured more coffee for Sarah and slid several perfect pancakes onto her plate along with a few sausages, and then did the same for herself. A bowl of beautiful fruit was already on the table along with butter and syrup. In case anyone still had room, a plate with small chocolate chip muffins sat nearby.

"Dig in," urged Lil, sitting down herself. "And I'll tell you what's happening."

Sarah took a bite of a light and delicious pancake.

"Is everything okay?" Sarah was beginning to worry why Cookie hadn't joined them yet.

"Oh, things are fine, but it's pretty doubtful that Cookie will be over this morning. She called before. I don't think food is high on her list at the moment. She feels a little green some mornings these days, and with all of the excitement yesterday and going to bed really late, this is one of those exceptionally off days."

"Oh, no." Sarah was concerned about her friend. And they had been so looking forward to seeing each other today. "I hope she'll be okay."

"She'll be fine, although she's plenty disappointed. Jim got on the phone and said that he wants her to take it easy today."

"Good advice," said Sarah.

"I agree. They've had a lot going on, and it's all good, but she needs to slow down a bit."

There was a brief silence as Lil paused to eat some of her pancakes while Sarah finished another delicious forkful of her own.

"Is there anything I can do for her or bring over to her?"

"Thanks. I don't think there's anything, but before you head home, just give her a quick call. Hearing your voice will make her feel better." Lil gave a reassuring smile.

Sarah grinned. "I'll feel better hearing hers, too."

"Join me in a few more pancakes?" Lil was already heading to the stove.

"I will if you will."

Tom soon joined them for a few minutes, wolfing down some pancakes and sausages while they chatted randomly about the latest neighborhood gossip. Soon, though, he stood up and poured himself more coffee.

"I'll let you ladies talk more while I go and catch up on the latest bad headlines."

Sarah sat back, certain she wouldn't need to eat another morsel for the next week. She and Lil remained at the little worn kitchen table chatting companionably.

"So, tell me what's happening with you, Sarah. Are you doing okay?"

Sarah could confide in Lil, but although morning sickness wasn't unusual, Lil was probably worried about Cookie. And Sarah wasn't sure if Cookie should know the whole story yet. If Sarah told Lil, then Lil would tell Cookie. It was time to edit a few details. She decided to begin on a lighter note, laughing about everyone chiding her for leaving Queens.

Lil nodded. "I get it." She lowered her voice. "Speaking of moving—and don't say anything yet because Tom isn't exactly ready for this idea—but Cookie and I have been talking. We think it might be a good idea for us to move out closer to them. There's garden apartments not too far from their house, and then of course we'd be close to the new baby."

"Sounds like a reasonable idea," said Sarah. Lil quickly added that Cookie's sister was on board with this, as well. She'd also moved out in that general direction not long ago.

Lil resumed her normal volume. "So, tell me, Sarah, what about this new job?"

Sarah sighed. "Oh, boy. It's complicated. So here's the thing. You know I needed a change from

Westervale. I was recommended to this employment agent who is like one of our old used car salesmen. Loud jacket, fast talk. You know what I mean."

Lil laughed. "You bet I do."

Sarah then described Dave's sales pitch that led to her current job.

"So do you like it, or should I be getting a sense that there's more to the story, and this isn't quite what you want?"

"I wanted a change, and I got it. But it might be time for another change, and now the employment agent says he's found something bigger and better."

Lil rose and got them some more coffee. "He sounds like a go-getter."

"You have no idea. He really should sell used cars on the side."

Lil grinned as Sarah continued. "Here's the thing. There's something I want to do before I leave this job. There's this homeless woman who usually sits on the church steps next door for a few hours most days. She's not a problem, and I've sort of gotten to know her. Umm, she's not the usual type of homeless person."

A small smile played on Lil's face. "It sounds as if you've been transferring some of your Westervale experience to your new location. And I'm not talking about the business part either."

"Well, yes, that's true, although at first I avoided her because I guess she brought back memories of Westervale. But that's sort of balanced off, and now I'm worried about the woman. You know, alone outside and with crime and all these days. Oh, and her name is May."

"So what do you and May talk about?"

"Well, the truth is that May has some sort of problem. She only seems to say a word or two from time to time. But she appreciates it if I bring her a donut or stop and say hi. And she points to Aunt Addie's old velvet scarf when I wear it. The one with the embroidered flowers."

"I sense there's more to this?" Lil studied Sarah's face carefully.

"Um, I'm thinking that she needs some sort of help. I asked Lorna at Westervale and the priest at the church if they could suggest anything."

Lil burst out laughing. "I swear, Sarah, you should have been a social worker."

"Oh, good heavens, no! I'm not cut out for that. I just want to help May while I'm still at the Butler Agency. But if there's anything I can do, I need to do it soon. You know, in case I might change jobs."

Sarah gulped some more coffee before continuing. "Truthfully, Lil, that job the employment agent is pushing is probably no more exciting than my current one, but it's in midtown and in a larger company. More people, more energy. You get the picture."

"Maybe more social opportunities, too?"

"Well, yeah, that too," mumbled Sarah, the image of an attractive, but off-limits detective flashing quickly through her mind. She reached for a small chocolate chip muffin and changed the subject in an effort to squash that mental picture.

Lil sat back. "I'd say there's plenty that's gone on since I saw you last. Some good changes, although I guess some of them, like your job, are somewhat transitional."

"That's it! Transitional. You're absolutely right."

Sarah bit into the delicious muffin.

"But let me get this straight. You want to do a good deed for May before you move on."

"Exactly."

Lil looked at the aging kitchen cupboard. "You think it's possible that May might have had a stroke or something like that? It could explain her not being able to speak much."

"Maybe. But she hums."

"What does she hum?"

"I haven't figured that out yet."

Tom shuffled into the kitchen for a coffee refill. Then, on second thought, he grabbed a muffin to go with it.

"You ladies doing okay?"

"Yup," said Lil.

He saluted with his cup and shuffled back into the living room and the rest of the newspaper that awaited.

Lil spoke first. "It's a strange coincidence that you're telling me about May right now. Maybe there's a little information I can get."

Sarah sat back in surprise.

"Remember Mrs. Grady from the library volunteers? And her daughter Bridget?" continued Lil. "I saw her just last week. Bridget is doing special research. Something to do with illness or injury in older people. It's for a graduate degree in speech therapy. Can't say as I understood a lot of what she said, but I can ask her. Maybe Bridget would have some ideas."

"That'd be great, Lil. Thanks."

"It's the old neighborhood network, you know?" Lil said. "People talk. Help each other. They keep links between the old and the new. If we move, I'll miss it."

"But then you'll build a new network, right?"

Lil smiled and nodded.

****

Sarah fumbled with her key, but by the time she opened her apartment door that afternoon, the ringing phone had stopped. Whoever wanted her would have to call back. She was tired. But it had been a lovely Thanksgiving and then breakfast today with Lil. She was just sorry Cookie hadn't felt well enough to join them.

Once she'd put Lil's leftover care package in the refrigerator, she kicked off her shoes and sprawled out on the blue couch. In a few minutes, she dozed off.

In what felt like only a few seconds later, the ringing phone startled her out of her nap. Hopefully this wouldn't be an involved conversation. With a groggy groan, Sarah reached for the receiver.

"Miss Quinlee?" The voice on the other end was familiar.

"Yes?"

"Detective Cahill here. Both Detective Rian and I have been trying to reach you today."

Ah, so the police had been at the other end of the ringing phone earlier.

"Yes. Well, I was at a friend's house for Thanksgiving and then out for a while today. You know, busy holiday time." And why did she need to explain her whereabouts to Cahill?

"Sure. Right. Uh, happy Thanksgiving." Cahill sounded awkward on the phone.

"Thanks. You too."

"So, look. We're sorry about the other day. It was an unfortunate emergency."

"That's okay. Happens," she said, quoting the desk sergeant.

Detective Cahill seemed to have a different attitude toward her since the day she'd drawn that sketch. Or maybe she was just imagining things.

"What was it you needed?" he asked.

"I wanted to give you an old write-up with a name. It's really not important."

A commotion in the background interrupted as someone yelled "Cahill."

"Look, can you drop it at the precinct on Monday?"

Again, "Hey, Cahill" sounded in the background. "Rian's already there."

Obviously, he didn't have time to listen to her ridiculous explanation about the ad, and Detective Rian was already off and running someplace.

"Monday's fine," said Sarah, feeling bad she'd started the whole thing in the first place.

"Is after you get off work okay? Both of us'll be tied up until mid-afternoon."

"Yeah, sure. I'll be there. Thanks."

Chapter Nineteen

"What is that woman mailing—a refrigerator?" The man ahead of Sarah on the line was clearly vexed. "Don't think we're going anywhere soon," he muttered.

Sarah had been determined to get to the post office early on Saturday morning to mail Gen's gift. The weather was decent, and she was looking forward to getting out in the fresh air and walking off the holiday meals of the previous two days.

Now, however, she began to question the wisdom of this plan. By the time she'd arrived, the predictable weekend mob was waiting to berate several hapless postal clerks. It was more crowded than usual. The official post-Thanksgiving start to the holidays had begun, with shopping, mailing, and decorating already in the air.

"I've been here twenty minutes already, and this line hasn't moved." The man continued to peer over a few heads. Sarah couldn't see much. The man was huge and blocked her view. His words only helped further agitate a number of people nearby. The diatribes soon began.

"Would it kill them to add an extra clerk today?"

"Budget cuts."

"What? Is the world getting cut?"

Ten minutes later, a minor revolt was in progress. Sarah realized the man had been right. The line wasn't going anywhere fast. Restless feet shuffled in place. The grumbling got louder. Still, she needed to get Gen's gift in the mail. She looked down, carefully checking her errand list to divert her attention.

What she really wanted to do was stop at the florist's shop that Amelia from the crafts fair had recommended and buy some flowers for her new pewter mug. She wanted to sketch it with lovely petals spilling over the top. True, there was a florist near her apartment, but Amelia said A Dozen Roses was exceptional. And it was quite close to this branch of the post office, too, which was why she'd come here in the first place. Plus, the walk had been nice.

Absorbed in her errand list, she jumped when she heard her name called.

"Sarah! What a great surprise."

She looked up to see Matt Andreuws from Rapid Printing. He must have been several spots ahead of her on the line.

"Matt, hi. You actually got to the front of the line? Good for you."

"Not easily. But it looks as if things are finally moving, so you won't have too much longer to go. I'll wait with you," he said in that nice, relaxed voice she remembered from when they'd met at the crafts fair last Saturday. He'd also been doing errands today and getting ready for tomorrow's party.

Matt was right. It didn't take much longer to reach the clerk and hand over her package, although spending a few minutes chatting together certainly made the time pass more quickly. Then the two of them threaded through the growing crowd in search of the exit.

By now Sarah had explained that she was heading

north to the florist's shop. Matt was pleased. It was across the street from Rapid Printing.

"I'll walk you there," he said. "But maybe we could stop for coffee on the way?"

Several minutes later, Matt and Sarah were chatting over steaming mugs of some welcome morning caffeine. The coffee shop was crowded, but they'd managed to squeeze into a snug corner booth next to the window.

"This gives me the chance to tell you what a nice job you did on that recipe book," Sarah said. "I'm really enjoying it."

"Thanks." Matt smiled easily. "The crafts collective was proud of it. They outdid themselves with the recipes and crazy local stories."

"The stories are pretty fascinating. And I've tried a couple of the recipes in the book."

Well, perhaps "going to try" might have been somewhat more accurate.

"Have you made the 'Amazing Ingredient Fruit Pie' yet? It's from Amelia at Crafty Crafts. I saw you went to her table last Saturday after we met."

Interesting that he'd noticed.

"Not yet. But Amelia was so nice. I bought some lovely gifts from her."

"Everyone knows Amelia. And her pie recipe is really good."

Since they were having a nice chat about recipes, why not see if Matt had any details about that page from the book she had so foolishly promised to show the police on Monday.

Was this the main reason she'd agreed to have coffee with him?

"I found a really nice recipe toward the beginning of the book," Sarah said. "It was for the goulash they used to serve at Two Violins restaurant."

Matt burst out laughing. "That was legendary. And so was the restaurant. Two Violins was way before my time, though. But when they closed, anyone who ever ate there insisted on knowing the secret ingredients of the goulash."

"Then it really must have been popular. The restaurant, too."

"It was. One of our old customers showed me pictures of it. The place was huge, with a dance floor. They had live music, too."

"With all of that and a killer goulash recipe, no wonder it was popular."

Matt grinned. "I guess it must have been. But it closed after World War II. Evidently things changed then. But hey, you should also try the recipe for the wonderful stew they used to make at the Zigeuner Café. Now that's the place I knew growing up. It was small and quiet. A nice place to relax."

Matt took a sip of coffee. His hazel eyes looked searchingly at Sarah as he continued. "Anyway, the Zigeuner was right upstairs in the same building as Rapid Printing's office. So I remember it very well. But like a lot of things around here, it closed a while ago, and everyone misses it. That stew was special, and so were their desserts. You should also try making the recipe for meringue cookies with chocolate bits, especially since you said you like chocolate." Matt smiled and continued reminiscing. "People liked the place for a quiet meal. They had live music, too. A zither player."

"I don't think I've ever heard a zither."

"Just wait till tomorrow. If you come to the party, you can hear one for yourself."

"So what's there now?" she asked.

"Just the remains of the old café. The owner retired in poor health and left everything. Just dropped all of it and left. No one ever cleared it out, took it over, or even rented the floor. I got permission from the building owner to use it for the party tomorrow. Basically, there's still some old-timers in the area who wanted to see it one last time before the building empties out."

"The building's going to be empty?" Sarah was confused.

"Yeah. The café's long gone. None of the apartments upstairs are rented anymore. I moved most of the business operations and most of myself out a while ago. There're not many local customers anymore. It's time to officially close here and go where more companies are moving into corporate complexes. In my case, it's an office park called The Cove, just a little north of the city. It's in a gorgeous setting, and there's a lot more potential business. I'm just wrapping up the final details here. Once the office itself is gone, the building will be empty."

"Oh." Sarah sipped her coffee thoughtfully. Just as the recipe book indicated, a lot of local places had closed.

Time to ask something important.

"So, Matt, speaking of your building going to be empty, I saw that the couple who owned Milaeve Engraving used to eat that goulash a lot at Two Violins. And then when I looked at the little historic story that went with the recipe, I realized their business was in the

137

same building you're in now. Small world! And you mentioned that the Zigeuner Café was there, too. Wonder if they ever ate at the cafe."

Matt looked into Sarah's eyes, curiosity forming in them. "Good question. You sure paid attention to those little stories in the book. All I know is, like the recipe book said, everyone remembered they loved that goulash at Two Violins. But they were gone, though, by the time the Zigeuner opened."

He paused to look out at the street for a minute, and then turned back to Sarah. "My dad rented Milaeve's space just before I was born. They'd already moved. Anyway, our location was the same, but my dad's business was strictly ordinary printing, no engraving. The Zigeuner upstairs opened when I was a kid, so I knew it growing up. But then I went upstate to college and only came back to run the printing business when my dad passed away. By then, the café was closed." He smiled. "My story in a nutshell."

There was a slight pause.

Matt looked directly into her eyes. "By the way, I hope you're coming tomorrow. You'll enjoy seeing what's left of the old café. Glad I'm able to use it."

"I'm looking forward to it."

Matt didn't have much information about the Milaeves, but he certainly seemed to want her to come to the party.

Sarah took another sip of her coffee. The place was getting more crowded, and they'd have to leave soon. She glanced out the window at the street. A busy Saturday.

But then her eyes widened as a familiar face hurried by.

The obnoxious, copper-haired teen.

The moment he caught a glimpse of Sarah in the window, his expression turned quickly into the one he'd worn when she and Gianni confronted him. Unmistakable fear.

****

Sarah was taken aback, but she didn't say anything to Matt. He probably never even saw the teen. Nevertheless, she was glad for Matt's company as they walked to A Dozen Roses. It helped lessen her alarm. And yet the teen's face had offered no threat. He looked genuinely distraught when he saw Sarah.

A Dozen Roses, as Matt said, was across the street from Rapid Printing. Both buildings were old, perhaps dating back to the turn of the century. The florist occupied a tiny ground-level space, crammed full of beautiful flowers, both inside and out. But the second floor of Rapid Printing's building immediately caught Sarah's eye. Its generous framed windows were distinctive, gently curving out from the main façade. Both places would make a nice sketch.

Matt brought her inside A Dozen Roses and introduced her to Jake, a young man whose family ran the shop. He was in charge that morning.

"I met Amelia at a big crafts fair," explained Sarah. "She said your flowers are wonderful. And, of course, so did Matt."

A smile spread across Jake's face.

"Anyway," she continued, "I want to buy a little bunch of flowers—something violet maybe—to put in a pewter mug I bought from Amelia."

"That had to have been the anniversary crafts fair," said the young man. "It was a big deal. We all know

139

Amelia. She stops in to say hello and chat with my family and even with the previous owner when he comes by. Amelia enjoys talking about the old days."

Ah, the old neighborhood network again.

While Matt exchanged a few quiet words with Jake, Sarah wandered among the flowers, picking out some fresh violets. The young florist packaged them for her as she and Matt chatted.

A mere few steps outside the shop, Matt and Sarah paused before she continued on her way.

"This is for you, Sarah." Matt handed her a delicately wrapped single, long-stemmed rose. He must have requested it while she'd been browsing. "See you tomorrow at the party."

Out of the corner of her eye, Sarah saw Jake, still inside, but very close to the door. He watched them with rapt interest.

****

That night, Sarah relaxed with her sketchpad. She'd already created a number of simple drawings of the people and places that had come into her life over the past few months. Now, she added a little shading to the one of Amelia, her sharp gaze still prominent in Sarah's memory. Next, she tried to capture the overflowing charm of the florist's shop and the captivating window in Rapid Printing's building. These were drafts, and she'd need to revisit them to focus on more of the finer details. She also began the first of what would be several sketches of her pewter mug, now with its intricate lacing of petals spilling gracefully over the top.

Then, there was Matt. Her pencil lingered over the page as she began sketching his profile, trying to capture the defining character of his face. She also created a simple likeness of the beautiful rose he had given her, now in a slender bud vase. It had been a sweet gesture.

Sarah vowed to return to all of these sketches soon. She'd choose her favorites and create more elaborate and polished versions of them.

Sighing contentedly, she flipped through each page again. Sketching was something she loved. It filled her leisure moments with joy and absorbed her attention when she was upset.

Now, though, she came to her sketch of Gil Rian. She quickly turned the page with a quiet whisper of sadness.

Chapter Twenty

"I'm so glad you're here." Matt greeted her the moment she arrived at the party. He now took a moment to admire her dress. "You look beautiful, Sarah."

Sarah had chosen a pretty burgundy sheath to wear and then selected a small pair of sparkly earrings to go with it. After all, it was a party.

Matt led her upstairs to the old, abandoned café. Guests were already gathered there. Despite a lingering musty aroma, the place had a true old-world appeal. Little tables and chairs dotted the floor. Sarah's eyes were immediately drawn to the vibrant posters of musicians, dancers, and vintage street scenes lining the walls. How charming this place must have been in its day, and now it had come to life for one more time.

The sweet sound of a graceful waltz floated gently in the air. It came from a discreet corner spot where a man deftly performed on an elegant stringed instrument resting on a table. A zither perhaps?

A long table with platters, heaped high with tempting little sandwiches and pastries, stood at one end of the room. Coffee and champagne were featured at the other. Matt wasted no time in bringing Sarah a slender flute of sparkling liquid. He touched his glass to hers.

"To new beginnings."

They moved closer to listen to the music and studied the posters in the background.

"Thanks, Matt. This is wonderful. And now you must tell me—is that a zither?"

Matt nodded. "He's one of the last of his kind around here. No one plays this anymore."

"Too bad. It has such a beautiful sound."

Matt smiled into her eyes as Sarah continued.

"What a lovely space. It seems a shame no one took it over. And now that you're moving, it will all be gone." She wondered if Matt was going elsewhere as much to avoid local changes and crime as for additional business.

"It's time," he said. "Building's been sold and will be torn down."

Another place to be torn down?

They were silent for a few minutes, standing side by side, listening to the music.

Then Matt placed a hand on the small of her back, leading her over to a tray of elegant tea sandwiches. "Here. Try some of these, Sarah. They're really good." He then pointed to a nearby silver dish filled with little cookies. "Those are the meringue cookies with chocolate bits I was telling you about. They're the best."

Sarah grabbed two little sandwiches and several cookies as Matt excused himself to greet an older couple who had just arrived. She tried one of the cookies first and had to admit they were exceptional.

More people were entering the room. Among them were Amelia and Grace from Crafty Crafts. Sarah walked over to say hello. "Hi, I'm Sarah. We met at the crafts collective's fair last week. I bought a lovely wooden jewel box and a little pewter mug from you."

A smile spread across the creases in Amelia's face, giving it an almost youthful glow. "Of course. You bought a gift for your friend and one for yourself. Some of those nice silver bookmarks, too."

The woman certainly had a sharp memory.

"You loved that little mug," she continued. "I hope you're enjoying it."

"Definitely. I went to A Dozen Roses yesterday, the place you recommended. And I took your suggestion and bought some purple violets. The flowers look perfect in the mug. I'm drawing some sketches of it. I'll bring you one."

"I'd like that." Amelia nodded, clearly pleased. "Oh, and I remember you won the peppermint basket in the raffle, but you exchanged it for our recipe book."

Nothing escaped Amelia.

Grace joined in, brushing away an escaped strand of her brown hair. "You looked relieved to give away all that peppermint. I don't know what I would have done with it either."

"Now if it had been chocolate…" said Sarah.

The three of them continued chatting amiably while sampling the delicious food. They admired the lovely windows high above the street, noting the singular angle of the view. The pleasant hum of party-like chatter and laughter filled the room as it became more crowded. Sarah recognized another face or two, perhaps from the crafts fair. She waved to Jake, the young florist, who nodded in return.

When Matt joined them again, Grace and Amelia wandered toward the coffee table, possibly to give Sarah and Matt a few private moments. Just as Matt had promised, he made sure she didn't feel alone, even though she came to the party by herself. Once more, he took her hand and led her closer to the zither player who now serenaded the room with an operetta medley by Lehar. On the wall behind him was a vibrant poster of a young couple dancing and another of an energetic young woman playing the violin. Sarah studied these closely.

"Sarah. Here we are—only just met—and I'm moving." He gave that casual smile again. "Can you drop by the office during the week? I'm going to put together a gift for you. A couple of smaller replicas of these old posters you've been admiring."

"That's so nice of you, Matt."

The party was in full swing now, and as Matt greeted a few more guests, Sarah was able to chat with several others and sample more of the food. In a little while, though, the room grew increasingly crowded. It seemed as if the entire neighborhood wanted to see the old café one more time. Sarah felt it was nearing time to leave. When Matt next joined her, she offered genuine thanks for inviting her to the event.

"I'm so happy you came. And I'd love to get together before I officially move. And afterward, too." Matt spoke softly. "I won't be moving far at all. And as bad a cook as I am, I'll even make the Zigeuner Café's famous stew for you whenever you'd like."

He pulled out a business card. "Here's all my contact information—my new business address and number at The Cove corporate park and all of my new home details. Maybe you can give me your number when you stop in this week." He pressed the card into her hand and planted a quick kiss on her cheek. Matt left no question about his interest in her, and it was obvious to anyone lingering nearby.

Sarah was at a loss for words for a moment, nice as Matt surely was. But Grace and Amelia approached just then, and Sarah tucked the business card deep into her dressy purse. All three women offered profuse thanks to Matt and then left the party together.

The fresh air outside was welcome. They walked and chatted until Amelia said goodbye a few blocks later when they reached the corner of her street. Sarah and Grace continued on. They didn't live far from each other.

"You're lucky. Matt really likes you," said Grace. She sighed, her next words filled with longing. "If I were only a few years younger…"

Sarah was embarrassed. "He seems like a nice person. The party was good, too."

Changing the subject, she said how delighted she was with her Crafty Crafts gifts and how well-loved Amelia seemed to be by the entire community.

Grace thanked her, but there was a tinge to her voice. "Amelia's a wonderful woman, but age is catching up."

Sarah nodded, thinking of the people at Westervale. "Happens to all of us eventually, I guess," she said. "But Amelia seems pretty sharp and energetic."

"So it seems, but I'm a little worried. Amelia loves talking about the old days. Maybe too much." She lowered her voice a bit, although no one on the street would have even cared about their conversation. "We all see people who look like someone else we used to know. Then we realize they just remind us of that person. But it's getting more frequent with Amelia."

Sarah wondered where this was going.

"When she thought she saw a former neighbor and it turned out to be someone else, I thought maybe her eyesight wasn't what it used to be. But back at the end of the summer, she swore the dressmaker's daughter from years ago was walking up some brownstone stairs nearby. It was a place that'd been vacant and was just torn down. Next, it was the old baker's cousin passing by our shop window. Oh, and a week later, it was one of the men from the singing society that folded way back. I assumed he'd have moved long ago." Grace frowned. "Then, back in October, Amelia insisted she saw the old engraver's son, Vincent, walking on Lexington Avenue with a friend. I mean, really! That whole family's been gone for decades. No one would recognize the son now, even Amelia." Grace shook her head. "To be truthful, I'm really worried that Amelia's losing her grip."

Sarah did her best to hide her shock.

Was Amelia falling victim to old age? Or was she just exceptionally observant?

Chapter Twenty-One

A small reindeer balloon completed its final dizzy sail through the air just as Sarah walked in the door. It deflated with a vulgar squeal, landing near her feet. Close by, a handful of young women in elfin hats stood clustered around a dwarfish Christmas tree. They were midway through butchering an *a cappella* rendition of "Santa Claus is Coming to Town."

It was Monday after work, and Sarah had arrived for her appointment at the police precinct. But now she wondered if she'd come to the right place. Venturing farther inside, she spied several half-empty cookie plates on a side table, a small knot of people dropping assorted crumbs nearby. The "donations" sign on the shiny, foil-covered box near the tree explained it all. It was the kick-off to an annual holiday toy drive.

Sarah side-stepped her way across the room to avoid some restless little kids, their mothers chatting at high decibel levels. A couple of hapless young cops in uniform had clearly been assigned to minimize the chaos. From the look of things, their efforts weren't too successful.

It was entertaining, though, compared with Sarah's previous trip to the precinct. By the time she reached an amused Sergeant Brushie, she'd almost forgotten her anxiety over the purpose of her visit—to give the two detectives the recipe page with the old Milaeve engraving advertisement. And now, she had additional information for them from her weekend.

Two small children zigzagged near the sergeant's desk until a mother plucked one from their energetic game. It was time for the boys to say their farewells.

"Bye, Mikey," said the boy who had to leave. "See you tomorrow."

"Bye," said his friend, walking over to the desk just as Sarah arrived there.

"Ah, Miss Quinlee," said Sergeant Brushie. "You're just in time to meet my little friend. This is Mikey."

The boy was probably no more than four years old, although Sarah wasn't a good judge of kids' ages. He looked at Sergeant Brushie, who nodded. Then the boy solemnly said "Hi."

Sarah smiled. "Nice to meet you, Mikey. I'm Sarah."

Sergeant Brushie invited them both to sit in the two chairs nearest him. "Start of the local toy drive. 'Tis the crazy season." He inclined his head in the direction of the inner room and addressed Sarah. "They'll be with you in a couple of minutes."

"My friend and I helped trim the tree," volunteered Mikey suddenly.

"You did a nice job," said Sarah.

At that moment, a jolt of recognition shot through her as she looked at Mikey. Could this be the same little boy who was with Gil Rian at the museum? The one who had hugged him? Sarah glanced at the boy's gently wavy hair and swallowed hard. She wanted to run.

But she had to keep on talking…or something. After all, the detectives were expecting her to meet with them. Running was out of the question. Her eye landed on a blank pad of paper in front of Sergeant Brushie, who was enjoying the holiday scene in front of him.

"May I?" She pointed to the pad and pencil. He nodded and pushed them in her direction.

"So, Mikey," she said, quickly dashing a few strokes on the paper. "What do you think? Did I remember everything?" The boy watched with growing interest, as Sarah swiftly created a simple tree and a toy collection box. A little teddy bear was trying to climb out over the top. A reindeer balloon flew low nearby, a few musical notes spewing from its mouth.

"Look." Mikey laughed. "The reindeer's flying, and the teddy bear's trying to climb out."

"I think they want cookies," Sarah said. "Would you like to have this?"

Mikey nodded as Sarah carefully removed the page and handed it to him.

Another familiar head of wavy hair appeared from the inside office. But at that moment, Detective Rian was intercepted by a woman who had been near the Christmas tree. It was definitely the pretty woman who'd been with him at the museum.

"Gil," she called, running over. She pointed to the group of singers as he whispered something to her. She smiled and nodded.

Sarah had no idea where to look as he approached the sergeant's desk.

Gil Rian's face lit up when he saw Sarah. Her heart plunged somewhere near her feet.

"Sarah, thanks so much for coming in."

Sarah nodded. She was beginning to wonder if she'd be able to speak at all now.

"Amanda brought some of her student nurses over to help us kick off the toy drive."

"That's great." Sarah barely choked out the words.

Mikey held up the sketch for Gil to see. "Look at what Sarah drew for me." And without taking another breath, he ran to over to his mother. "Mom, Mom. Look at this."

Just then, someone blew into a pitch pipe that was two tones higher than Sergeant Brushie's ringing phone. The student nurses, perhaps not sure which sound was their rightful cue, broke into a spirited and wildly off-key rendition of "Rudolph, the Red-Nosed Reindeer."

Sarah sat back. It was a relief not to have to talk for few moments.

Applause marked the end of the song. Then the remaining visitors headed for the door as the nursing student choraleers waved enthusiastically to their departing audience.

Now what?

Mikey dashed back at high speed. Amanda was close behind.

The little boy looked up. "We have to leave now, Uncle Gil," he said.

Uncle Gil?? What?? Uncle??

That might explain the same wavy hair.

"Sarah, this is my sister, Amanda."

Amanda had the same smile as her brother and grasped Sarah's hand warmly, while Sarah tried putting a coherent greeting together. She was convinced her face had turned several colors during the previous thirty seconds.

"We better catch up to our student nurses, Mikey."

Then she turned to Sarah and Sergeant Brushie. "They're all coming to our apartment." She looked frantic.

"We're going to have pizza," Mikey announced. "And I'm going to show them this." He pointed to Sarah's sketch.

Sarah grinned as the two of them rushed off. Now she struggled to breathe and sort out the events of the past few minutes.

"It was lovely meeting your family, Detective Rian…"

"Gil," he said to her with that beautiful smile.

Sergeant Brushie ended yet another phone call. He turned to Gil and Sarah. "You're wanted inside. Ho, ho, ho!"

****

"Miss Quinlee. Good to see you." Detective Cahill seemed in a jolly mood. "Hope you enjoyed the festivities."

They all sat down. "That I did." Sarah was still in a fog of amazement.

"So, you have some information for us?"

Sarah handed him the folded pieces of paper from the crafts fair recipe book and described how she'd come by this information. Cahill studied the pages carefully.

"You wanted to give us a recipe for Hungarian goulash?" There was a slight hint of humor in his voice.

"Good grief, no! Please, look at the description in the text with the name and the location. And I copied the page that said where it was printed, too. But now I'm figuring you probably knew about this, so maybe it's not all that important," said Sarah.

Cahill looked up at Sarah as he quietly passed the pages to Gil. "Actually, we didn't know all that much."

"Oh, well, then I'm glad I came in. But that ad was from a long time ago and it still might not mean anything. And I was feeling really foolish for even trying to bring this in last week. But you said you wanted to know if anyone had heard that name. Umm, now there's a little more."

Both men looked at her patiently.

"Well, as of the weekend, there's more." Sarah looked at the top Cahill's desk, waited a beat, and then plunged ahead. "Believe me, things just sort of started happening."

There was a flicker of something on Cahill's face at her statement. Perhaps it was the start of the coming explosion that was sure to erupt at some point.

Beginning with the post office and running into Matt, she mentioned her shock at seeing the obnoxious teen through the coffee shop window. Then she emphasized that her main goal had been to go to A Dozen Roses.

They both listened intently as she continued.

"Uh, the lady at the crafts fair said the florist was excellent." Sarah then outlined her brief visit there. She specifically added that she really did buy some flowers to sketch.

Best to edit out the part about the rose.

Cahill leaned back as the rest of her story unfolded.

Then came Sunday's party. "Oh, and here's the invitation. Matt said it'd be interesting to see the old café upstairs that also had a recipe in the book. I mean, I was curious. It was in the same building where Milaeve's business had been."

Cahill carefully looked at the invitation before handing it to Gil.

"Invitation for two," said Cahill. "So you grabbed a date and went."

"Umm, no." Sarah couldn't look at Gil, although she was curious about his reaction. "I went by myself. But then at the party, I ran into Amelia and Grace. You know, the nice women I told you about from that table at the crafts fair. So we ate a lot of food and talked and admired all the old decorations. It was nice to see a sort of landmark, since they're going to tear down the building. Then Amelia and Grace and I left together."

"And that's it?" asked Cahill.

Sarah took a deep breath. "Not exactly. There's more."

"More? You're one busy person."

Sarah recounted the story about Amelia thinking she'd recognized some people on the street, including a very much alive Vincent Milaeve.

A heavy silence followed. The detectives looked at each other and then back at Sarah.

"Maybe Amelia's not quite as imaginative as Grace might think," Gil said.

"Yeah. That's what I thought, too. Look, nothing adds up here. I feel like I walked into the middle of a movie and got lost. You probably think I'm a lunatic, but there's too many coincidences since I started this job. And Amelia could just be having problems with aging. I used to work in a senior facility, so I've seen this before. But *everything* feels off." Sarah hesitated before adding something that had been on her mind. "I know that Vincent Milaeve's death might be a random street crime but, umm, could it be more?"

Cahill looked at the ceiling. "Anything's possible. They say there are no coincidences. And sometimes people and things aren't what they appear to be. Some really hardened criminals can seem quite nice. And even sweet old ladies can be sharper than we think."

Gil chimed in. "You're right. Something doesn't add up. And we don't think you're a lunatic." His eyes were serious. "And we definitely don't want you getting into any danger."

It was Cahill's turn now. "Miss Quinlee." He took a long, deep breath, as if for strength. "Sarah, if I may, since you seem to have become a frequent visitor here."

Sarah nodded. And waited.

"Look, Sarah, we don't want you walking into a hornet's nest. And we know you know that Gianni remembered about the Milaeves, too. He came in today about an hour before you."

"Right. He told me when I went in to say happy Thanksgiving last week." Sarah paused. "I keep thinking about Amelia. She seems so observant. And everyone knows and likes her."

Cahill chewed his lip in exasperation. "And that's probably all true."

"But she could also be in trouble for mentioning the name of a murdered man, mistaken identity or not," said Gil. "Whether or not she knew he'd been killed after she saw him." He continued, his face etched with worry. "We really appreciate your coming to us with everything. We'll follow up on all of it. But please, Sarah. Don't put yourself in any danger."

Cahill picked up from there. "Look, Sarah. You're an honest and good person. I can see that. But even honest and good people can get into real trouble trying to be Nancy Drew."

Funny, but she really hadn't thought of it that way until now. But maybe she really had been trying to do some amateur sleuthing. Just from curiosity, though.

Could there really have been more to Milaeve's death?

Cahill closed his eyes as if trying to shut out a memory. "Believe me, I've seen trouble happen. Especially with decent people like you."

"Thanks for your compliment, Detective Cahill, about being honest and good and all that. But when we first met, I really thought you believed I murdered that man and that I was awful."

Gil looked pained, and Cahill more so. "No, Sarah. I never believed that." Cahill glanced quickly at Gil before continuing. "I need to apologize for that day. There had just been another case…" Again, he closed his eyes. "Look, you were there early on a desolate street not unknown to a crime or two, and I could see how things might not have turned out so okay. I was frustrated and my nerves got the better of me. The timing wasn't good."

"Okay, I understand."

There was a pause before Gil spoke. "Sarah, please come to us first if something doesn't seem right. We don't want anything to happen to you."

Cahill continued. "And Sarah, *please* cut the sleuthing. I should lecture you more, only he'd get upset." He nodded in Gil's direction.

"I'll do my best." Sarah grinned, and so did Gil. And it almost appeared as if Cahill came as close to a smile as was possible for him.

Cahill had some paperwork to finish, so Gil and

Sarah headed out the door together. They chatted for a minute or two, each unwilling to say goodbye. Finally, Gil turned directly to her. "Sarah, if you're free, would you like to go out for something to eat now? I promise, no more talk about the case or police business."

"I'd really like that."

****

True to Gil's word, they didn't discuss any police business as they lingered over enormous burgers, fries, and beer at a pub in Sarah's neighborhood. They got caught up in each other's life stories. By the time they'd started eating, any previous awkwardness started to fade, replaced by a sense of ease in their conversation.

"You wanted to go to law school?" Sarah asked, incredulous at this intriguing admission.

"No Perry Mason stuff. I come from a family of cops. They probably wouldn't speak to me if I'd done that." He laughed. "I'm just kidding actually. We all cheered my brother on when he decided to leave and get into corporate security management. In my case, I switched from law into a graduate program in police science instead. I'm almost finished. We'll see where it goes from there, whether in the department or for something else. But that's all in the future."

"Sounds like you have a good plan," said Sarah. She then confided about her jobs and her eventual wish to add art into the mix somehow.

"You should. You have real talent, Sarah."

They shared details about family, friends, interests, and even though it was getting late, they both ended the evening reluctantly, continuing to chat as Gil walked Sarah home.

On the way, they stopped abruptly in front of a new

demolition site—a diminutive, old building recently gone. Dust and decay were heavy in the air, a last remnant of the hopes and dreams of the people whose lives had once been entwined with the place.

"They're coming down more these days," Sarah said, peering at the debris behind a restraining fence, some still visible despite the darkness. She had an urge to sketch it, to capture the passing of the old neighborhood. If only she'd paid attention to the place before it was gone.

"Probably the last tenant moved," commented Gil. "Then the building owner either abandoned it or dumped it on a speculator."

"The last tenant?" Sarah remembered her conversation with Matt about this.

"Sometimes an owner just runs it down, hoping everyone will move out. And sometimes they make it hard for the last renter or business to stay. Or the owner just can't keep it up. Three or four floors out of five will be empty and that's the signal the place won't be there for long. Especially these old buildings if they haven't been repaired."

They stood and scrutinized the rubble for a couple of minutes before moving on.

"Thanks for having dinner with me, Sarah," said Gil. "I'm glad it worked out."

"Thanks for asking. I really enjoyed tonight."

"Can we do this again?" He hesitated a beat. "Maybe Saturday?"

"That'd be great."

"I've wanted to ask you out before, but people were always around, and…" He halted for a second. "I wanted to be sure it was okay to ask." There was almost a question in his voice.

Ah, he had definitely sensed her backing away after she'd misinterpreted that family scene at the museum. No wonder he'd hesitated.

Sarah smiled. "It's definitely okay."

Chapter Twenty-Two

Sarah caught up with Father Haney after a brief visit to the church on her way to work.

"Father, could I come to the library sometime this week and take a look at those old photos on the library wall again?" Something was nagging at her about the photos.

"Of course."

They both looked over at May on her usual step.

"I didn't forget about our friend," said the priest. "I'm waiting for some people to return my calls. It's been slow because of Thanksgiving. I'll let you know as soon as I hear something."

Sarah thanked him and then walked over to sit briefly with May before heading to work.

"Hi, May." She reached into her shoulder bag and took out a small individual sketch she'd drawn of the woman. "Here. I made this for you."

May took the drawing and studied it carefully. Sarah had shaded her hat, highlighting the texture of the finely woven applique and arranging the escaping strands of hair to emphasize May's soft expression. The sketch made her look younger and brought out the sweetness that Sarah knew the woman possessed.

She looked up at Sarah with tears in her eyes. "May?" she whispered.

Sarah nodded, stunned she had said her own name.

May must have said her name to the city social worker, too, the one the cops mentioned. How else would they have known it?

"For you, May," said Sarah, squeezing her hand, again aware of the worn, yet stylish gloves the woman wore. May squeezed her hand gently in return.

"I have to go to work now. I'll see you soon." Sarah smiled.

****

Mrs. Butler seemed to trill as she flew into the conference room that morning where Sarah and Kelly were deep into her organizing project. Old files, loose papers, books, correspondence—there was a lot to go through and put in reasonable order. They agreed to work on it at least two or three times this week.

"Fabulous job, girls!" Mrs. Butler circled the table and stared at the neat piles they'd made on the floor against the wall. "Would it be better if we had boxes that could be labeled? It might be easier to organize everything this way, uh, temporarily."

"Sure," said Sarah, wondering about how temporary this arrangement might be. Or would everything stay in those boxes according to some other plan? "It would be more…organized."

Kelly nodded with a questioning glance at Sarah.

"I promise I'll order some," Mrs. Butler said, while producing a box of another sort and setting it on a side table.

"More candy?" asked Kelly.

"From Urban Woodwork. Another thank you gift."

"If these are thank you gifts," said Sarah, "I can't imagine what Christmas will be like."

Edgar appeared. He always seemed to know when

there was food or candy around.

"Help yourselves, all of you," said Mrs. Butler, grabbing several pieces for herself before fluttering out the door.

****

After sampling Urban Woodwork's candy, Sarah wasn't hungry for her sandwich at lunchtime. Besides, she had questions that were bothering her, and Gianni might be able to help.

The twinkling chimes alerted the man that someone had come to visit.

"Hi, Gianni. How was your holiday?"

"It was perfect, Sarah." Gianni beamed and pulled his chair from behind the counter. "How about you?"

"Wonderful. But it seems like ages ago." Sarah sat in her now familiar spot.

They spent several minutes catching up on holiday dinners as well as the adventures of Gianni's family. Finally, Sarah told him she needed to talk.

"It's about Edgar. You mentioned how shy he was as a kid. And kind of frail and always wearing glasses. And you said he was sick a lot and couldn't eat some kinds of foods?" Sarah cleared her throat. "This is going to sound silly, but would you happen to remember what foods he couldn't eat? I know this is ancient history, but…" Sarah's voice trailed off.

Gianni studied her carefully before speaking. "It was a long time ago, but you know how sometimes a crazy little memory sticks with you?"

Sarah nodded as he continued.

"Way back when, there was some sort of special holiday event in the school cafeteria. At the end, each kid was given a small bag with a few trinkets and candies. But they weren't supposed to open the bags until they got home." Gianni shook his head. "A few of us parents volunteered to be there, and we were talking as the kids lined up. A couple of them palmed a piece or two of their candy and gobbled it up."

Sarah laughed. "We all did stuff like that."

Gianni smiled. "But then there was Edgar. He always obeyed the rules, but you know kids. Anyway, he was eating a small piece of candy. Well, his mother saw it and ran screaming at him to put it down. We thought she was mad because he broke the rules."

"Kids will be kids," said Sarah, sort of happy that Edgar had chanced walking on the wild side a little, even if only for a treat.

"Yeah, but later on we found out that he was only supposed to keep the trinkets when he got home and not eat the candy. He had a really sensitive stomach. There were some foods he needed to stay away from, and candy was one of them. He just didn't tolerate it well. But he was still a kid and probably figured this was his big opportunity. I felt sorry for him."

Gianni cleared his throat. "Well, Mrs. Frainie was upset. Then Edgar started looking a little green and they left. By itself, it wasn't unusual. Kids get into candy, and it backfires. But later, word spread that no one should give Edgar candy. There were a couple of other things, too. I don't really remember. But that candy incident sticks out in my mind."

Sarah studied her hands for a moment before speaking. "Gianni," she finally said. "Did Edgar's twin have any issues with food or candy?"

"Not that I can recall. You have to realize, though, that this was a long time ago. And Edgar and his brother were older than my boys." His gaze was quizzical. "Why do you ask?"

She felt she could trust Gianni. "This will sound weird."

"Go ahead, Sarah. It's okay."

For the next few minutes, Sarah confided how Edgar regularly gobbled up candy with gusto at work, even to this morning with that new box of chocolates. Then she described seeing him at a distance that Sunday morning walking out of the church service without his glasses. Finally, she confessed how she'd retrieved his dropped glasses at work and could have sworn they were clear, non-prescription lenses.

"I mean at the office, he seems shy, well-meaning, and sort of sad. It fits the description of him as a kid. But the glasses and the food really keep bothering me."

Gianni looked over at the shelves for a long moment and then back at Sarah. "I suppose people can outgrow food sensitivities. You're sure about those glasses?"

"Not a hundred percent. And I know people wear contact lenses now sometimes. But when I put it all together, I started to wonder. Umm, Edgar's twin brother died, right?" Sarah hesitated, scrunching up her face in anticipation of her next words. "But is there a possibility that *our* Edgar might not really be Edgar at all? I feel weird saying it, but could it be his twin brother?"

"You mean still alive and posing as Edgar?" Gianni looked stunned. "But why?"

"I was just going to ask you the same thing."

****

Sarah couldn't concentrate all afternoon. She was

relieved to have confided in Gianni. But she felt silly, too. Her suspicions seemed farfetched when she'd actually voiced them out loud. By the end of the workday, she'd gotten distracted and lost track of time, cutting things too close after missing the first downtown train to get to the bank interview Dave set up for her.

When she arrived, she flew down the hall past a group of young people and pushed through the glass doors marked Human Resources. Yes, it was a real business in a real building with lots of people and social opportunities. Right now, though, Sarah just caught her breath, smoothed her hair, and announced her name to the receptionist.

Soon, an impeccable middle-aged man in a blue, three-piece suit and glasses whisked her into his office. She thanked the man for agreeing to meet with her after regular business hours. It was hard to stop staring at his glasses. Were they real or not?

Suspicions about Edgar were definitely getting to her.

"It's quite nice to see a candidate who's responsible to their current job," the man said. "No making excuses about a dentist appointment to sneak away during the day."

Why was the dentist always the culprit?

The man was nice enough. He outlined the job— writing benefits descriptions, talking to new staff, handling forms, learning the ropes—whatever those ropes were. It was an exciting work environment, room for growth, and so forth. At least he didn't twirl a cheap ballpoint pen.

Then the inevitable question came up. "So, I see

you've only been working a few months at the Butler Agency. Any particular reason you want to leave now?"

What could she say? Perhaps now wasn't the perfect time? *Not until helping a homeless woman, sorting out the lunacy at work, and trying to solve what she now believed to be a real murder. Maybe because she'd been the one who found the body?*

"Dave and I discussed it carefully," Sarah began in her most professional voice. "We both feel there's a real chance to grow here and that I'd be able to contribute more in a larger environment such as this one. Of course, if I come under serious consideration for the job, then I would do everything to make leaving the Butler Agency as smooth as possible for them."

But suppose it wouldn't be smooth? Suppose something was terribly amiss?

The man seemed satisfied. "All right, I'd like to set up an interview for you with the department manager. If I can swing it for this time, would that work? Perhaps next week?"

"Sure. I'd appreciate that."

****

The day had been nonstop. But after Sarah got home and had barely finished a dinner of quickly heated canned ravioli and green beans, the phone rang. It was Cookie with an invitation to visit on Sunday. And she begged Sarah to bring both her sketchpad and her stories.

No sooner had they signed off when Lorna called.

"Tried you last night," she began, "but you must have been out partying."

"That's in the right ballpark," said Sarah with a smile. "Will tell all when I see you."

"You better. But in the meantime, I found someone you can talk to about that homeless woman. It's a start anyway. Grab a pencil. I'll give you her name and number."

After her calls, Sarah sank back, exhausted, on the blue sofa. The crafts collective's recipe book was still there, and she couldn't resist picking it up and leisurely turning its pages once more. There was that goulash recipe from Two Violins, the dish that the Milaeves had loved so much so long ago. The couple with the same last name as the murdered man.

The quotes from the Gaspar family who owned the restaurant and from the headwaiter, Lel Vandert, were a nice touch. Sarah read everything on the page again and then chuckled to herself. Maybe the reason she kept coming back to the page was because she was curious about the goulash and why it had been so popular. She should try making it soon.

This brought a pang of guilt as she thought of Matt and his offer to make the Zigeuner Café's delicious stew recipe for her. Nice as he was and flattering as his attention had been, she just wasn't drawn to him the way she'd been drawn to Gil. But she still needed to figure out how to spare Matt's feelings and graciously decline any future overtures if he got in touch.

Chapter Twenty-Three

With a cheerful thumbs up the next morning, Kelly motioned Sarah over to her desk.

"Dave is really getting things going." Kelly spoke in an excited whisper. "He's setting up a couple of appointments. You know, I might need to 'go to the dentist' for a few hours."

They both smiled at this well-worn code for a job interview.

But weren't most employers on to this ploy by now?

The moment Sarah got to her desk, the phone rang. As she could have predicted, the familiar voice on the other end was Dave.

"Just checking in. First, thanks for sending Kelly my way. She's a great candidate."

"You're welcome."

"Next. The personnel guy at the bank loves you. If all goes well after you meet with the department manager next week, I think I can smell an offer."

Sarah imagined him twirling his ever-present ballpoint pen. Circling in on the deal.

"Look, Sarah. I know it doesn't sound like the most exciting job, but there's some hidden potential there, and I think you'll find this one particularly intriguing, given all we've discussed about your goals. And it's a steppingstone."

Hadn't he said this about the Butler Agency, too? The stepping stone part anyway.

"Just go for the next-level interview and check it out."

"I will," said Sarah. "And I really do thank you."

****

Sarah was growing uneasy around Edgar. She tried hard not to stare at him. He seemed just as shy and unassuming as ever. And he was always sincerely nice to her.

But what about the candy and the glasses? Was there a reasonable explanation? Maybe he'd outgrown the candy issue, and she might have been mistaken about the glasses.

Edgar wasn't the only person on Sarah's mind. There was also Amelia. Sarah decided to pay her a visit at the Crafty Crafts shop. She'd promised to bring Amelia a sketch of the little pewter mug with its overflowing flowers, and if Amelia or Grace had another intriguing comment or two, that would be nice. Could it really have been Vincent Milaeve who Amelia thought she'd seen, or was it just a case of mistaken identity from a woman growing older?

Sarah pushed aside an image of Gil's look of concern, along with Detective Cahill's caution to stop playing Nancy Drew. *This really wasn't sleuthing, was it?* She'd be following through on a promise to bring a sweet elderly lady a little handmade sketch.

With this rationale in mind, Sarah left at the end of the workday and headed for Crafty Crafts. She enjoyed walking almost everywhere within a reasonable distance instead of taking the subway, at least when the weather was decent. Now she hoped to catch Amelia before the shop closed for the evening.

A couple of blocks from Crafty Crafts, she literally collided with Matt. She was surprised, even though she shouldn't have been. Rapid Printing's office wasn't far away.

"Sarah! This is wonderful. I was hoping you'd stop by." Matt was his casual self, even a bit more relaxed than he'd been at the party last Sunday. "I just closed up, but we can go back or, even better, go out for a bite to eat. And I still have those replicas of the posters for you."

She tried not to let dismay show on her face. "Matt! I didn't forget. But I'm rushing right now to deliver something, and I'm running really late. It's been a killer week already!"

"Busy lady." He laughed.

"Hey, thanks so much for inviting me to the party on Sunday."

Matt placed a hand on each of her shoulders and gazed directly into her eyes. "I was so happy you came." He smiled. "Okay, you need to run now. But soon? I'm clearing out the office by the end of next week. You have all my contact info on the card so we can stay in touch."

Right, the card. Buried somewhere in her dressy purse.

"You bet. But I have to hurry now."

"Take it easy, Sarah. Please stop by soon," he called out as she sped down the street.

Sarah needed to let Matt down kindly, and soon. Subtlety wasn't going to be an option.

She flew around the side street a few minutes later and headed into Crafty Crafts. The sign indicated it would be open a little while longer, and Amelia and Grace were both still there.

"Hi everyone!" Sarah called out, breathless after half running down the block. She quickly glanced around. Light gleamed from a little hanging mobile of silver gondolas, and an old-fashioned gingham doll sat contentedly on a high shelf. The place was crammed with handmade gifts and novelties and charm.

The two women greeted Sarah enthusiastically.

"I know it's getting near closing time. But, Amelia, I wanted to drop off the sketch I promised to make for you. Of the little mug with flowers."

And maybe find out if there are any more tidbits, real or imagined, about the past?

Sarah pulled the sketchpad out of her shoulder bag and laid it on the countertop. She found the page with the sketch of the little mug and flowers and carefully removed it.

"Keeping it in the sketchpad was the easiest way to make sure it stayed flat," she said, handing the sketch to Amelia.

"Why, thank you." Amelia carefully studied it and then broke into the brightest of smiles. "This is lovely. Grace, come here and take a look."

Grace joined them. "You're a real professional, Sarah."

Although Sarah protested, both women praised the sketch as one of fine quality.

"I'm going to frame this for you, Amelia." Grace immediately headed for one of their frame displays.

Amelia pointed to the sketchpad. "Can I see some of your other work?"

"Oh, sure. But these are pretty basic," said Sarah.

"Just some people and places I've gotten to know since I started working at my job. I love trying new subjects. It helps me improve my technique. I'm even hoping to take some more courses so I get better at this."

Sarah turned to some pages she thought might interest Amelia. There were sketches of places—an attractively decorated doorway near her apartment, the unique second-floor window in Rapid Printing's building, and the bustling local newsstand near work. And there were some people Amelia knew, Matt and Jake among them, and probably some she didn't.

"You have a perceptive way of capturing the heart of a person or a place. Or an object," Amelia commented.

Sarah was flattered by this observation.

Amelia then called Grace over once more. "I told you, Grace. Remember? I told you I saw some people from way back when. Here are two of them."

Sarah caught Grace's familiar eye roll.

Amelia pointed to the first. "This is the dressmaker's daughter I saw a few weeks ago walking up the stairs to the old shop."

She turned to Sarah. "They just tore down that building."

Then she chose another sketch. "And this is the man who was walking with Vincent Milaeve, the son of the old engraver."

Sarah was unable to utter a sound.

Amelia had pointed to May—and then to Edgar.

****

To anyone looking at the contents of Sarah's shopping basket that night, it would have seemed she'd be eating mostly ice cream for dinner. It might help her think. Or at least relax.

Grace thought that Amelia's stories were getting fanciful. Hadn't Sarah's days at Westervale taught her to seriously consider such possibilities? Still...

"One of those days?" asked Hilda as Sarah placed down two substantial containers of strawberry ice cream, dwarfing a can of tuna fish and the fresh tomato that followed.

"It was like five days crammed into one."

Hilda laughed heartily as Sarah grabbed a package of gum and added it to her order. Could it help with her nerves?

"So, Hilda. You know Amelia, right? From the crafts collective? I saw her for a couple of minutes today. She said she recently saw an old dressmaker's daughter climbing the stairs to a brownstone that was recently torn down. Do you know what dressmaker she meant?"

Hilda set her lips in a straight line. "Amelia's a wonderful person, but Grace tells me she's been having some age problems recently. So I don't know. Plus, that's really a little out of my territory up there. I know both of them mostly through the crafts collective." Hilda packed the ice cream carefully at the bottom of the bag. "Are you interested in finding a dressmaker?"

"No, no. It's only curiosity. Just wondered who that dressmaker was and who else might have had a business in that brownstone. I've started to sketch a few old buildings and some of the demolitions. It's all pretty fascinating, and I'm trying to improve my technique." Sarah rattled on. "In this case, all I can draw is the demolition. Still, a little history is nice, and sketching these types of things is part of a portfolio I'm putting together for some art classes I'd like to take."

Really? Well, maybe. Although some classes might not require a portfolio. But it was good to be prepared just in case, wasn't it?

"I'll ask around about the dressmaker next time we have a crafts get-together."

Sarah thanked Hilda and headed home, pondering what to do with Amelia's latest information. She'd already told the cops about Amelia thinking she'd seen people from the past, including Vincent Milaeve. But that was before Amelia actually pointed to the sketches and identified Edgar and May. On the other hand, this was no guarantee that they were truly the people Amelia thought she'd actually seen. Both Grace and Hilda insisted that age was a big factor here. And since Sarah didn't really know Amelia, she didn't know who or what to believe.

But later on that night, she studied her sketch of Amelia. The woman's whole expression was keen and observant—the set of her mouth, the lines on her forehead. And yes, especially, her eyes.

Chapter Twenty-Four

Sarah visited the church the next day at lunchtime to talk to Father Haney. She wanted to take another look at the old photographs on the church library wall.

The priest was waiting for her. "It's good to see you, Sarah. Come on into the library."

He led her to the place with the small collection of photos. "I did find a magnifying glass in case you'd like to see the young Mr. and Mrs. Butler up close."

"I appreciate it."

Father Haney handed Sarah the magnifying glass and said he'd be in his office when she was finished. "Maybe we can talk for a few minutes when you're through."

Sarah thanked him and turned to the photos. Magnifying glass in hand, she carefully studied the class photos, finding the Butlers once more. Yes, Mr. Butler might have been in his early teens, but his facial expression was the same. Hard to tell with the girl she assumed was Mrs. Butler, though. She angled the magnifying glass another way. Young Mary Vandert, who'd won an award for spelling, looked far happier than the woman Sarah now knew. Well, the years could put a lot of care on a face.

Sarah looked at other graduating classes and found a photo with the Frainie twins. They really did look exactly alike, although Edgar had those glasses and you could see by his posture that he was shy. Funny, though, he'd won an award for arithmetic, but now he didn't have any confidence with numbers. He was always asking her to check things. But his twin, Elwyn, stood straight and tall, a natural for those acting and elocution awards.

Other students had won awards, too, and it was fascinating to study those young faces and read of their special talents. Truthfully, she wanted to see if Vincent Milaeve was there somewhere. He would probably have been around the same age as the Butlers or maybe the twins, give or take a year or so. But his name wasn't there at all.

Sarah studied many of the faces and matched them to their names and the awards they'd received. What did the boy who won the athletic award look like? Could she guess from the photo? Or the girl who won for cooking? Some, like Elwyn, had won double awards. And again, she looked at Edgar. *Could her crazy theory have any basis?* It would be impossible to conclude anything from old pictures.

She revisited a few appealing faces, returning to one girl in particular. She was in a later graduating class than the Butlers. She'd received awards for both sewing and music. It was an expressive, pretty face. Sweet. Something familiar about it, too. Her name was Eliza. Eliza May Kieran.

Sarah looked closely at the face once again, angling the magnifying glass back and forth a dozen times until she was almost sure. Until it took her breath away.

Eliza May?

It was May.

****

Sarah flew down the hall to Father Haney's office.

"Please come quickly. There's something you have to see…"

Stunned, the priest ran after Sarah, who was already halfway back toward the library.

"Look!" She handed Father Haney the magnifying glass and pointed to the small photo. Then she read off the name.

"Eliza *May* Kiernan… *May*! It's *our* May. I'm sure of it."

Father Haney scrutinized the photo, remaining skeptical. But he promised to pull out any early school records he could find to get some more details about Eliza May Kieran, whether or not she was the May they knew.

Sarah then told him about Amelia recognizing the sketch of May as an old dressmaker's daughter. "And, look. She won awards for sewing and for music." This might shed some light on May's humming, too. But they just needed more information now.

****

That afternoon, Sarah and Kelly mumbled quietly in the conference room as they continued with Mrs. Butler's organizing project.

"Why do they need everything organized, neatened up, and marked open or closed back from the Stone Age?" Kelly checked to be sure no one was nearby listening.

"Could they really be selling the business?" Sarah wondered out loud.

Kelly shrugged. "Anything's possible. Maybe moving the business?"

They continued speculating as they carefully pruned the files, putting together those that had gotten out of order and sorting stray pages that had been misfiled. After the time they'd already spent on this project, they were now dipping back into the much earlier days of the firm.

A little while later, Kelly stopped, scrutinizing one file closely. "Hey, Sarah." She lowered her voice as she approached. "What was the name of that man? You know, the dead guy?" Kelly was still scared to mention him.

Sarah moved closer. "Milaeve. Why?"

Kelly inclined the open folder in Sarah's direction. Wide-eyed, the two of them paged through. There were several basic policies under that name. They were from way back in time and ended in the 1940s. No claims had ever been filed. At least there was no evidence of that. But there were two pages with beautifully engraved letterheads in the file. They were addressed to Mr. Butler's father and sent from Theodore Milaeve. *Vincent's father who loved eating at Two Violins?* In both letters, the older Mr. Milaeve thanked the older Mr. Butler for his understanding of the situation with Vincent and his associates and for his discretion. The second letter offered assurances that details would be settled with all due speed.

"Mr. Butler never said anything about knowing the name when the cops asked." Sarah almost choked, thinking back to that morning. "But he said he'd look through the files and see if anything came up. He was looking at his shoes the whole time."

Kelly's eyes were wide. "Do you think this is why we're doing all of this organizing?"

"But no one told us to look for that. And this is *Mrs.* Butler's project," Sarah said. Immediately the image of Mrs. Butler at the police precinct flew into her mind. "This account looks like it was closed decades ago. And the letters were written to Mr. Butler's *father.* Maybe the Butlers forgot about it. Or didn't even know about it." Now came an excellent question, one Kelly was quick to ask. "What do we do now?"

"I guess we need to say something to them," said Sarah.

"Which one?" asked Kelly.

"Probably both? It's Mrs. Butler's project, but the letter was to Mr. Butler's father."

"I guess. And then they can tell the cops." Kelly looked hopeful. Then she stopped. "I know this will sound awful, but suppose they don't go to the cops?"

Sarah's voice was now a hoarse whisper. "I know this is going to sound awful, too, but maybe we should copy anything that looks important in here first. Just in case. I mean, if they don't tell the cops, umm, then I guess we probably should?"

Kelly's bottom lip quivered. "I want to get this over with. Let's do it now."

There wasn't much in the file, so they made copies of the two letters and the cover pages of several policies. Folding these in half, they stuffed them into Sarah's shoulder bag.

Kelly looked at Sarah. "Now?"

Sarah nodded.

Together they walked up the stairs to Mrs. Butler's office, the original file folder in hand. Since this was her project, it seemed only fair to go to her first.

They needn't have worried. She was standing in

the doorway of her husband's office when they approached. Two for the price of one.

Mr. Butler sat at his desk, papers spread on every portion of the surface. They both looked up in mild surprise as the two young women approached.

Sarah assumed that Kelly was letting her do the talking.

"Umm, Kelly and I were working on that organizing project, and we came across something we figured we should show you…both. It's a really old file, but we thought you'd like to know."

Mrs. Butler spoke without hesitation. "Old files? Well, thanks, girls. But that's Mr. Butler's domain." She walked out into the hall. "I'll let the three of you talk. And don't forget to have more of that candy downstairs." Sarah and Kelly stared at her retreating figure in shock.

They turned to Mr. Butler.

Sarah handed him the file. "When the cops asked if we'd ever heard the name of the, umm, dead guy, you mentioned you'd check the files. Well, we saw the last name just now…"

It was hard to read the expression on Mr. Butler's face as he paged through the papers in the slender folder. The silence was oppressive.

"I noticed that the first name isn't the same as the man…" Sarah trailed off.

Kelly had been quiet up until now. "We thought you should know."

Mr. Butler sighed deeply and looked up with a weak smile. "Okay, thanks, ladies. Don't worry about it. This was so long ago that it probably wouldn't help the cops now anyway." He slid the folder into his bottom desk drawer. "Thanks again." He turned back to his work.

All Sarah and Kelly could do now was leave. They rushed back to the conference room and exchanged hushed whispers.

"He's not going to tell the cops, is he?" Kelly wrung her hands.

"Doesn't look like it." Sarah studied Kelly's grave face. "I mean, it may not be important, but I guess we should tell them? They asked if anybody had ever heard the name. Plus, I have more to tell them." She looked at Kelly earnestly. "After work? We can go together?"

Kelly nodded, but she still wrung her hands.

"An hour and a half," said Sarah. "Let me call and see if one or both of the detectives will be there later on."

****

Sarah managed to make a furtive call to Gil who, she hoped, wouldn't worry she was going to back out of their Saturday date. He had the patience and good grace, though, to hear her real reason for the call—a halting request for an after-work meeting with Kelly and her.

For the next hour and a half, it was almost impossible for the two young women to concentrate on anything, even on their organizing project.

Later, on their running walk to the precinct, Sarah filled Kelly in on additional details from the past twenty-four hours.

"Good grief, Sarah. You should be a private investigator."

"Please, no!"

When they arrived, they were greeted by a friendly

Sergeant Brushie, who immediately waved them inside.

"So good to see you both." Detective Cahill was in an upbeat mood. Gil joined him in greeting, and he and Sarah exchanged bright smiles.

"You first, Sarah," said Kelly, her eyes moving warily over their surroundings.

In a rush, the first part tumbled out of Sarah, from Edgar's inconsistencies to Amelia's identification of the sketches. Then they both told their story about the old Milaeve file and Mr. and Mrs. Butler's reactions. Sarah handed them the copies. When they finished, Sarah gripped the arms of her chair, and Kelly clutched her hands into fists. Were they betraying their employers? But they had to come to the cops.

Gil leaned forward and cast a compassionate look at the two of them. "We appreciate this. Please don't worry. You both did the right thing."

"Okay," said Cahill. "We really do thank you." He nodded at Gil. "And we probably owe you both a little more information in case it helps connect the dots to some other details. This is what we're able to tell you about Vincent Mileave. Gil, you want to start?"

"Seems as if Vincent grew up in the neighborhood, although not quite as close as where you work. As you know, he was from a family of engravers. Then something happened, and given the tone of these letters and from what we've heard, Vincent might have done something shady or illegal as a young man."

"Whatever he did," Cahill said, "it caused a rift between Vincent and his father, Theodore. Then Vincent enlisted during the war, as did a number of others. And as you already know, his parents gave up the business and moved. Everything seemed quiet after that."

"Until Vincent was murdered a few weeks ago," added Gil. "It's like he sprang up out of nowhere after thirty-five years. Well, not exactly nowhere. He had an ex-wife and two grown kids near Chicago. The wife said that Theodore, who wrote these letters, was quite old, and they got word from a lawyer that he died in upstate New York this past spring."

Sarah and Kelly looked at each other, eyebrows raised in surprise.

"Given a lot of this random information, we're sure the Butlers and possibly Edgar might have known, or at least have known of, the family back in the day," said Cahill, "But we don't have a lot to go on." He paused. "And much as I hate to say this, but given all of the circumstances, Amelia's story about recognizing Edgar and Vincent still doesn't sound solid enough to pursue."

"Oh," said Sarah, still totally unwilling to discount Amelia's story.

"What do we do now?" Kelly asked.

Cahill spoke first. "Both of you just keep your eyes and ears open. And *do not* talk to anyone about this."

Gil looked at both of them. "And please stay safe."

Chapter Twenty-Five

Sunday was Sarah's delayed get-together with Cookie, and she had the entire subway ride out to Queens to think. Events were moving quickly, but at least some of them were quite pleasant. She stared at the graffiti-covered interior of the train and replayed her date with Gil the previous day.

Their afternoon trip to an art show in the afternoon was followed by a leisurely dinner at a quiet restaurant. It had been the best time, much too short, although hours had passed. And just like their meal at the pub the previous Monday night, they'd became absorbed in their conversation. They made plans to go to a local holiday concert midweek, and Sarah promised to cook dinner beforehand. Now she smiled, still savoring the memory of Gil's warm hug when they said goodnight at her door.

Now, the moment Cookie opened the door for Sarah, she was beaming, her red curls dancing and her face glowing with enthusiasm. Lil and Tom had invited them for a traditional Sunday dinner of a delicious roast with all the trimmings. After this, Cookie and Sarah planned to catch up. Then Cookie and Jim promised to drive Sarah by their new house. They were set to close on it in a few weeks.

"Seems to me," said Cookie's dad, Tom, "that a house is a pile of work." But then he chuckled at his observation.

While Lil doled out huge helpings of food, Cookie and Jim outlined their plans for fixing this and that after they moved in, especially the baby's room.

"Okay." Lil broke in. "And here's the other news. Tom and I are going to move soon, too. What's the use of staying here in Queens when our new grandchild needs us?"

"Hmpf," said Tom with a hint of amusement. "Garden apartment. And since when did I ever garden?"

"You'll love it, Daddy." Cookie grabbed his hand and squeezed it.

Lil shook her head and laughed before changing the subject. "So, Sarah, I have information from Mrs. Grady. Her daughter, Bridget, wants to talk to you. You probably remember her from a long time ago. Just remind me to give you her phone number before you leave. Like I said, she's doing specialized research into some sort of speech and cognitive problems for adults with health issues, and she's extremely interested in your homeless friend."

"Thanks, Lil," Sarah said. Between Bridget Grady and Lorna and Father Haney's contacts, May might have a really good chance of getting some sort of help. Especially now that it was possible she might have graduated from the old church school.

When everyone was bursting with food, Jim and Tom pitched in to help Lil clean up. They shooed Cookie and Sarah into the living room to talk.

"You brought your sketches?"

"Yup. I promised and here they are." Sarah pulled her sketchpad from her shoulder bag.

Cookie began paging through immediately.

"This has to be May," said Cookie. "You're right about one thing, I think. There's more to this woman than being homeless. Look, Sarah. Look at how sweet and how aware her face is."

Cookie had always been intrigued by faces as portrayed on a page or on canvas, and she was perceptive about what those faces revealed. Sarah thought back to their many trips together to museums as well as the sketching classes of their youth. Now they continued looking at the sketches, and when Lil joined them, Cookie returned to the obnoxious teen. She studied the first sketch, but also the second after he'd dropped the scowl before running off, genuinely frightened.

"Hmm, almost looks like two different people, but it's the same guy. The scowl is very theatrical. He's scared. Even with the scowl." Cookie looked up from her curious admission. "I figure he's part of the story?"

"Sort of, yeah." Sarah hesitated, but Cookie knew her too well. "I wasn't going to tell you some stuff because I didn't want to upset you."

Cookie almost jumped out of her seat. "What? You better tell everything!"

"I will. And believe it or not, something very good came out of something not so good."

Both Cookie and Lil looked at her quizzically. Then she told them her story, editing a little bit and softening a few details here and there to lessen some of the impact.

At the end, they both sat back, stunned.

"Thank goodness you're okay," said Lil.

"That's for sure." Cookie put her arm around Sarah

for a quiet moment. "So much for a job in the boring insurance industry, as you've called it."

"True." Sarah was relieved to have shared her story, more than she realized.

"Okay, let's look at each sketch again," Cookie said, as Lil peered over her shoulder.

Sarah wanted Cookie's objective thoughts, her usual sensitive and perceptive responses to faces. Cookie immediately caught the worry on Mr. Butler's face and the suppressed anxiety bursting from Mrs. Butler.

But Sarah was especially interested in her friend's take on Amelia.

"Look at how keen and observant her eyes are," said Cookie.

"I know." Sarah was thankful for Cookie's reaction. "But it seems as if everyone keeps writing her off as old and confused."

Lil studied the sketch thoughtfully. "Seems as if everyone should keep an open mind."

"Okay." Cookie pointed to another sketch without hesitation. "That's got to be Gil. His picture matches just how you described him."

"And," added Lil, "we want to meet him."

"You definitely will."

Cookie turned a few more pages. "Matt?" She waited for Sarah's nod. "You haven't been able to define him yet, have you?"

"You're amazing, Cookie. No, I haven't. He's friendly and has a casual way about him, but he seems a little desperate to have more togetherness pretty quickly."

"He's probably on the rebound," said Lil.

"Although I'm getting the sense that it really doesn't matter, does it? I think Gil is the guy who's close to your heart."

Chapter Twenty-Six

Kelly came in late Monday morning from her "dental appointment." She was all smiles. It had been a good interview. She and Sarah exchanged thumbs up as Kelly went to her desk.

The morning was quiet and at lunchtime, Sarah wanted a breath of fresh air and a change. Gianni's shop was closed today. Even May wasn't in her usual place. She ran up the church steps, hoping Father Haney was around. He was just coming out of his office.

"Sarah. I thought I heard someone. I was about to lock up, but I'm glad you're here."

"Father, I didn't want to bother you, but could I look at those school photos again? Just one more time? I'll only take two minutes."

"Don't worry. Take as much time as you like."

The priest led the way to the library. "I left the magnifying glass here, just in case." He picked it up and handed it to Sarah with a quizzical expression.

"I'd just like to check Mrs. Butler's photo again," Sarah said, still not sure why.

Once more she angled the magnifying glass on Mrs. Butler's—Mary Vandert's—face. It was happy and glowing with youth. She was, no doubt, pleased at having received a spelling award. What was bothering Sarah about the photo?

"Thanks, Father." She handed the magnifier back to him.

"Is everything okay, Sarah?"

"I guess. I'm just looking for a few missing pieces."

"I'm here whenever you'd like to talk," he said.

****

Sarah headed back to work and, with a jolt, spied Matt coming out the door of the Butler Agency. Even though she needed to talk with him, now wasn't the time or place.

"Matt!"

Once again, Sarah hoped her dismay didn't show too clearly.

"Sarah, I just left the poster copies with the secretary. I'm clearing out everything from the office, and there might even be a few more things you'd like." He paused. "I hope you'll come to my place soon, so I can make dinner for you. The Zigeuner's stew or even the Two Violins goulash. Whatever you'd like."

Those dinner recipes. What was it she couldn't quite remember?

"Matt, thank you. This week is becoming impossible…"

"Sarah!"

Someone else called her name. It was Edgar, poking his head out the door.

"I'll be right there." Sarah turned back to Matt. Despite the cold air, there were beads of sweat on his forehead. He was nervous and probably sensed she wasn't able to return his feelings. Maybe dropping off the poster copies at work was rooted in a bit of desperation.

190

"I have to go, Matt. Thanks so much for bringing those poster copies."

"Soon, Sarah." Matt took her hand, gave her a quick kiss on the cheek, and walked away.

No doubt Lil had been right. Matt was probably on the rebound and wanted badly to connect with Sarah. She felt terrible. Now she ran inside.

Edgar and Kelly were standing in the entranceway.

"Sorry to interrupt, Sarah," said Edgar. "But Mr. and Mrs. Butler seem extremely anxious to meet with all of us."

Kelly and Sarah exchanged startled looks as they followed Edgar into the conference room. The Butlers were already at the table and invited them all to sit. Mrs. Butler's face was puffy as if she'd been crying. Mr. Butler looked somber. The air felt still, almost stagnant.

Mr. Butler cleared his throat. "We wanted to tell you together when it became official."

Mrs. Butler whimpered softly.

There was a crack in Mr. Butler's voice when he finally spoke. He ran his hand over his hair before beginning.

"We're going to close the agency. The business has changed over the years, and I'm sorry to say we haven't changed with it."

Mr. Butler looked down at the table. Edgar did, too. Kelly grasped Sarah's hand tightly under the table. The air pulsed with tension.

Mr. Butler continued. "Plus, the building's management..." He trailed off for a beat. "...is making it more difficult for us to stay here."

It was happening all over, so it was no surprise that

it was happening to the Butlers. Those top floors weren't for the agency's old papers and such. They were pretty much empty. She and Kelly had figured this out a while ago.

"Please, this has nothing to do with any of you. We've appreciated your hard work. And we're going to make sure that each one of you has a place to go. We're turning over our clients to several places, and we're already making inquiries, so not one of you will be out of a job."

A thick silence followed.

Edgar spoke first, in formal, theatrical tones. "I appreciate all you've done for me, and I think I speak on behalf of all of us when I say we've enjoyed our time working for both of you."

Sarah and Kelly nodded in agreement, both unable to speak.

"We're still working out the details," continued Mr. Butler. "This will happen after New Year's. So please don't worry. We'll be sure you're all taken care of."

So much for worrying about honoring the employment agency agreement.

When Mr. Butler was done, Mrs. Butler called Sarah and Kelly over and gave them each a hug.

"Later," said Kelly to Sarah when they left the conference room and neared Kelly's desk.

Then she handed Sarah the envelope with the poster copies from Matt.

The envelope was heavy, as heavy as her heart was for the Butlers.

****

Holiday lights twinkled around the city that

evening, but Sarah wasn't in much of a festive spirit as she left work. She truly felt sorry for the Butlers. Why were they closing the business at this particular moment? Did it have anything to do with Mrs. Butler's trip to the police precinct? Or with Mr. Butler's strange reaction to that old Milaeve file? Or with the disagreement between the Butlers that Kelly had overheard? *Or with Vincent Milaeve's murder?*

And Edgar? Was he really Edgar, having outgrown his food sensitivities? But what about the glasses? There could be a simple explanation. Still, nothing was making sense. Things really seemed different after Vincent Milaeve was killed. A coincidence?

Detective Cahill said there are no coincidences.

Sarah pushed open the supermarket door. She needed ingredients for the dinner she was making for Gil on Wednesday night, something she could have ready immediately since they'd be going to that neighborhood Christmas concert afterward. She was looking forward to it and trying hard not to let her troubling thoughts interfere with her anticipation of their date.

Now she gathered the ingredients for a simple lasagna. She'd make it tomorrow night and then heat it up when she got home on Wednesday so it would be ready when Gil arrived.

"Look at all these groceries," Hilda said when Sarah began unloading the items from her basket. "Not just an ice cream dinner then." She carefully packed the box of flat noodles, meat, a jar of sauce, and some salad fixings safely inside the bag.

Sarah laughed. "I'm having a friend over for dinner this week. And a main course of ice cream just wouldn't do, much as I'd like it myself."

"By the way," said Hilda. "I ran into a woman from the crafts collective who lives in Amelia's neighborhood. We got to talking about some of the building demolitions around here, and I mentioned the one where you said that old dressmaker used to be."

Sarah's pulse quickened. She thought back to Amelia who'd been so certain that May was the person she'd seen walking up the steps to a building before it was torn down. She'd identified the sketch of May as an old dressmaker's daughter.

Hilda grabbed a piece of paper from the drawer under her register. "Here. I was saving this for you. The dressmaker's name was Julia Kieran. Of course, she's long gone by now."

Sarah froze. So Amelia had been right. Eliza May Kieran, in the old photo at the church, must surely have been Julia Kieran's daughter. And that daughter had to have been May.

****

May. Sarah couldn't get May off her mind when she got home, along with everything else that had happened. She'd need to find help for May quickly, since Sarah was not going to be working in the area much longer, now that the Butler Agency would be closing.

There was one thing she could do right now. She needed to call Mrs. Grady's daughter, who was doing that special research project. Sarah took out the phone number Lil had given her yesterday and dialed Bridget Grady. As the young woman answered, Sarah fervently hoped she could help open some new doors for May.

Chapter Twenty-Seven

Sarah was now certain that Amelia had been accurate about all she'd seen. And if Amelia had correctly identified the sketch of May as the old dressmaker's daughter, then she was probably right about Edgar being the person she'd seen walking with a very much alive Vincent Milaeve. But no one except Sarah seemed to take Amelia seriously, even the cops.

Everything swirled around in Sarah's mind on the way to work, including last night's talk with Bridget Grady, who was anxious to meet May. In addition, Lorna said her social worker friend had been in touch with additional ideas and also wanted to meet May. At least some things were moving in a positive direction.

Sarah's thoughts were interrupted as she walked past the old school. The workmen were there again removing more boxes. She waved. By now they recognized her and seemed to appreciate Sarah's cheerful greetings whenever she passed by.

"This is it," said one of the men.

"Any word on what's next?" Sarah asked, stopping to watch for a minute as they shoved the last boxes into the back of the van.

"No idea," said the second guy. "We just deliver these to some law office near us and we're done."

He pulled out his *Two Guys from Grenleah* business card and handed it to her. "If you or your boss ever need small movers, give us a call. We're not far, and we service the tristate."

Maybe the Butlers might need their services.

Sarah thanked them and put the card in her shoulder bag.

Gloom was heavy in the air as she pushed open the door to the Butler Agency. "Nothing new," said Kelly as Sarah approached the young woman's desk. "The Butlers are upstairs."

"Edgar?"

Kelly nodded in the direction of Edgar's office. "Where else?"

Sarah tried hard to smile. "I don't know about you but, under the circumstances, all I have concentration for is our organizing project. It's probably the most helpful thing we can do right now."

"That's the best suggestion I've heard in a long time," Kelly said.

"Besides, it'll give us a chance to catch up."

****

The young women took a break at lunchtime, and Sarah ran over to the church. When she found Father Haney, he was pleased to share his news.

"I just heard from one of my contacts. She's interested to learn more about May," he said.

"That's great news. And I have some things to tell you, too." First, she told her story about the sketch and the dressmaker, both increasing the possibility that May was, very likely, that young girl in the school photo. Then she filled him in about Bridget Grady and Lorna's social worker friend.

"Sarah, would you like me to set something up here with all of them?"

Sarah was relieved. "I'd be so grateful if you did." She'd hoped he'd be willing to talk with the others, but his offer to take the lead was even better. It would be a good mix of professional and spiritual expertise, more than anything she could possibly offer. Perhaps Father Haney felt responsible toward May since she gravitated to the church steps and, likely, had attended the school so long ago.

They chatted for a few more minutes. Sarah thanked him and then handed him a sheet of paper with everyone's contact information, including her own.

****

It was too quiet for the rest of the day. After work, Sarah trudged over to the downtown train. Today she was scheduled to meet with the head of the benefits department at the bank, her second interview with that institution and the last place she felt like going at the moment. But she knew she needed to stoke up some enthusiasm for the job, now that the Butler Agency was going to close. They might have promised to help everyone find new positions, but Sarah wasn't waiting around to see what they came up with. The bank job had a sense of urgency now. It might not be what Sarah wanted in the long run, but she was soon going to need a job. Unlike last week, she made sure to leave enough time to get to the interview without arriving breathless.

The Benefits Department was on a different floor than Human Resources and in a more serene setting. The manager was an older woman, trim in a deep green suit, with nicely groomed graying hair. But an open and welcoming face was her most outstanding feature. As soon as they were settled in her office, Sarah sensed that this was not going to be a textbook interview.

"I'd ask you why you'd like to work in benefits," said the woman, whose name was Clare, "but I've spoken with Dave, and I think I have a better idea of your situation right now."

Sarah's eyes widened. "Well, Dave spoke highly of the bank and this job…"

Clare smiled, thankfully interrupting before Sarah needed to struggle on further.

"Look, Sarah." She leaned forward and spoke kindly. "Dave filled me in on the Butler Agency's plans to close."

How did he know already? Ah…Kelly. Then again, Dave seemed to be up on everything in the employment world.

"And I know he was trying to place you here before the news about this broke." Clare swiveled back easily in her chair. "Dave's placed a number of my colleagues in the past, and he's been a valuable contact. We're good friends, too."

Good friends? Sarah tried to picture the conservatively suited Clare having lunch with Dave in his wild sports jacket.

Sarah just nodded, wondering what was next. Clare was obviously prepared to say more, and Sarah guessed it wouldn't be along the lines of the usual interview-speak.

"I'm sure you'd be a great person for this job—a hard worker, willing to learn, good references, and all that. Dave usually fills me in pretty thoroughly about an exceptional job applicant." She leaned forward again, a hint of humor on her face. "But from what Dave's told me, this probably isn't what you had in mind for the long haul."

Sarah felt the need to respond. "So, are you telling me I'm no longer a candidate?"

"Not at all." Clare smiled. "You're definitely qualified, but I'm assuming it wouldn't be for the long term." She paused. "But here's the story. You'll be needing a job in January. And I need a person I can rely on, and fairly soon. Unfortunately, there was someone on staff who wasn't a good fit, and things didn't work out."

Sarah raised her eyebrows. Clare continued without giving any further details.

"There are several things I'm going to suggest, and you can think about them over the weekend. Then we can talk again."

"All right," said Sarah, still a bit stunned by this unusual twist.

"First, I'll outline all the components of the job today. And just so things are totally clear, here's a summary sheet of everything." She handed Sarah a piece of paper.

The woman certainly was organized and direct.

"And, yes, I'm interviewing two others. But your résumé shows you're highly qualified, and Dave gave you a strong recommendation. I sense that this would work out well."

"But you said you believed I wouldn't stay long." Sarah was confused by the woman's total honesty. This was unlike most, or just about all, interview situations in her experience.

"True, although in general, many young people tend to move more frequently anyway, even during these times. Most do it for more money, more prestige, a better commute, whatever. But I happen to know about your interest in art. And I think you'd move because of a specific passion in that direction, and that's a genuinely first-rate reason. And, from what Dave tells me, you'd fairly honor any commitments to the job you'd be in before making a move." She looked at Sarah carefully and continued. "And there are also numerous other opportunities to consider here at the bank as time goes on, as well."

All Sarah could do was nod.

Looked like Dave had spilled everything.

Clare smiled at Sarah's amazement. "I like helping people reach their goals. Long story short, people have helped me many times in the past, and I'm appreciative."

"Okay," said Sarah.

"In the meantime," continued Clare, "if this becomes a reality, you'd have a secure job here and you'd add a few notches to your work experience. At the same time, I'd be filling an immediate need in my department with a qualified candidate." She smiled. "And totally aside from this, I know a board member at a community arts and cultural outreach, and I believe that you might be interested in exploring this group. Maybe you'd like to use your art talents for one of their projects, even for just a few hours a week. They deal with local organizations and individuals who would be grateful for your input. And there could be some good contacts for the future. Whether or not this job here materializes, I'll still put you in touch with them."

Sarah was further stunned. "Thank you."

"So, should we go over the job content now?"

****

Sarah sat for a while when she got home. This had

been one of the most unusual interviews she'd ever experienced, but refreshing, too. Clare had gotten to the heart of things, discussing all aspects of the job and promising to call Sarah after the weekend. Things might work out well with this. And Sarah bet that Dave would be in touch soon to fill her in more.

Now she needed to make the lasagna for tomorrow night's dinner with Gil. She'd add a salad and some crusty bread for the meal, too. Gil had promised to bring some wine. After dinner, they'd go to the little concert and walk around afterward to see the growing number of neighborhood holiday decorations. Gil had been especially happy that the concert was this week and not next, since he'd be working a later schedule then.

Lorna called just as Sarah was finishing up in the kitchen.

"Just checking in. How was your date? I want details."

Sarah burst out laughing. "It was wonderful." She gave Lorna a run-down of their gallery visit and dinner the previous Saturday and their plans for tomorrow night.

"So should I be loaning you my wedding planner?"

"Not so fast," said Sarah, glad that Lorna couldn't see the slight blush growing on her cheeks. "I'm taking it nice and easy. But he's a really good guy."

Then she told Lorna about Father Haney's offer to coordinate a team to help May.

"He's as good as his word," Lorna said. "I wanted to let you know that my friend Alison, the social worker, just called to tell me he was in touch with her late this afternoon. He's already setting up a group meeting."

"Fantastic! Thanks, Lorna. I'm thrilled that Father Haney is coordinating things."

After the call, Sarah sat down with a cup of tea. The crafts collective's recipe book was still on the blue sofa next to her, just where she'd left it the other night.

Smiling, Sarah picked it up. By now, it opened on its own to the Two Violins page, the place where old Mr. and Mrs. Milaeve had loved to dine. She practically knew the page by heart. One of these days, she would make that goulash recipe.

Her eyes fell again on the quotes from the owner and the headwaiter from so long ago. They'd obviously loved the place. She gave their words a second look.

And the moment she did, she knew why those old school photos at the church nagged at her. And not just the one of May, but also the one of Mrs. Butler as a girl. Sarah had studied the face in the photo carefully just to be sure it was, indeed, Mrs. Butler. She was the girl who'd won the spelling award and whose maiden name was listed as Mary Vandert.

Sarah now stared at the page in front of her—especially at the quote from the man who'd been the longtime headwaiter at Two Violins. His name was Lel Vandert.

Chapter Twenty-Eight

The phone on Sarah's desk rang promptly the next morning at 8:35. *Dave*. At least he'd given her a few minutes to take off her coat before calling.

"I guess we really don't have to play the twenty questions phone game anymore, do we? And in case you were wondering how I knew about the agency closing, Kelly told me when I was setting up an appointment for her."

"That's what I figured," said Sarah.

"And you probably figured that Clare and I had a nice phone conversation last night."

"Somehow I'm not surprised. And let me say that she's a lovely person, although it certainly wasn't a traditional interview."

"Clare doesn't do things by the book."

"Obviously."

"First, she's honest," Dave said. "I've known her a long time and can safely say this. And, second, she is really impressed with you and when she heard about the agency closing, I knew it could be a win-win situation for both of you. And, yes, I told her about the art."

"Okay, a question. What didn't work out with the previous person in the benefits job? She said it wasn't a good fit and left it at that."

"Off the record, Sarah, and only because I don't want you to worry that it had anything to do with either

Clare or the job itself."

"Scout's honor," replied Sarah.

"Look. The guy who had the job developed some very complicated personal issues. It affected the quality of his work, his reliability, doing the team player thing. 'Nuff said?"

"Yeah. I get the picture."

"Good. So, Sarah. This might have all come at a very good time. The job could work out well for you in a lot of ways. Not that I don't have other possibilities, but I had a feeling to begin with that you and Clare would be a good match. So, you two talk again next week. Oh, and I'm sure Kelly will fill you in on her story."

Sarah grinned. "I'm sure she will."

****

Sarah looked at her desk that morning. There was the catalog envelope from Matt with the poster miniatures he'd brought to the office. She carefully slid the pages out and studied them with their lively dancers and musicians and strolling couples in old-fashioned costumes, all in vivid color. This was a thoughtful gift, prompted by her admiration of the originals at the party. He'd also included a quick note and yet another card with his new contact information. She returned everything to the catalog envelope to study more carefully later. Sarah bit her lip. She knew she had to face Matt and decline his ongoing offers to get together. She didn't want to hurt his feelings, but she needed to be fair, too.

Right now, though, Sarah needed to turn her attention to the organizing project that she and Kelly were working on. It was clearly apparent that the files and papers they'd been so carefully assembling weren't going back in the cabinets at all but, rather, staying in the file boxes to be transferred or discarded when the business closed.

Regular paperwork was grinding to a halt, and Sarah realized how much of it had been of a basic nature. What had she truly learned about insurance, despite her jokes to friends? And what had she gleaned about the inner workings of the Butler Agency? Did they just hire her to help with the wind-down of the business?

Was Edgar still as busy? And exactly what caused him to always be slavishly chained to his desk? Had there really been that much insurance business or did those special client reports occupy a larger majority of his time?

"Sarah?" Kelly interrupted Sarah's thoughts, moving closer so they could talk privately.

"I have another interview later today. You know, for the job I really liked."

Kelly had been busy with numerous interviews. Dave was never idle.

"I think this is the one. Dave says he smells an offer coming soon."

Dave was always smelling offers. But Sarah had stopped looking askance at that recently.

"Sarah, I feel bad for the Butlers. But if I get an offer, I want to take it, even if it means leaving before they close things down."

"Do whatever's right for you, Kelly." Sarah didn't hesitate a moment with her response. "I've got a feeling there's not too much more we're going to be able to do here anyway. And I might not be too far behind you myself. We'll just do all we can while we're here." Sarah offered a smile to her friend who smiled back with relief.

****

Sarah was not looking forward to what she'd planned at lunchtime. But it was the right thing to do now and in person.

She ran the short distance to Rapid Printing. Taking a deep breath, she opened the door. Matt looked up with enthusiasm.

"Sarah!" He rose and walked over. "What a great surprise! Would you like to have lunch?"

Before he could go any further, Sarah shook her head. "Matt, thank you so much, but I can't. I'm sorry." There was nothing else to do but forge ahead with the little speech she'd been preparing over the past couple of days. The one where she thanked him profusely for the party invitation and the lovely poster replicas. The one that ended with her confessing she had just started seeing someone.

He was quiet while she talked, his face melting. "We could still have lunch now as friends," he offered, trying to inject some hope into their conversation.

Sarah felt wretched as she declined.

There was an uncomfortable pause.

"If things don't work out..." He was struggling now to choose his words. "I'll always be glad to see you. I'm just here till next week." He waved his hand over the small office/shop. "Then I'll officially open the business at The Cove. It's only a short train ride, and it's in a beautiful town. I have a nice apartment nearby. It's pretty country with rolling hills, a lake, lovely shops. Sarah, you know I'd always look forward to

206

seeing you and getting together anywhere."

Before things got any more awkward, Sarah smiled, extending her hand.

"Thanks, Matt. Good luck." They shook hands. He held on a moment longer, just as he'd done when they first met at the crafts fair.

"And before I move, if I find any more memorabilia you might like, I'll let you know."

Sarah smiled again and left. She felt bad. Matt was no doubt on the rebound, as Lil had observed. She hoped he'd meet someone nice in his new location.

Jake, the young florist, was standing outside A Dozen Roses across the street, tending to the numerous displays with admirable dexterity, in spite of his gardener's gloves.

Sarah hurried over to say hi.

"Good to see you, Jake." They'd last seen each other at Matt's party.

"Hey, Sarah. In the market for some new flowers for that pewter mug? Amelia showed me your sketch. It's perfect."

"Thanks, Jake. But I'd like that little bunch of tea roses. It's a small gift for a friend."

Jake packaged up the flowers in record time as Sarah stared out the window, preoccupied.

"Having lunch with Matt now?" He grinned.

"Umm, no. Running off to do another errand."

They settled for the flowers and Sarah dashed away.

****

As Sarah hoped, May was on the church step. Sarah joined her.

"I brought you some flowers, May," she said,

handing May the cheerful little bag holding the pink tea roses, similar to those on Sarah's scarf.

May accepted them as if they were the most precious things she'd ever seen. "For-r…" The woman pointed to herself. "…May?"

Sarah's smile was huge. "For you, May," she said, giving the woman a hug.

****

May was still very much on Sarah's mind when Gil came for dinner that night. They'd been laughing over a funny anecdote and catching up on things. It was midway through their meal when Sarah changed the subject.

"Look, I know we've sort of agreed not to talk about official things on our social time, but part of this isn't exactly official. The rest is."

Gil took a sip of wine and grinned with good humor. "Sometimes it's hard not to talk about official things, Sarah. There's a lot going on these days."

"True. But I swear this will only be five minutes. No more."

"More than five, if you need it. I can listen and enjoy this great lasagna at the same time."

"Well, the first part really isn't official," she said. Then she recounted how she'd been looking for help for May and how Father Haney offered to organize the team of people.

"You're right. It's not really official, but it's nice of you to reach out to all those people and try to help May." He looked up, fork poised in mid-air with a small wedge of lasagna. "I hope this works out. And I agree. She doesn't seem like a typical homeless person, although sometimes it's hard to define typical."

Sarah nodded as she finished a mouthful of salad. "Now for the more official part, although even a little of that is unofficial, too. And you can time me," she said, noting his amused look. "I promised it would only be five minutes, so here goes."

Gil accepted a second helping of lasagna and listened about the church photo, the Butler agency closing, and the name link between Mrs. Butler and the long-time waiter at Two Violins.

"Five minutes on the nose," announced Gil when she was finished. "You sure can pack a lot into a few days and into five minutes!" They both burst out laughing.

"That's my story. The more or less official part, I guess," said Sarah. "You can figure out what it all means, but I needed to tell you everything. I just can't seem to let go of the possibility that there's more to all of this than meets the eye, especially Vincent Milaeve's murder."

"You've got a lot of intriguing details, but we still need to figure out how they tie together. You're right. There's a lot of things that don't add up, but until there's more hard evidence or a way to connect it, there's not a lot we can do right now."

"Yeah, I know," Sarah said. "I guess it could still have been a street crime. But it doesn't feel like it."

"Believe me, Sarah, I'm not discounting anything you're saying or that you've found out. And unfortunately, we have a lot of pending cases now, too. Don't worry, though. I'll fill Harry in on everything you told me."

"Uh-oh. Then I'm in trouble."

He smiled and then spoke seriously. "How about

your other unofficial part of the story, Sarah? You'll have some more changes pretty soon with the agency closing."

As they walked over to the concert, she filled Gil in on her meeting with Clare and the possibilities that particular job might hold. Then they went on to talk of other things, their time together always flowing.

The holiday brass quartet concert was excellent. It was just what Sarah felt she needed to get in the spirit of the season. Afterward, they walked for a little while, admiring the lights and decorations in the crisp winter evening. Then they made plans for a movie and dinner on Saturday, saying goodnight at Sarah's door. Gil left her with a soft and gentle kiss.

Chapter Twenty-Nine

It was a few weeks since Sarah had last seen the entire Westervale crowd for drinks. A lot had happened since then, and she felt like a different person. Now, the gang would assemble for the first of several pre-holiday celebrations and, also, to toast Julie's birthday. Sarah had promised to stop by, despite the fact that it had already been a busy week.

Fortunately, work that day consisted mostly of the organizing project. Sarah and Kelly were forging ahead at an easy pace, stopping to eat a sandwich together at lunchtime. The Butlers and Edgar were quiet and stayed to themselves. By the time Sarah left work, she felt that, for once, the day had been reasonably serene.

Fiddler's in midtown was Julie's choice because of its festive holiday atmosphere. It was fun with the Westervale staff, but the place was predictably crammed with people. Soon, they had to shout to hear each other as jubilant patrons, fueled with holiday spirits of both the literal and figurative kind, cranked up the noise level. Eventually, Sarah wished everyone well and left.

Rush hour had thinned out by the time she boarded the uptown local. It was after work hours, and the cocktail crowds were still making merry. Serious commuters were already on their way home. Although the subway wasn't empty, it wasn't totally full either or as packed as the interior of Fiddler's had been. Sarah smiled as she thought about the enthusiasm of the Westervalers and how glad she'd been to see them.

At the stop before hers, a figure slid into the car and grabbed onto a pole nearby. Sarah's eyes were immediately riveted. The hand holding it sported a long, slender tattoo.

The obnoxious, copper-haired teen.

She forgot about her stop being next. Swinging around, she grasped the same pole the teen held. They were now face to face.

It only took a second for him to register her identity. His fright was unmistakable.

"Who are you?" Sarah came close and lowered her voice just enough to be heard over the rumbling accompaniment of the fast-moving train. "And why are you trying to scare people?"

She sensed he was going to bolt. Perhaps shoving aside anyone standing in his way to chance jumping between cars of the moving train until he could find another door and run out at the next stop.

In a spontaneous move that surprised even her, Sarah clamped her hand over his on the pole. He could easily break free of her grip, but the move startled him, just long enough to freeze, to answer a question. A second later, she realized she could be taking an awful risk.

"Don't even try to run, or I'll yell," she threatened. Of course, even if she did, it was doubtful anyone would respond. She'd said it for shock value, hoping to get a reply from him.

Surprisingly, the teen spoke. "I swear, I didn't know who you were…and who you knew."

"The cops?" Sarah shot back.

He half shook his head. "Please, lady. Please leave me alone. I just made a couple of bucks doing a few things. I don't know nothing."

He looked at her pleadingly. The train rattled on, making yet another stop. If anyone was listening to their conversation, they didn't let on.

"Where do you come off, threatening old people? And threatening me? If you didn't do anything wrong, then tell the cops your story. They're looking for you."

Were they?

"It's not the cops...I'm sorry. I didn't know who you were. I'm sorry I yelled at the old lady by the church. I didn't want to." His words were halting and his face etched in panic.

As another stop approached, the train screeched to a halt. Abruptly, the teen wrenched his hand free and bolted out the door. Sarah ran after him.

But she was wearing heels, and there were a few people in the way. The teen was fast and wily. He flew up the steps, pushing past everyone. Sarah made it halfway up the stairs, but she knew she'd lost him.

Leaning against the railing, she stopped to catch her breath, her lungs filled with the putrid stink of neglect and decay. She looked around. Suddenly, anyone who'd left the train was gone. The platform was empty. In her zeal to squeeze information out of the teen, Sarah had gone a couple of stops too many. Perhaps he had, too, while he pleaded with her.

An unearthly sound came from far off. Somewhere up on the street. An awful chill erupted from deep inside her. She was alone in a desolate subway station. Missing those extra stops had brought her firmly into the boundaries of gang territory.

****

Sarah fled up to the street. *Safer? No.* The atmosphere of threat refused to evaporate. The air was suddenly punctuated by a primal cry. Then dead silence, as if the world was waiting for chaos. Several individuals slithered into view at the corner near some burned-out buildings. Sarah's breath came quicker, more shallow. There was no other choice but to hastily descend the rank stairwell across the street on shaky legs to the almost empty downtown platform. Only a shadowy figure or two lingered at each of its far ends.

She studied the platform's surface, random puddles gathering here and there. Litter stuck in corners near the grimy walls, their tiles cracked and vandalized. A lone shape appeared on the stairs, an indistinguishable form that descended and moved close to the edge of the platform, peering into the darkness in search of the promising beam of an approaching train.

Ten minutes? Perhaps fifteen? More? It finally emerged like an apparition out of the inky emptiness. Sarah felt the train's deep vibrations before hearing or seeing it clearly. Then it pulled to a stop with an ear-splitting screech. She boarded, wedging into a corner of the car and fixing her eyes on the blue and yellow and crimson graffiti splashing its interior, as if it was of utmost importance. Although aware of them, she did not look directly at the very few other travelers there.

An eternity of minutes passed. Additional passengers began trickling on at intervening stops. Finally, and with a sigh of relief, Sarah arrived at her own.

She barely remembered the walk from the subway

and, once home, she closed the door to her apartment firmly and stood with her back to it for a moment, shutting her eyes. She'd been lucky tonight. Of this she was sure.

In a short while, Sarah clutched a mug of hot tea. She curled her legs under her on the blue sofa, a small blanket of Aunt Addie's tight around her lap for comfort. Wherever the teen escaped to, Sarah had no clue. Her intuition told her he didn't belong in the area where he'd fled any more than she did. He'd just tried to run from Sarah. In a panic. *Why?* What had he meant by he didn't realize who she was? Who she knew? The cops were the obvious answer, but that didn't seem to fit. Did it have to do with Vincent Milaeve? How? Why was Sarah a threat? And why had he had apologized for yelling at May?

Now something else occurred to her. The detectives. She had to tell them.

Chapter Thirty

The teen's words echoed in Sarah's mind throughout her entire sleepless night.

I didn't know who you were...and who you knew.

In the morning, Sarah called Kelly to say she might come in a couple of minutes late. She had to tell the detectives first thing and shuddered to think what they'd say.

Sweeping into the precinct before her own starting time at work, Sarah hoped the two men would be in by now. Maybe even in early. Or even in at all.

Sergeant Brushie greeted her cheerfully.

"So good to see you again, Sarah. You're quite the early bird."

"Good to see you, too. I was sort of hoping there might be some other early birds today?"

They were just getting their coffee, and Sergeant Brushie told her to go on in.

"Sarah!" Cahill's eyebrows raised in surprise, but he seemed in a good mood. Then again, criminals might just be waking up themselves and not have started on their busy day.

"Coffee, Sarah?" asked Gil. He smiled, but concern crept onto his face. She shook her head and smiled back.

"Thanks, no. Umm, I have to get to work. But I need to tell you something that happened last night."

She hesitated. The three of them stood. Waiting. "It happened quickly." She eased into a chair. "Uh, maybe what I did wasn't the best idea, but it might have brought out a new detail or two…"

The two men sat, a whiff of apprehension in the air.

"Are you all right, Sarah?" asked Gil. She nodded, to his visible relief.

"Why do I suspect we're going to get the latest chapter in another Nancy Drew adventure?" Cahill sipped his coffee and sat back.

Sarah took that as her cue and plunged into her story, finishing in record time. Pain spread across Gil's face. Cahill stared at the ceiling as if for strength.

There was a momentary silence.

Gil put his coffee cup down and leaned forward earnestly. "Thank God you're okay."

Cahill took another gulp of coffee and shook his head. "Sarah, Sarah. What are we going to do to keep you out of trouble?"

"Actually, I don't try to get into these situations."

"Imagine if you tried." Cahill was clearly frustrated. He opened his mouth as if to go further, but Gil gave him a look and then interrupted.

"Thanks for coming to us. For telling us the truth."

"Why wouldn't I tell you the truth?" Sarah asked.

"Because not a lot of people do." Cahill gave a long sigh.

"Every detail helps, and we're grateful," said Gil. Then he looked at her, pain spilling into his voice. "But, Sarah, you've got to stay safe."

"I'm working on it."

"*Keep* working on it," said Cahill.

****

Gil walked her to the front door of the precinct.

"Did you tell him not to get mad at me?" Sarah asked.

"Actually, yes. A while ago. But I also figure that Harry's become quite absorbed in your sleuthing adventures."

"And you?"

"Absorbed? Yes. Scared? Totally." He turned to her as they stepped outside for a brief moment. "Sarah, I'm worried. I want you to be safe."

"Thanks. Me, too."

Gil waited a beat before going on.

"I'm really looking forward to tomorrow," he said. He hesitated another moment. "Sarah, I have another invitation for you, if you're free and might be interested. I was going to call you later on."

Seemed as if Gil's sister just put together a last-minute, tree-trimming party on Sunday afternoon. Some family, a couple of neighbors, and so forth. He'd love it if Sarah could come, if she was up for two dates in one weekend.

"You can let me know, but I wanted to ask…"

"I'd definitely like to come." She returned that warm smile with one of her own.

****

"You weren't even two minutes late." Kelly met her at the door. "I didn't say anything to anyone."

"Thanks, Kelly," said Sarah. "I had the weirdest experience. Actually, a lot of weird stuff's been going on. Any chance of coffee after work today?"

"I'm counting on it." Kelly's voice was bright. "I need to tell you things, too."

When Sarah reached her desk, she studied the papers there. They weren't piled nearly as high as they'd been in the past. It was obvious that the business was winding down.

Edgar walked out of his office, prompting Sarah's growing unease in his presence.

"Hi, Sarah." At least he was wearing another jacket, not the one with the hanging thread. "Not a lot for you today. Just some follow-ups." He laid the folders down.

In an out-of-character move, he sat down in the chair next to her desk. "I feel so bad the agency's closing. I just wanted to tell you that Lou and Mary are doing all they can to be sure the three of us have jobs to go to.

Sarah nodded. Unease lingered at the back of her throat.

"Everything's changing around here," he said.

This was odd. Edgar randomly passing the time chatting?

"Even the old school just got emptied out."

Sarah nodded. "You went there, right?" Then she couldn't resist. "And your brother, too?"

Edgar raised his eyebrows slowly, a movement that was a mixture of surprise and wariness. Sarah wondered if she might have ventured too far.

"There were some old photos in the church library," she explained quickly. "I sometimes go there to say a prayer and borrow a book or two from the library."

"Yes, my brother and I did go there." Edgar's voice was somber. "But I didn't realize there were any old photos around."

"Just a few of some of the classes. Actually, I like vintage things and happened to take a look one day when I was on my way out of the library."

Sort of passing by. By pre-arranged plan. And with a magnifying glass.

"I only saw a couple of people whose names I knew, including the Butlers. Gianni's boys went there, too, but I guess they were much younger." Now Sarah ventured further, pushing the word "sleuthing" from her mind. "You know what else was interesting?" she continued. "The lists of achievement awards. I saw you got one for arithmetic, and your brother got one for acting. And the two of you looked so much alike, except for your glasses, of course."

Edgar looked down at the desk and then spoke in a perfectly measured cadence, not in his usual shy, often stumbling delivery. "That was a long…long time ago."

Suddenly, Sarah felt she had crossed the line. That he might be aware of her suspicion that he really wasn't Edgar at all.

He looked at her closely. Yes, she was almost sure. Those glasses were just a prop.

Was Edgar the person the teen meant when he said, "I didn't know who you knew?" Was he guilty of something? And had Amelia been right, despite what everyone said?

A moment later, however, he lapsed back into his usual way and rose from his chair. "I just wanted to let you know that while I'm interviewing for jobs, I'll also be on the lookout for you and for Kelly, too. We're all going to come through this."

"That's really nice of you, Edgar. Thanks."

****

Lunchtime couldn't come fast enough. Sarah grabbed her shoulder bag and ran in the direction of Crafty Crafts. She'd brought her sketchbook with her, hoping Amelia might be free to chat for a few minutes. When Sarah flew in the door, Amelia was sitting behind the counter. Grace was tending to something in one of the aisles.

"Sarah!" Amelia broke into a huge smile. "Look." She pointed. "There's your beautiful picture. Everyone's been admiring it."

Sarah's sketch of the little pewter mug, complete with flowers overflowing, was displayed in a place of honor. Grace had nicely matted and framed it.

Sarah was truly pleased. "Thanks so much! It looks lovely there."

"You should sell your sketches. Maybe get some commissions."

"That's so kind of you to say. But I'm not advanced enough yet."

"You're quite advanced." Grace joined them.

"Tell you what," said Sarah. "I'll make a sketch of your shop for you. Then if people like my work and might want their own sketch, you could let me know."

"Good idea," said Amelia. Grace nodded enthusiastically.

The door opened abruptly, and an older couple bustled in. Grace approached them, and Sarah seized this hoped-for opportunity to talk with Amelia privately.

"Could I show you something?" She pulled out her sketchpad and pointed to sketches of the teen. "By any chance, do you know this guy? Or have you seen him?"

Amelia scrutinized the teen's face and pointed to

the drawing without the scowl. "I've seen him around delivering things. You should ask Jake. He might know more because he's got a good view of the whole world when he's at the flower shop. Or possibly Matt would know." Amelia looked at the sketch again. "But yes, I've seen him."

"Thanks, Amelia." Then, noting that Grace was still occupied with the couple, she turned to Edgar's picture. "Last time I was here, you said you'd seen this man walking with a friend?"

"Sure. I saw him with the old engraver's son a while back. Were you looking for him?"

"Oh, no. I was curious. The old engraver's name was in the recipe book on the page about the restaurant he used to go to. I've sort of gotten intrigued by the history of the area."

Amelia was more than willing to talk. "Grace tells me it couldn't have been the old engraver's son. That I'd never recognize him after all these years. But I knew it was him. He was the spitting image of his father."

But would anyone, except for Sarah, believe Amelia? Including the cops?

Amelia sighed. "That old engraver must be long dead now."

But hadn't the cops said something about the old engraver having died not long ago?

****

"It's looking good." Kelly spoke after having barely removed her coat and just before sliding into one of Dexter's red plastic seats after work that afternoon. Long before the waitress brought their coffee mugs, Kelly was halfway through a recap of her job interview with a large publishing company the previous day.

"Dave called me this morning. He said he smells an offer early next week."

"I'm guessing this is a good smell." Sarah laughed, imagining Dave waving his cheap ballpoint pen while delivering this favorite among his numerous punchlines.

"Definitely." Kelly's voice was confident. "It looks as if I could be giving my notice to the Butlers soon. Except, Sarah, I feel bad about leaving you before the agency closes."

"Don't, Kelly. There's a chance I could be leaving, too." Then she told Kelly about her own interview with Clare. "But so much other stuff has happened in the meantime."

Sarah quickly updated Kelly on recent events, including the story of the subway incident with the teenager and what he'd said to her that had been so perplexing.

"Who you *were* and who you *knew*?" Kelly's face scrunched in confusion.

"Yeah. I can't figure it out." Sarah pulled out her sketchpad, opening it to the two contrasting images of the teen.

"You're right," said Kelly, pushing aside her coffee mug and carefully studying them. "When he's not scowling, he looks scared. And you still don't think he killed that guy?"

"No, not really. Despite him being obnoxious at first, I get the feeling that his tough exterior thing is all an act. Plus, he's really scared of something or someone."

"You mean besides you?" joked Kelly as she began

scrutinizing the next sketch.

Kelly paged through more sketches as Sarah continued. "Could it be someone else? Or someone I don't realize I know? He said he didn't realize who I *knew*," repeated Sarah. "Makes no sense, unless it's the cops. And he seemed to brush that off."

Kelly looked up for a moment. "Could it be because both the detectives we know are plainclothes guys? And the kid only thinks of a cop as someone in a uniform?"

"I never thought of that," Sarah said. "But then who does he think they really are?"

"That's anyone's guess." Kelly shrugged and continued looking at the sketches.

"I've tried to buy the whole idea that Vincent Milaeve was just the victim of a street crime. But there's too much going on."

"Like the kid," said Kelly. "And Mr. and Mrs. Butler acting weird, especially Mr. Butler with that file. Although maybe they just don't want to get involved."

"Yeah. But what about Edgar?" asked Sarah.

"Amelia could still have been mistaken that it was Vincent walking with him. Even if she is sharp, her eyesight may be getting poor," said Kelly. "And everyone seems to think she's losing some grasp on reality, too."

Sarah grimaced as Kelly continued leafing through the sketches. "And it can't be May or Father Haney—or me! At least I hope not." Kelly chuckled.

Sarah shook her head. "So who's left? Not Amelia or Grace. Neither one of them looks like they could pull a gun on someone."

But didn't the cops say that sometimes people

weren't what they seemed?

"What about Matt?" Kelly asked, studying the page with his sketch. "I mean his father took over old Mr. Milaeve's space."

"Yeah, but Matt was a baby then. The Milaeves were gone. And his dad's business was just printing. Matt took over after college when his dad died, and now he can't wait to go to that pretty suburban business park. He's not going to miss much around here."

"Yeah," said Kelly. "I only met him once when he brought those poster ᴄopies to the office, and he didn't seem like the type to wield a gun."

"Jake either." Sarah pointed to the mostly bland face of the young florist.

"Still, if Vincent's murder isn't a random street crime, then there's not only the question of who but, also, of why? Why would someone kill him on purpose?" Kelly looked up.

"I wish I knew. Money? Revenge? Status? Hiding something?" Sarah shook her head.

"Like Edgar hiding his identity? Or Mr. Butler ignoring that file from years ago? What are the real motives here?" Kelly turned back to the sketchpad, studying one face in particular.

When Sarah looked down at that page, she burst out with an emphatic, "No!"

"Look, Sarah. I don't even want to think it, but we have to consider everyone."

Sarah was horrified. "It couldn't possibly be Gianni. And like I told you, the teen talked back to him that Sunday afternoon on the street, too."

"Yeah, but it didn't bother Gianni, did it? And he's been around here for a long time, and you said he grew up in a tough area. Old as he is, he's got street smarts. Gianni could probably handle things way better than any of those younger guys." Kelly kept studying the sketch.

An image of Gianni coolly and without hesitation coming to her aid with that pipe flashed through Sarah's mind. She caught her breath.

But lots of guys had street smarts. Hadn't Gianni said that as a kid, Edgar's twin, Elwyn, could take care of himself on the street? But did you need street smarts to shoot someone? And then it all came back to the original question. Why?

Sarah felt a sharp pain deep inside. "What's the motive? No, I can't believe it's Gianni."

Kelly sighed. "I can't either, Sarah. I'm just trying to think of something we missed."

They sat for a moment before Kelly finally turned to Sarah's sketches of the cops.

"Well, it couldn't be Detective Cahill. He's too busy committing the crime of being grumpy to have done anything else." Kelly appeared to be trying for some humor after she'd brought up the subject of Gianni and saw how much pain it caused Sarah.

"And," she continued, "we know for certain it's not Detective Rian. At least not since I suspect you two have started dating."

Sarah blushed, and Kelly grinned. "It was only a matter of time. You should have seen the way he looked at you whenever he came into the office."

Chapter Thirty-One

Sarah spent early Saturday morning working on the sketch of Crafty Crafts she'd promised to give Amelia. She even made a quick trip there before the store opened, squeezing onto the step of an old building across the street, a perfect vantage point to study the place. One by one, she decided the shop's little flaws added up to an appealing whole. She admired the gently lopsided steps down to the door and subtly humorous lettering on its sign. For the first time, she realized that the store's diminutive windows artfully camouflaged security bars. Nothing was ordinary about this place.

She still had some time before needing to return home and get ready for her date with Gil. But as much as she tried to shake it off, curiosity took hold after her last conversation with Amelia, coupled with a random fact the detectives dropped when she and Kelly talked to them. Just curiosity. That was all.

Now, Sarah pushed open the door to the local library, a venerable branch close by to Crafty Crafts and not far from the office. She was greeted with a respectful hush. Then again, the place was more than half empty.

Sarah approached the desk. "I have a sort of unusual request," she said, realizing she had no idea of how to find this information herself.

The young reference librarian looked up eagerly.

Perhaps it was a new job for her. She still smiled, even after Sarah explained what she was looking for—an obituary for an elderly man somewhere in upstate New York who had probably died earlier in the year.

"Here," said the young woman, offering paper and pencil. "Why don't you write down what you need and give me your daytime phone." She promised to see what she could find but confessed it might take a few days to get back to Sarah.

With profuse thanks, Sarah headed home, asking herself why she was doing this. She tried not to think of the detectives pleading with her to be cautious. Still, she had only requested some information from a public library.

No harm in that. Probably too dull for Nancy Drew.

****

Sarah and Gil lingered over a glass of wine before dinner at a small Greek restaurant. They were talking about the plot of the movie they'd seen that afternoon.

After a slight pause, Sarah changed the subject. "Five minutes? I promise."

"Another sleuthing confession?"

"Sort of."

"Go ahead, Sarah. I'm sure Harry will be sorry to have missed this." He grinned.

"Oh, please! I can still hear Harry…I mean Detective Cahill…lecturing me."

"You're turning into one of his favorite people." Gil tried unsuccessfully to suppress a laugh.

"Never thought I'd see the day."

"Seriously, Sarah. If you need to talk, you don't have to hold it to five minutes. You know that.

Whatever's on your mind."

"Thanks." She took another sip of her wine and then launched into the gist of her talks with Kelly as well as her recent visit to Amelia.

"You do manage to keep busy." Again, Gil spoke with a good-natured glint of humor.

"I try."

"Look, Sarah." His voice grew serious. "Everything you've said about things not making sense—makes sense. I agree there's a lot of loose ends here. And I'm sorry we really can't verify Amelia's stories. But Vincent Milaeve's murder could still be just a street crime. And I'm not saying it is…"

"But you think I might be looking for trouble where there isn't any," interrupted Sarah.

"Truthfully, I'm worried that you're looking for trouble period. As in putting yourself in danger if there's a more complicated backstory. I'm still recuperating after hearing about your subway adventure the other night. And the kid's story might be an altogether separate and dangerous issue, totally unrelated to the murder." He took another sip of his wine. "And let's not forget that if the murder *was* a genuine street crime, then there's still someone else on the loose who you need to worry about." Gil put his hand over her outstretched one. "Sarah, please stay safe."

Best not to mention her library visit this morning.

"We're still looking for more details about Vincent Milaeve and, sad to say, we have a lot of other cases pending in the meantime."

"I know, Gil. And thanks for listening." She squeezed his hand, which was still over hers. "Okay, enough about police business. Please tell me about tomorrow."

As their dinners arrived, Gil filled her in on the informal tree-trimming party that his sister and her family were holding the next day.

"My family is grateful for good people and happy occasions. They don't take any of it for granted now. It's been a challenging year or two." He explained that his mom passed away last year after an extended illness. Then his brother-in-law, a firefighter, had been injured.

He looked up. "I'm happy you're coming tomorrow. By the way, so is Mikey. He hasn't stopped talking about your drawing of the donation box with the teddy bear climbing out."

Sarah laughed. "Can I bring something?"

"Nothing really. They've only asked people to contribute an ornament for the tree if they want to, but don't worry. I'll have some with me when I pick you up tomorrow."

"Thanks." Sarah was suddenly struck with inspiration. "But I'm going to bring a special ornament, too."

****

Sarah pulled out three cardboard boxes from way back in her clothes closet when she got home from their date that night. These were among the last of Aunt Addie's things. She'd pushed off going through them. Now she rummaged through their contents, looking for a small collection of Christmas ornaments in there somewhere. When she finally found them, they were exactly as she remembered.

Smiling to herself, she unwrapped the small teddy

bear, wearing his tiny Santa Claus hat, a candy cane tucked securely under his arm. She wanted to bring it to the party to add to Amanda's tree, making sure that Mikey would have it for Christmases to come. Pushing the boxes neatly to the side, Sarah left them out on the floor, vowing to go through their remaining contents soon. It was time. Then she carefully re-wrapped the ornament and put it by her purse, so she wouldn't forget it the next day.

****

Amanda and Mike's building was a brief walk from Sarah's apartment. Gil came to get her at four o'clock on Sunday. Their lighthearted conversation never touched on crime and murder and was only interrupted as they got off the elevator at their destination. The scratchy sound of an old record floated into the hallway. The tune grew louder as Gil's dad, Ben, opened the door. His curly-ish graying hair belied his youthful zest. He didn't waste a second before welcoming her.

"Sarah, it's great to meet you. Come on in." Ben grasped her hand.

"I love that old song," Sarah said after greeting Ben and listening to a few strains of "Have Yourself a Merry Little Christmas."

"It's an original recording. Vintage. From 1945," said Ben with a smile. "You know who's singing?"

"Judy Garland. She sang it in a film in 1944. And 'The Trolley Song,' too."

"At last!" Ben was beaming. "Someone who appreciates good old-fashioned music!"

"Careful, Sarah," Gil said. "If you encourage him too much, he'll insist on playing his entire thousand-record collection for you."

"Now *that's* impressive!" said Sarah, joining in their good-natured banter.

"If it wasn't the holiday season, I'd play you some of my rare recordings of Cole Porter and Noel Coward singing their own work. I just found them the other day. Misfiled. You'll have to visit again soon and listen to them."

"I'd love to," said Sarah.

Noel Coward? Hadn't she just heard an old favorite or two of his on the radio?

Amanda and Mike's apartment was filled with light and music and friendly faces. Sarah felt their warm hospitality before she was barely a few feet inside the door.

Ben continued with a grin as Mikey ran over to say hi. "Word has it you're a fine artist, in addition to being a music lover. My grandson here is your biggest fan."

With Ben's help, Mikey then introduced Sarah to his best friend and his family. Then Amanda joined them, continuing the introductions from building neighbors to the student nurses who'd been at the precinct's toy drive. Warm and friendly chatter competed with Ben's vintage-78 holiday records. Sarah basked in the energy of it all and, especially, in Gil's obvious joy at her presence.

Before dessert, the tree-trimming began. The guests gathered near the lush little pine, glowing with twinkling lights in its special corner of the room. The student nurses, full of energy after numerous trips to the loaded buffet table, broke into an eager rendition of "Frosty, the Snowman" and other favorites as everyone took a turn hanging the ornaments they'd brought.

When it was Gil's and Sarah's turn, she asked Mikey to help. His face lit up when he saw the teddy bear ornament and, together, they added it to a special place on the tree.

Chapter Thirty-Two

Several papers blew off Sarah's desk Monday morning as Kelly ran over to her.

"Do I smell good news?" Sarah asked with a grin, doing her best impression of Dave.

"Excellent news. I got it!" Kelly was so jubilant that she couldn't stop hopping from one foot to the other. Sarah wondered if she might soon fly around the room.

In hushed whispers, Kelly revealed that she had a firm job offer and could start the Monday after New Year's. This would allow her to give proper notice to the Butlers and leave a few days free during the holidays for herself. And her new department even invited her to their holiday cocktail party the following week, just to get to know everyone. She thanked Sarah profusely for introducing her to Dave, who'd brokered the deal.

Sarah hugged her friend. "I'm so happy for you! When will you break the news?"

Kelly suddenly stood still and grimaced. "Sometime today. Whenever I can tell the Butlers together."

"It's all good. We'll go out and celebrate soon," said Sarah.

Kelly's good news lifted Sarah's spirits in the now gloomy atmosphere of the Butler Agency. It kept her afloat until lunchtime when she ran over to the church. Father Haney had promised to fill her in about his own recent talks with Bridget Grady and the others to discuss May. He had certainly taken the lead in coordinating the group. Sarah was grateful.

"Bridget's going to call you again and talk further, but I think we have an excellent chance of really helping," said the priest. This was the most enthusiastic she'd ever seen him.

"There's a new pilot program we're looking into. Bridget will explain it better. We still have to figure out a little more about May's background and what, if any, family she might still have. But this is a good team, and I think something positive will come from it."

"That's wonderful news," said Sarah.

"Bridget is taking the lead. She even stopped by to talk to May this morning. She told May she's an old friend of yours."

Ah, the old neighborhood network in Queens, as Lil always said. And as Sarah remembered Bridget, she was sure to handle all of this quite well.

"Bridget thinks May could have had some sort of health situation or trauma that affected her speech. And it might have caused her to gravitate toward comforting places she remembered growing up. That would account for her coming here. The humming probably means something important to her, too. Bridget believes that May understands far more than she's given credit for, but she needs to relearn how to express it. And Bridget would like to work with her as part of her ongoing research project."

When Sarah left the church, she stopped to chat with May. Once more, May's eyes were drawn to

Sarah's scarf.

"The flowers are pretty, aren't they?" Sarah watched how the woman's eyes were transfixed. And once again her fingers gently touched the little embroidered flowers on the panel. Sarah wondered if May's mother, or even May herself, might have done embroidery such as this. She'd mention this to Bridget.

"My friend Bridget was so happy to meet you this morning when she went to church. I know she'll come and visit again."

May responded with a sweet smile.

****

Mr. Butler was putting on his coat as Sarah walked in the door after lunch. He gave a brief nod to Sarah before he spoke.

"I guess you've heard that Kelly found a new job." He ran his hand over his hair.

Sarah nodded. Kelly must have broken the news just a little while ago.

"We're happy for her, of course." Mr. Butler then reassured her that they would do everything to help Sarah and Edgar with jobs. "I'll be gone for the afternoon with a client. When you have a moment, Mrs. Butler said she wanted to talk to you."

"Oh, sure. Thanks."

As he left, Mr. Butler hunched over as if he had the weight of the world on his shoulders.

****

Sarah's footsteps echoed as she headed up the stairs into the all-too-quiet office there.

"Mrs. But—"

The woman never gave Sarah a chance to finish. "Sarah, please come join me." Mrs. Butler patted the place next to her on the worn leather couch against the wall. Obviously, this was not a day for the formality of the desk and visitors' chairs.

Sarah sat down and studied the deep circles under Mrs. Butler's eyes. It looked as if she hadn't slept enough for a while. She grabbed Sarah's hand and held onto it as if for dear life.

"Kelly just told us the news. And, Sarah, you know that Mr. Butler and I are doing all we can to make sure you and Edgar will have jobs to go to when we close the agency. You've been so good to us and worked so hard. We want you to find a job that will make you happy."

Sarah didn't know what to say, so she smiled and nodded, her hand growing uncomfortable in Mrs. Butler's tight grasp.

"I think there could be something you might like that's coming up. It's at a medium-sized insurance firm, and we'll be turning over some clients to them."

More insurance?

"The manager visited us just about an hour ago, and I thought we might catch you and grab a quick sandwich and talk about the job. But you'd already gone. He'll be back later in the week, though, so maybe we can set something up then? I'm so sorry we missed you today."

Sarah felt obligated to give an explanation for her whereabouts at lunch, even though it wasn't really necessary. But Mrs. Butler seemed to be waiting for Sarah to say something.

"I'm sorry I missed you, too. Umm, but I ran over to see Father Haney. You know May? The woman who sits on the church steps? We're all trying to get her some help, and Father Haney wanted to fill me in on the latest developments."

"Well, Sarah… That's lovely." Mrs. Butler was flustered. But why?

Sarah continued, wondering if she should say any more. "We think May went to the old church school years ago. There's a few photos of the first classes on the wall. Uh, with names and the awards students got for things and all. Umm, it looks like May got awards for music and sewing. And we wanted to look into this further…"

"School photos?" Mrs. Butler interrupted, genuinely surprised. Just as Edgar had been.

"Nice ones of some of the graduates. I saw Mr. Butler's picture and, I think, one of you, too. That's so nice you both went to school together. Your name was Mary Vandert, right? I was sure that was you in the picture."

Mrs. Butler's face congealed in shock. Her abrupt silence was unnerving. By now, though, it was too late. Sarah couldn't stop herself.

But was it dangerous to continue?

"And can I ask you something?" Sarah didn't wait for a response before plunging ahead. "I have this recipe book from a local crafts fair with neighborhood stories. There was this goulash recipe from Two Violins restaurant with quotes from the owners and from the headwaiter, Lel Vandert. I, umm, just wondered if you were related? It's such a small world and all."

Sarah stopped, a sudden chill creeping through her. Mrs. Butler stared at her, wide-eyed after these last words. Stone-still, not moving a muscle. What would happen now? Would she yell? Deny she'd ever heard of

Lel Vandert? Throw something? Pull out a gun and shoot Sarah?

But what happened next was even more stunning. After an awful silence, Mrs. Butler burst into crushing sobs. In a moment, she was leaning against Sarah. What else could Sarah do except put her arm around Mrs. Butler and let her cry?

A few minutes passed. The woman was wretched.

"Can I get you a glass of water? Or something?"

"No, thank you. I just need to tell you…" she said in between gasping sobs. "I told some of this to Detective Cahill, but not everything." She looked up at Sarah with a tear-stained face, makeup blotched, some of it smeared on Sarah's sweater.

"It's all right, Mrs. Butler."

Sarah snatched a nearby box of tissues and waited for the latest wave of sobs to pass. Mrs. Butler grabbed a tissue and blew her nose with fervor.

"Lel Vandert was my father. He was the headwaiter, an excellent headwaiter, at Two Violins." She halted a few seconds to catch her breath. "When I was a girl, I used to go there with him sometimes. It was nice seeing the people and hearing the music. I'd do my homework. Work on my spelling. I liked that."

Sarah murmured soothing noises, hoping this would urge the woman to continue.

"And old Mr. and Mrs. Milaeve would eat there a lot. They'd always say hello to me and ask me about school. Mr. Milaeve was a fine, fine engraver. He did specialized work for the important people in the big mansions and town houses and at the private clubs over near Fifth Avenue. He was in high demand, and his business did really well."

Sarah hadn't said a word about the Milaeves. This had just spilled out.

She patted Mrs. Butler on the shoulder, encouraging her to go on.

"All I told Detective Cahill was that a long time ago I met old Mr. and Mrs. Milaeve where my father worked. Because the cops wanted to know if any of us had ever heard the name. But I couldn't tell him the rest."

There was more?

"About their son, Vincent. He was a little older than me, and he went to another school. He would come and eat once in a while with his parents. I got to know him." This last statement was punctuated with a sob. "I…I…oh, Sarah, I guess I had what you young people today call a crush on him."

Sarah struggled to envision the sobbing woman next to her as a girl, one drawn to a long-ago youth who turned into a murdered man on the church steps decades later.

"When I got out of high school, we went out a few times. All very innocent, please understand," continued Mrs. Butler.

Stunned, Sarah nodded, wondering what revelation was coming next.

"And then… And then, he and a couple of high school friends pulled some sort of deal to make money. They weren't poor. Vincent's family was very rich. But he wanted to prove himself on his own. He always was sort of rebellious. It was part of his charm." She took a deep breath. "So he sold some sort of fake securities and all. Things he beautifully engraved himself, of course, because he grew up learning the art. And then he and his friends did some people out of money. I'm not sure how many or how he did it. One of them was my husband's father."

This explained the old letters that were in the files.

"Old Mr. Milaeve found out. He was furious. He said Vincent had ruined the family name. The war was on, and Vincent and his friends ran off and enlisted. That was the last anyone saw him. Mr. Milaeve discreetly made what amends he could, left his business, and they moved."

Mrs. Butler looked at Sarah and spoke as if pleading.

"Sarah, I couldn't believe Vincent came back after all these years and that someone…murdered him." She stifled another sob. "I was afraid to tell the cops any more than just knowing the family's name. I was afraid they might think I killed him or that Lou did because of his father."

Motives. Revenge on behalf of Mr. Butler's father? Or maybe Mrs. Butler felt jilted somehow? *There was another motive for the list.*

"That was all so many years ago. No one could think you or Mr. Butler are at fault."

"I didn't tell Lou I went to the cops. Then I overheard you and Kelly tell my husband about the letters you found from old Mr. Milaeve." Mrs. Butler twisted the tissue in her hand.

She eavesdropped that afternoon? Seemed everyone was doing it these days.

"I asked him later, and he didn't want to get involved. We didn't talk about it anymore."

Sarah's stomach was in knots. At least it seemed as if Mrs. Butler was coming clean.

But what about her husband? Could Vincent's scam have had long-term implications?

"Mrs. Butler." Sarah's words were gentle. "You could share the full story with the cops. They'd probably appreciate it, and I think you'd feel better, too. I'm sure they'd understand and would never think you did anything wrong. And maybe Mr. Butler would want to join you?"

The cops already knew about that old file anyway from Sarah and Kelly.

Mrs. Butler looked down at her hands, clenched tightly in her lap. Finally, she spoke.

"Maybe it's best I speak to the cops first. And, Sarah? Please don't say anything to Mr. Butler right now. I want to tell him myself."

"Okay. Would you like me to call one of the detectives and see if we could set up something for you to talk with them?"

She looked at Sarah with tears in her eyes, but she nodded. "Thank you, Sarah. You're so kind. You're probably right. I would appreciate it if you'd do that. I need to talk to them."

"Why don't you go and splash some cold water on your face while I make some calls."

As soon as the woman left the room, Sarah called the precinct, hoping at least one of the detectives would be there. She wanted to get this going before Mrs. Butler lost her nerve. Thankfully, she got through right away.

"Gil?"

"Sarah?"

"You're not going to believe this."

****

Sarah walked Mrs. Butler to the precinct and made sure she was settled in with Gil. He said he'd call later. Then she ran back to the office and filled Kelly in. Edgar was buried in paperwork. And Mr. Butler was still away with his client, unaware that his wife was spilling some intriguing tales to the cops.

And what about Mr. Butler, anyway?

Later on, Gil called her at the office. "Mrs. Butler's okay. We had a uniform bring her home. She was still a bit upset."

"I can imagine."

"Maybe you could fill me in on what prompted this? Just so I can reassure Harry that you're keeping up with your regular sleuthing duties." Amusement tinged his voice.

As Sarah told her story, she did confess to having asked a few leading questions. "But she was definitely ready to talk."

"She did seem relieved to tell us everything," agreed Gil. "Any sign of Mr. Butler?"

"No. He said he was out with a client for the afternoon."

"Okay. Just keep on the lookout for anything strange. And, Sarah, please call me anytime something doesn't seem right. Or just anytime."

Even over the phone, she could sense his concern.

"I'm afraid to ask if you have any more sleuthing planned," Gil asked.

"Better you don't ask. Things just seem to erupt spontaneously anyway. Tonight is all about sketching, though. Generally."

"Hmm. It's the 'generally' that scares me."

Chapter Thirty-Three

After work, Sarah decided to visit Crafty Crafts. She was anxious to give Amelia the sketch of the shop. And she was hoping Amelia might have a few more bits of information. No matter what anyone else thought, Sarah still believed in Amelia.

The moment she came through the door, Amelia greeted her like an old friend.

Sarah smiled at this warm welcome. "Hi, Amelia. Just like I promised, I made you a picture of the shop." She pulled out her sketchpad. "I hope you like it."

"I already know I will," said the woman.

Sarah carefully removed the sketch from the pad.

Amelia examined it closely. "Beautiful. You caught all the little details. How the steps have a slope. How the sign is slightly unusual." She looked up. "Thank you, Sarah. This is really special. Grace will frame it and we'll hang it where everyone can see."

Sarah hoped Amelia might comment more about the past, but they were interrupted. Jake arrived, carrying a gorgeous potted plant.

"Hey, Sarah!" He nodded in her direction. "Amelia, here's the holiday plant Grace wanted for her friend." He placed it on the far end of the countertop.

"Thank you, Jake. She'll be back soon. Come take a look at Sarah's latest sketch. We're going to display it, and then if any customers are interested in hiring

Sarah for their own sketches, they can get in touch with her."

Jake praised Sarah's sketch as Amelia continued. "You should do a sketch of the flower shop, too. That would be even more advertising for you, Sarah."

"Excellent idea," agreed Jake.

A customer entered the shop, and Sarah realized she wouldn't have any more opportunity to chat with Amelia. She promised to visit again soon and do some holiday shopping there. Both she and Jake said their goodbyes to Amelia and headed for the door together.

Jake reached to open the door for Sarah. She stifled a gasp.

Was she mistaken?

Outside, darkness quickly enveloped the street in the few moments it took them to reach the corner.

"Jake." Sarah swallowed hard. "Can we talk for a minute?"

"Sure." They stopped near the isolated cross-street, a nearby light illuminating their faces. Jake reached into his jacket and withdrew a pack of cigarettes, offering one to Sarah.

"No, thanks. Umm, Jake…"

He quickly lit up, casually taking his first puff. He exhaled in the direction of the moon, a sliver of its surface barely visible over the jagged outline of buildings. The smoky aroma was unmistakable, even in the cool night air.

Yes, she was sure of what she'd seen.

Jake now turned to Sarah, his expression different, with a hint of something ominous.

Her sketch of Jake had been quick, in need of more time to clearly define it. It had been a bland face until now. More accurately, it was a blank canvas of sorts. But now, lines and shadows, more definition, were filling in that blank canvas.

"What's on your mind, Sarah?"

The mark was unmistakable. His right arm was crooked, the hand eloquently angled as he moved the cigarette slowly to and from his lips. His face had taken on a sly and almost shrewd look. It was pointless to beat around the bush. Jake knew she wanted to talk about more than just a sketch of the flower shop.

"Your hand, Jake. I noticed your tattoo." She hadn't been aware of Jake's hands until tonight. He'd always been busy with something, wearing his gardener's gloves, or else there was something to distract her. But now, the slender, wavy line was clearly obvious. Discreet as far as tattoos went, but still unmistakable.

Jake gave a half-smirk as he turned his hand for a quick gaze, almost as if to confirm the mark was still there. Then he took another drag on his cigarette. He didn't say anything. He wasn't going to make this easy for Sarah.

Now what? Nothing like the truth.

"Look, Jake. A teenager hassled me a couple of times. He had the same tattoo on the back of his hand. I just wondered what it means. I don't even know who he is…"

"Dek?" His face turned into one of feigned interest. "He's just a dumb neighborhood kid." Then he gave a mirthless laugh. Jake held up his tattooed hand. "A copycat. A wannabe who's done a few stupid things."

Sarah started to ask something else but Jake stopped her.

"You seem like a nice lady. Maybe a little too curious lately, though. My advice? Stick to your drawing. Go downtown and do some more holiday shopping. Meet your friends for dinner. Forget about tattoos. Some of them, like this one, are meaningless." He briefly held up his hand and then tossed his smoke into the gutter, just as the teen, Dek, had done on that first evening not so very long ago.

Then with one swift motion, he pushed up his sleeve to reveal a threateningly inked forearm. "And some of them aren't."

Sarah stared, speechless. But as swiftly as Jake made his revelation, he yanked down his sleeve and assumed the blank-canvas expression on his face.

"Looking forward to that sketch of the flower shop," he said pleasantly. "'Night, Sarah."

She watched Jake's figure retreat into the darkness. Only then did Sarah realize how badly she was trembling. How could she have been so wrong about Jake?

She'd sketched his face as bland, a blank canvas. But eventually, something always emerges on a blank canvas.

****

Sarah had to walk off her terror, or at least try.

I didn't realize who you are…or who you knew…

The teen's words—Dek's words—echoed over and over in her mind. Could the person he meant have been Jake? Had he seen her talking to Jake on some random occasion? Had Dek been following her? But why?

She needed to tell Gil. He was on a late schedule this week and should be at the precinct. Even a lecture from Detective Cahill would be welcome right now.

The air was quiet, heavy with sinister chill as the early winter evening settled in deeper, colder. The streets seemed almost devoid of people. Sarah walked faster, almost breaking into a run. When she reached the heavy door of the precinct, she was close to breathless.

There was chaos inside. Sergeant Brushie wasn't on duty, and the desk officer in his place looked unhappier than the two captures being marched in by uniformed cops.

"Cahill and Rian are out on a call." He gave her a perfunctory glance. "Message?"

"I'll call them tomorrow," she said, suddenly anxious to leave. If they were out now, it had to be for something urgent and, unsettled as Sarah was, she knew her story could wait. And everyone here was a stranger to her now.

Back on the street, she hesitated. Then on impulse, she headed toward the block where she worked. Still walking fast. Still anxious.

It was eerily silent. The church steps were empty, and the few remaining businesses were closed, including the Butler Agency. Only a smattering of lights shone in apartments up and down the street, not as many as one might have imagined.

Sarah stopped in front of Gianni's shop. Of course, it was shut. But he'd mentioned having a small apartment there. She entered the tiny vestibule, shocked to discover that the only name next to any of the handful of buzzers was Gianni's. Did everyone else wish to stay anonymous? Or was he the only remaining tenant, similar to some other buildings nearby?

Sarah pressed the buzzer. No response. Maybe he

was visiting his sons. Or eating dinner and didn't want to be disturbed. She pressed the button again, several times, while Kelly's questions drifted through her mind. But Sarah was resolute. Gianni was her friend.

But hadn't she misjudged Jake as harmless? Maybe she was wrong about everyone.

Not long after finally hearing a response, she identified herself, and the inner vestibule door opened to reveal Gianni's startled face.

"Sarah! Are you all right?"

"Yeah, I didn't mean to bother you, but could we talk for a couple of minutes?"

"Of course. Come into the shop. I'm better equipped to entertain there. It's where I keep my best tea kettle, and you look like you could use some tea right now."

As soon as they were settled and sipping their tea, Sarah filled him in on everything about tonight's frightening episode.

Gianni breathed out a long sigh. "The teen, Dek, sounds like a gang wannabe."

"You said the same thing when we met him that Sunday afternoon, and Jake said it, too. Well, he just said 'wannabe,' not gang."

Gianni shrugged. "Random tattoos don't necessarily mean an affiliation, but having one on the back of the hand can be a way to look tough. Ready for more. It hurts to get inked there. Maybe Dek was doing a copycat thing to prove himself, although Jake didn't sound too impressed. Maybe all Dek's guilty of is getting a few bucks to harass people. That's not any sort of initiation. But I suspect he's having second thoughts about wanting in at all. He's scared."

"But what does it all mean? Is Jake the *who* that's so frightening?"

"Possibly." Gianni frowned. "Did you notice what Jake had tattooed on his arm?"

"No. He pulled his sleeve down quickly, and I was too stunned to concentrate."

Gianni nodded sympathetically. "Look, Sarah. No matter what, stay clear of Jake. We don't know what his story is. And as far as the dead guy, Vincent Milaeve, is concerned, whether or not he was mugged or intentionally killed, you might be getting too close to something. Let the cops handle it." Gianni looked at her directly now. "And please get a job out of this neighborhood as quick as you can. Something's not right around here."

"I know. I'm working on it." Sarah paused. "And I'm still wondering why Dek needed to scare people away on *this* particular street. Whether or not it was connected to the murder."

"Yeah, I wondered that myself," said Gianni.

"And I keep thinking about what Dek said: 'I didn't realize who you *are* and who you *knew*.' Jake could be the person I *know,* but what did Dek mean by *who you are?*"

"I have no idea, Sarah."

They sat for a few quiet moments, sipping their tea. Sarah was feeling calmer now. Gianni's presence was comforting.

"Sarah, over the weekend, I came across one small detail that might or might not help with May's situation. Today I went to visit a sick friend uptown, so I was planning on bringing this over to you at work tomorrow. But here you are instead." Gianni smiled.

"Anyway, it's the name and address of an old family of seamstresses my wife once knew when she did that type of work. It was in some of her old papers. Looks like they moved to another neighborhood a while ago and maybe they might not even be there anymore. But it could be worth a try to get in touch if they're still around. Just in case they might have some detail that could help with May, since you mentioned her mother could have been a seamstress."

He reached under the counter and gave her a piece of paper.

"Thanks, Gianni."

When they'd finished their tea, Sarah rose to leave.

"I'm walking you to the corner and waiting till we can hail you a cab home. You've had enough excitement for one night."

****

When Sarah got home and was safely inside, she breathed in deeply, grateful for the warmth and security of her apartment. And grateful, too, that Gianni had spent time talking with her and insisted on waiting until she got into a cab.

Dropping her coat on a chair, she walked slowly into the kitchen. All she wanted was to burrow into the blue couch with a small glass of wine, a comforting wedge of cheese and some crackers, and then process everything. Should she phone Gil? Probably not. If he'd been out on a call, it must have been urgent, and he'd have plenty to do by the time he returned late to the precinct. And she didn't want to call him at home and bother him when it would really be late. It could wait until tomorrow, much as she would have felt comforted hearing his voice.

Now, though, she turned on the radio and settled into the couch, pulling her feet up under her, sipping her wine, and nibbling at her snack. She wasn't even in the mood for ice cream. As the soothing radio music played some sweet orchestral waltzes, Sarah picked up the recipe book, still on the couch. She idly thumbed through, coming across the tailor's holiday bread she'd vowed to try. And now, near Christmas, the local bookstore manager's ginger cookie recipe was a close second. The little book offered some diversion, helping her unwind.

Sarah cut a piece of cheese for herself and continued to leaf through the book. There were more cookie recipes, including the Zigeuner Café's tasty meringues with chocolate bits. It was well-known as a dessert treat at the café and had been one of several items boxed and sold to take home. It was a true favorite of the local butcher's huge network of relatives, the dry cleaner's entire staff, and a must at the singing society's post-rehearsal coffee hours. The printer and his family always brought some when visiting friends who'd moved. No wonder everyone missed the café, Sarah thought. They were in love with its food.

The phone rang. She stood up reluctantly and reached for it, smoothing out the perpetually tangled cord and knocking over some papers piled on the end table in the process.

"I know it's getting late," said Lorna. Sarah smiled in spite of herself.

"Never too late for a friendly phone call." Sarah took comfort in Lorna's upbeat voice. "I was planning on calling you this week anyway with some updates on a few things."

"Good. And I hope there's a few *social* updates."

"Well, that, too."

"Any chance of dinner on Wednesday? I'm dying to hear what's going on. Besides, I need a shoulder to sob on."

"Sure. New episodes in 'As the Bride Cries?' "

"You know it," sighed Lorna. "Now my sister Keesha tells me that the flowers we picked clash with the dresses. And my aunt is suggesting, and not too subtly, that her rowdy two-year-old grandson would be a perfect ring bearer. I'm telling you, Sarah, take my advice and elope."

Sarah was laughing now, and it felt good. "I'm nowhere near having to worry about that."

"Ah, but I have high hopes."

They signed off after setting the time and place for dinner after work on Wednesday. But not before Lorna had clarified a few more specific details about Gil—his full name, precinct where he worked, where he lived, height, age, hair and eye color, and so forth. She even wanted to know why Sarah was only seeing him on the weekend and not during this work week. It was a fun conversation, and Sarah basked in the lighthearted banter, especially since she had no intention of telling Lorna about today's serious events until they got together.

Exhaustion finally took over. Sarah was thoroughly drained. But despite craving sleep, she walked over to her shoulder bag and pulled out her sketchpad, turning to her portrait of Jake. A sort of morbid fascination propelled her.

She studied the picture. Her sketch had been a

quick one of a bland face, a blank canvas. Not revealing anything of him or his inner self. But tonight, he had shown another face, fleeting but far more complex. Then in the eerie glow of the streetlight, that face resumed its bland expression once more.

What was the real story behind that blank canvas?

Chapter Thirty-Four

The next morning, Sarah's phone rang soon after she reached her desk. It was Clare, following up as she'd promised about the benefits job. Sarah was overjoyed to hear from her, and they set up a meeting for after work on Thursday. Right now, that job sounded like the most attractive thing on the planet.

Then came the question of what was left to do on the job she did have. Most of Mrs. Butler's files had been organized. There were fewer and fewer forms and letters to deal with, now that the agency was closing. Things were winding down quickly.

Sarah shook her head as the phone rang again.

Matt.

"Hi Sarah. I really didn't want to bother you at work, but I wanted you to know that I came across some old menus from the Zigeuner Café you might like. They're so beautifully artistic that I thought you'd appreciate having a few of them."

"Oh, Matt, don't you want these for yourself? You told me you loved the place growing up, and it's such a really nice memory for you."

Matt gave a small laugh. "I definitely loved it, but there are a lot of duplicates, and I wanted to share some of them with you."

"That's so nice of you, but you already shared those lovely poster replicas. And by the way, that artist was superb."

There was an awful pause when neither one of them knew quite what to say.

"How about this?" continued Matt, to Sarah's chagrin. "You could stop over after work in the next couple of days and pick them up. The office will officially be moving to The Cove at the end of the week. Whatever I can't take or give away is going to be demolished along with the building."

"Thanks, Matt. I'll give you a call if it could work out."

There was disappointment in his voice as he spoke. "I'll wait to hear from you."

Sarah signed off in frustration.

****

Sarah and Kelly planned to clean up any last random files and miscellany in the conference room that afternoon and talk, too. Edgar waved on his way to the coffee pot and then buried himself in his office with the door closed. Mr. Butler was out to a late lunch, and he'd said that Mrs. Butler was a bit under the weather and not coming in today.

Near lunchtime, Sarah checked to be sure that no one was in earshot. Then she picked up the phone, hoping that with his later schedule this week, Gil would be in by now. It was a relief to hear his voice.

"Sarah, how's everything going at work today?"

"Beyond quiet. Mrs. Butler's out and not feeling well."

"Not surprising."

"Gil, I have more to tell you. Just quickly. I stopped by the precinct last night, but both of you were out on a call. And I didn't want to bother you later, so I

256

waited until today. Sergeant Brushie wasn't there either, and the guy at the desk looked a bit, umm, overwhelmed."

"Nicely put," said Gil. "We never heard that you came in. Is everything okay?"

"Sure, but there was something a little, uh, weird, and I figured you should know."

Sarah lowered her voice and launched into her capsulized story about Jake, hopefully told in a way that wouldn't make Gil worry too much. Then she mentioned coming to the precinct and seeking out Gianni.

There was a catch in Gil's voice when he finally spoke. "Sarah… Thank goodness you're okay." She heard him draw a deep breath before continuing. "Please stay away from Jake. I don't care how nice his flowers are. And Dek? Gianni's right. He's probably a garden-variety delinquent who could be getting cold feet."

"He really did seem scared. I'm almost starting to feel sorry for him," said Sarah.

Gil's voice was serious. "He's a street punk, Sarah. And you don't need more trouble."

"I guess not. But Jake could certainly be the person I know who's scaring him."

"Anything's possible." Gil paused for a moment. "Sarah, I'm really worried about you. You know you can call me anytime. Please, if I'm not here, tell the desk to get hold of me. Call me at home. It doesn't matter what time it is. I just want you to be safe."

"Thanks, Gil. Umm, I try to stay safe, but things just seem to happen. It's all okay now, though. Actually, it's pretty boring today." She wanted to make him feel better. He sounded so worried. "I'm going home after work, watching TV, and catching up on a phone call or two."

"Okay," said Gil, anxiety still in his voice. "You could use the relaxation after yesterday."

"Please don't worry, Gil. I'm really fine. But I just figured you should know."

"To quote someone we both know well—please, no more Nancy Drew." He was trying for a lighter tone. "Seriously, Sarah. Just be careful."

****

Kelly was horrified when Sarah filled her in on the events of the previous evening.

"Sarah, you've got to get out of here." Her face was lined with concern.

"I'm hoping that will happen sooner than later," she said, trying to console Kelly. She then told her about Clare's call and their upcoming appointment.

"Best thing," said Kelly. "If she offers you the job, take it on the spot."

"If you'd said that two weeks ago, I'd have made a face. Now? I'd snap up an offer from Clare in a heartbeat."

Sarah and Kelly continued pulling together the last of the remaining files and papers.

"Oh, and I meant to tell you. I'll be taking off tomorrow afternoon to sign some paperwork for my new job. With Mr. Butler's blessing. No need to do the dentist appointment routine now."

Boring was the best way to describe the rest of the afternoon and that was not necessarily a bad thing. When Sarah got home, she immediately ate dinner and lingered over a large dish of ice cream. Then she cleaned up her dishes, made a cup of tea, and turned on the TV as background. But the ringing phone interrupted her quiet evening.

It was Bridget Grady.

Chapter Thirty-Five

Sarah slid into a church pew early the next morning. After breathing a short prayer, her thoughts turned to her phone conversation with Bridget last night. She'd explained the scope of her research project and how excited she was to be able to work with May along with Lorna's social worker friend, Father Haney, and the priest's church administrative contact. She was thrilled when Sarah told her about the lead from Gianni. This might offer even more help.

"I'll be happy to follow up on that, if you'd like," Bridget offered. "Sarah, I believe we can make real strides on May's behalf soon." The only other thing that Bridget thought might help was the name of the city social worker who had checked up on May when she first began sitting on the church steps. Sarah promised to get that information from the cops.

Now, Sarah rose, hoping to catch Father Haney before heading to work. She wanted to thank the priest for his efforts in gathering the group and helping to get it started on its mission.

****

Gil called again that morning. "Just wanted to be sure everything's okay."

Sarah was pleased. "Absolutely fine. And I was going to call you with a question." She told him about Bridget's request for the name of the city social worker.

"I'll get that for you by tomorrow. I'm glad things are all right after your eventful week."

Sarah burst out laughing. "Things are pretty un-adventurous now. Work is slow, and tonight, I'm meeting my friend Lorna for dinner. So, it's more or less normal." Sarah paused a beat. "But when we see each other on Saturday, I have another five-minute monologue for you."

"Looking forward to it, Sarah. In the meantime, please take an intermission from any new adventures. The dangerous kind, I mean."

"I'm planning on it."

"Oh, and one thing I need to tell you. Dek, or at least someone who looks like him, has been seen around in the past couple of days. No one's reported any crimes, but it seems as if anyone looks at him too long, he runs. His description keeps coming up."

"Hmm, that's interesting."

"I just wanted you to be aware he's out there. He's not accused of anything. But he's skittish, and we'd like to talk to him. Just be on the lookout. And please stay away from him."

****

Sarah started to go through her desk drawers to organize and sort their contents. There really wasn't a lot left to do otherwise, and the office was beyond quiet. She even began going through some items in her shoulder bag. She'd recently thrown far too much into its generous interior. Now she fished out a few items in the hope of discarding anything that wasn't necessary and leaving ample room for her sketchpad and pencils.

She found the business card from those movers—*Two Guys from Grenleah.* Sarah remembered how cheerful and friendly they'd been. Maybe the Butlers really could use their services. She set the card aside.

Then she pulled out the catalogue envelope with the miniature posters from Matt. Studying them once more, she was again impressed with their vibrant color and energy.

The extra business card that Matt had included in the package fell out on her desk. Sarah realized that she'd never taken out the one she'd buried in her dressy purse on the day of the party. Now she looked at Rapid Printing's new office location at The Cove, that lovely new corporate office park. Matt had written down his new personal address, as well. Both were located in the same town…

Sarah jumped when the phone rang. It was the nice reference librarian she'd spoken to on Saturday.

"I think I found what you're looking for," the young woman said, sounding elated at her revelation. She was doubly happy when Sarah promised to run over to the library on her lunch hour.

****

Later, Sarah sat at her desk, eating a cheese sandwich and thoughtfully reflecting on the information she had just received along with everything else. She made a mental note to bring the young librarian some holiday cookies soon to thank her for her cheerful and very illuminating help. Sarah re-read Theodore Milaeve's obituary that the kind young woman had been so delighted to have found for her. Theodore Milaeve—Vincent's father.

Theodore had been rich and generous, helping a lot of people over the years. He must have tried hard to fill the void in his life that was left by Vincent. The story became clearer now, all the little remote facts coming together. One by one. Little details—Sarah's sketches, random conversations, the recipe book details, individual reminiscences, the obituary, and, now, the items spread out on her desk. Past and present. All starting to tie together.

Sarah didn't like the result. Vincent's death had been murder. That was sure. The pieces of the puzzle were fitting together with alarming accuracy.

Now, picking up a paper on the desk was impossible. She shook so badly. Sarah was almost sure she knew who'd been responsible and why. She needed to call Gil. Immediately.

She attempted to reach for the phone, but a shadow loomed over her desk.

"Sarah."

Edgar's voice made her jump. "I didn't mean to startle you."

He slid into the chair next to her and sat quietly. Sarah balled her hands into fists and crossed her arms to hide their trembling.

"Got a minute?" Edgar didn't sound like Edgar right now. Of course not. Most likely, he wasn't really Edgar. As if to confirm this possibility, he removed his glasses and placed them on her desk, looking at her carefully. If he'd pulled out a large chocolate bar, it would have sealed the deal.

"Okay." Sarah shifted in her chair. The two of them were alone now. Kelly had left earlier to sign the papers for her new job. The Butlers were both out. Sweat formed on the back of her neck. If only she'd called Gil five minutes ago.

"We need to talk," he began. "And I have a feeling

you've figured out some of this already."

"All right, Edgar."

"And I realize you know I'm not Edgar."

An uncomfortable silence followed. She hadn't expected him to admit this.

Finally, she spoke. "You're Elwyn."

He nodded. "Look, Sarah, you were the one who found the body on the church steps and that started you getting curious, asking questions. Drawing conclusions. Although you probably have no idea why I've posed as my brother."

"Whatever the reason, it's none of my business. You don't owe me any explanations."

"I think I do. For your own safety."

A tiny shiver crept along her spine. *Was this a threat?*

"Look, Sarah. I told the cops some of it. But not about the blackmail yet."

Why did it seem as if everyone had only been telling the cops half a story?

Sarah remained silent, not sure if she was scared or just numb.

"Vincent Milaeve and I met in high school, and we got caught up in the thrill of pulling a con. He engraved fake securities certificates and a few other things, and we sold them."

So he was one of the "friends" Mrs. Butler had mentioned.

"Vincent hit up old Mr. Butler. My twin, the real Edgar, worked for him and innocently mentioned to me that the man had some cash to invest. It really was naïve on his part. Believe me, my brother was as honest and diligent as they come."

Sarah hugged her long sweater around her more closely, clutching it so tightly that her hands hurt.

"We hit up a bunch of other people, too." He paused to wipe his forehead with a handkerchief. "Most of them aren't around anymore and neither are their families."

"That was a long time ago, Ed... ur," she stammered.

"Edgar's fine. That's sort of who I am now."

The only thing Sarah believed was louder than the ticking of the clock in the front hall was the beating of her heart. It intensified with each of Edgar's revelations.

"Sarah, we were young and stupid. But we made a lot of cash."

Why was he telling her all of this? *For her own safety, he had said.*

"Old Mr. Milaeve found out and was furious. He cut Vincent off completely. We got scared and ran. Joined the army. You know, it was wartime. They were going to get us anyway, I suppose. And then my poor brother was drafted."

The phone rang in Edgar's office. He ignored it. Yet, he waited until it stopped before speaking again. In the meantime, Sarah lowered her eyes to everything on her desk—the business cards, the obituary, miscellaneous items from her shoulder bag. *And, yes, she knew...*

Edgar continued. "When Vincent and I got out, we pulled a few more, uh, jobs out in the Midwest. We got caught but got off light." Edgar studied his hands now. "By then, my brother, the real Edgar, was permanently admitted to a veteran's hospital. He'd developed some serious health complications after being wounded. From there on, it was all downhill."

Edgar looked away, letting out a half-choked sigh. Sarah was sure he was going to break down. But after several deep breaths, he continued.

"It should have been me, Sarah." His eyes looked more pleading without the glasses, watery, his face more drawn.

She had no idea what to say.

"Vincent and I parted ways. I was sorry I'd ever met him. I moved near the veteran's hospital and got a factory job. Spent all my free time with Edgar. I'd read to him. We'd listen to music together."

Music. Yes, one more piece of the puzzle. Now she knew what May was trying to tell her. It all fit.

Edgar went on. There was no stopping him now. "We had time to talk. I confessed everything. Before he died, I promised him I'd turn my life around and make everything right with the Butlers. He somehow felt responsible because he'd let those details slip, and he worried that old Mr. Butler's loss of that money might have hurt his business."

Edgar revealed how he'd come back years later and looked up the Butlers. "No one had seen my brother or me for years or even knew what happened to us after the war. Or even remembered too much about us. Old Mr. Butler was gone, but Lou Butler hired me. I posed as my brother Edgar, saying that it was Elwyn who'd died. It was easier all around."

"You won an acting award at school," Sarah said, absorbed in his story for the moment.

He nodded. "Yeah, the acting did come in handy. But all I wanted was to put my past, and my real identity, behind me. And I needed to do something good for the Butlers to keep my promise to my brother and make amends somehow."

Sarah continued to listen, putting these additional details together with things she'd just learned or remembered or realized as she gazed at the assorted papers and cards on her desk.

"It all went well for years," he said. "I even made up a few fictitious customers along with the real ones and developed business plans in their names. Lou didn't know some of them weren't real. He was happy to let me build the business plan aspect of the firm. Then I paid the agency from the money I'd stashed away from the bad scams in the old days. It was the least I could do."

Good grief!

"Edgar, why are you telling me all this?"

He looked at her directly, concern mingling with the sorrow on his face.

"Because, Sarah, you've accidentally gotten yourself in the middle of some ugly things. You've asked a lot of questions, talked to a lot of people, and it's gotten around. It's dangerous for certain people to realize this. But you deserve to know the whole story before I go to the cops with the rest of it. I wanted to get one last bit of proof so they wouldn't think I was guilty. But there might not be time now."

"I think I know..." began Sarah, but Edgar was intent on finishing his story completely.

"Old Mr. Milaeve died earlier this year. He was *very* rich and very generous. He made a lot of money as a master engraver. He really was one of a kind. And after he moved, he bought and managed real estate both here in the city and out of town where he lived."

Sarah glanced down at the obituary on her desk. It had told her as much.

"He felt he could never make it up to people for what Vincent did." Edgar sighed, noting Sarah's confusion. "All right, I told you about my fictitious clients and how I pumped money into this business. But Old Mr. Milaeve also sent money semi-annually to the Butler Agency. Oh, it was supposed to be as payment for some sort of services rendered to his real estate firm which, by the way, was never officially connected with him. It was in a generic name and handled by a lawyer. Old Mr. Butler knew the story, but I don't think he ever told Lou. It lasted for years. Old Mr. Milaeve did this for others around here, too. Some of it was to make amends for our scam, and some just to help people and fill a void in his life. His good reputation meant everything, and he spent years trying to overcome the damage he felt Vincent had done to the family name."

Sarah was quiet for a long moment, as Edgar took a deep breath and let his gaze sweep the room.

"When old Mr. Milaeve died, he still had a large estate. His wife and daughter were already gone, and the daughter's family inherited a large sum, even though they weren't in contact with him much. Even after bequests to charities, there was a huge amount left."

"And that's why Vincent came back here? To claim his inheritance?" Sarah's voice was almost a whisper.

"More specifically, he came back to go after the person who was going to inherit what he felt was rightfully his portion and owed to him by birth. And he threatened to blackmail me by telling everyone and the authorities who I really was if I didn't help him by whatever means, legal or not, to overturn the will. To make it worse, Vincent only found me by accident. He was coming to see Lou Butler."

Why had Vincent come to seek out Mr. Butler?

Edgar misread the look on her face. "I didn't do it, Sarah. I would have faced up to everything, but I wasn't going to do anything bad ever again. I promised my brother. And I told Vincent I wasn't giving in to his blackmail. He could've told everyone the truth about me. Sarah, please believe me. I didn't kill Vincent."

"I know that, Edgar," Sarah said finally. She was shaking again, pulling her long sweater tight around her. She knew her suspicions about the real murderer were correct.

He looked at her with deep anxiety on his face. "I'm telling you this for your safety. You've started to figure out too much. We're both in danger. It's all going to blow up."

"Go to the cops right now, Edgar. With or without the final proof. And please tell me the rest quickly. I need to hear it from you, but I think I know—"

But the abrupt sound of the front door opening stopped both of them.

Mrs. Butler.

Chapter Thirty-Six

"So, you two are still busy working away?" Mrs. Butler sounded cheery, but her tired and worn face said otherwise.

Sarah and Edgar exchanged glances.

"Edgar, can I talk to you now about that company that wants to hire you?"

Edgar hesitated, and Mrs. Butler took this as a "yes."

"I know it's getting late, Sarah, but when Edgar and I finish, could we talk for just a couple of minutes about that job I mentioned the other day?"

"Umm, sure, Mrs. Butler. Thanks. I just need to run over to the church for two minutes. I'll be right back. I'll leave my things here."

Sarah hoped May was there now. She hadn't seen her this morning. Sometimes this meant she'd be around later on.

Mrs. Butler headed up the stairs, slightly out of earshot.

Edgar whispered to Sarah before following. "Be careful. I'll be down as soon as I can."

Sarah nodded. Then she grabbed the sketchpad out of her shoulder bag and tore out two pages, leaving everything else on her chair. Hugging her long sweater close along with the two sketches, she ran out the door. She was counting on May being there.

It was later than May usually stayed, the same as the day they'd first encountered Dek, the night before Sarah discovered Vincent Milaeve's body on the church steps. The night when Sarah's part in this really began. But it wasn't until now that the pieces of the puzzle began to fit.

May could confirm what Edgar didn't have the chance to finish telling her. Then she'd run back to work, get Edgar, and rush to the police precinct. Now. Today. But she had to talk to May...even though Sarah already knew.

Breathless, Sarah ran to the church steps and sat down next to May. She smoothed out the two sketches. Why hadn't she done this before? Why had it taken her so long to identify the little part of the song May always hummed and realize what she was trying to tell Sarah?

The song had been on the radio. And then Ben had randomly mentioned the composer's name. Sarah should have recognized it long ago. Like that toy shop she'd joked about with the same name as a song. Only this was a different place with the same name as a different song. And it was nothing to joke about.

"I need to show you a picture, May." Sarah placed the first sketch in May's lap. A slight breeze gently played at the edge of the page as she turned to look at the woman.

As soon as May saw the image, she pointed, her worn glove showing a slight tremor. The lines in her face deepened. If Sarah sketched her now, those lines would be ones of fear.

"Sing me your song again, May. Please."

May hummed the handful of notes.

Sarah whispered the title to May and gave her the

271

other, hastily drawn sketch of a place. Same name as the old Noel Coward song, the one whose few distinctive notes May had done her best to hum. The place associated with the sketch that had just brought such fear to her face.

"You were trying to tell me, weren't you?"

May nodded. She must have seen or heard something but didn't know what to do or who might believe her…except Sarah.

It all added up now. Old Mr. Milaeve had more than made amends for his son's actions. He had also generously reached out to additional people and places. Had he and Vincent ever tried reaching out to each other? No matter. In the end, they both followed their primary motives. Mr. Milaeve's was generosity, probably to fill an aching gap in his life. Vincent's was money, which filled some deep need in his own life. But then, everything backfired.

There are no coincidences.

"May, please hold these sketches. I have to get Edgar. I'll be right back. The three of us need to go to the police."

Sarah ran, hoping to grab Edgar, whether or not he and Mrs. Butler were done. She glanced at Gianni's shop. Closed. Was he away? In his apartment? No lights were on in the building.

The sky already turned to an early dusk. The street was empty. She pulled her long sweater tighter around her. But it offered little protection from the chilly air. And from her fear.

All was still. Too still. Except for a slight change in the shadows. Sarah didn't notice it until she was closer. Too close. Too late.

Suddenly, she was yanked into a vise-like grip.

Chapter Thirty-Seven

"Let go!" she yelled.

Even before Sarah saw the face and felt the sharp jab of metal in her side, she knew who it was.

There are no coincidences.

"Sarah." The casual voice, once so friendly, was now dense with threat. "I was worried when I didn't hear from you." His arm was firmly around her.

"Matt! Let go!"

The door to the Butler Agency was tightly closed. Mrs. Butler and Edgar were probably still upstairs, unable to see or hear anything out on the street. Why wasn't there anyone around?

Matt continued drawing her to him with one arm, as if they were on familiar terms. And there was no doubt about what he had shoved into her side with his other hand, the side closest to him. Something artfully concealed. A gun. Was this the evidence that Edgar wanted to find?

Matt pressed it close into her long sweater, invisible except to the most closely observant. Had May seen her look of horror? Seen her struggle and then quickly grow still at the feel of the weapon jabbed in her side?

"Come with me to the shop." Matt propelled her down the street. She didn't have much choice. "Everything else can wait. And please don't do anything foolish." His voice strove to keep the same casual tone, while his grip around her shoulder tightened and the metal dug deeper into her side. If she screamed or tried to run, he could shoot her at startlingly close range.

To anyone passing by, they might have been on their way to a romantic evening. He with one arm protectively around her, the other placed with suggestive intimacy at her side. Perhaps trying to keep her warm since her only outer garment was the long sweater. Whispering to her, lips grazing her chestnut hair. An amorous couple. Unless, of course, someone caught the look of terror on Sarah's face. But it was a rare individual who looked into the face or the eyes of anyone they passed on the street, especially in this city. And there were only a few people who were anywhere nearby now. They had their own business to attend to. Besides, it was almost dark.

In a few terrible moments, they were at Rapid Printing. Sarah glanced quickly across the street at the flower shop. There was no sign of Jake. *Would it have mattered?*

Then Sarah caught a reflection in the window, just like the one she'd seen after her trip to the grocery store a mere few weeks ago. She was sure this time. It was Dek. *Had he been following her all along?* Gil said he'd been spotted more frequently around the neighborhood lately. Why? But the reflection quickly vanished.

Once inside, Matt kicked the door shut and motioned to the stairs leading up to the Zigeuner, the abandoned café. A neighborhood fixture. Its name was the same as the old Noel Coward song, a phrase of which May had always been humming. A phrase Sarah had finally discerned. Too late. It was the only way the woman probably knew how to voice her suspicions.

If only Sarah had realized earlier what May was trying to tell her. The song had just been on the radio. Why hadn't Sarah recognized that one little haunting phrase?

"Please, Sarah. Let's walk upstairs now."

Should she try to push him off balance as they climbed? *But the gun was too close.*

"Matt. If you tell your complete story to the cops, whatever it is, it could work out all right."

"Oh, Sarah. It could only work out all right if *you* didn't know. You were asking so many questions about the old days, the people, and the Milaeve name. Talking to everybody. And let's be honest. You were the one who found the body, so it wasn't exactly a shock when you started sniffing around."

How did he know this?

They began their ascent, Matt diagonally to her right. Barely a step behind Sarah.

"You killed him." She stated this as a fact. "You killed Vincent Milaeve."

His voice had a thick layer of distress. "Yes…I did."

Slowly. Another couple of steps.

"Why?"

But she'd just about figured it out. Motives, both basic and complicated.

"When we first met, Sarah, I hoped you'd never suspect. Never find out. I could have put it behind me. Then we could have made a great couple. Could have really gotten something going. I wanted that badly.

We'd move to Grenleah and start over. A new life together."

With a murderer?

If she'd only looked at Matt's address card right after the party, instead of burying it in her dressy purse. Of course, she now knew that The Cove corporate park was in the town of Grenleah, same as Matt's new apartment, same as old Mr. Milaeve's longtime residence as noted in the obituary, same as the movers, and probably same as the lawyers who they'd delivered the boxes to.

And same as where "the printer and his family" brought those meringue cookies with chocolate bits from the Zigeuner Café as gifts when they visited friends who'd moved. Their friends, the Milaeves.

But Matt was continuing with his bizarre explanation now. "People already thought we were a couple when they saw us at the party. They believed you were my girlfriend. No one would have ever thought I'd done anything except spend all my free time with you."

What had Dek said? *I didn't realize who you were…who you knew.*

Who you were? Matt's girlfriend? Who you knew? Matt?

Bile rose in Sarah's throat. And what had Dek's part been in this?

Had he been paid a few dollars to follow her? To get information?

Matt continued. "But then you turned me down, and I found out you had a thing for that cop. And all the while, you kept asking questions of everyone, and you wouldn't stop."

Slowly, two more steps up. "But why, Matt? You have a great business, right? And you were all set to move to the beautiful new place…" Sarah faltered now.

"Why did I shoot Vincent?" Matt finished her question. "Because he was going to take all of it from me. You don't think the business could have continued without financial help, do you? Even while my father was alive, it wasn't possible. Vincent's father, old Mr. Milaeve, died at a ripe old age a few months ago. He'd given us money all along the way, and he included me in his will. Money, this building, and a big interest in the The Cove corporate park. I visited him for years with my own father. Gained his trust. Even went to college upstate near him. I filled a gap in his life in a way that his daughter and her children didn't even try to do. And certainly not Vincent. He just showed up thirty-five years later and threatened to sue me, or worse, over the will. Then he accused me of forcing his father to change it when he was old and feeble. He said that he had a witness from the old days who could swear to it."

Two more steps. Slowly.

"It was about money, Sarah."

At least she'd gotten that part right. But had he cared about old Mr. Milaeve or not?

"I didn't mean to do it, Sarah. It's not me. I wanted things to be normal. For Vincent to leave me alone. Never even met him till a couple of months ago. I just wanted to have a nice life with someone like you." He was pleading now. "That's why I needed to bring you here now. To talk to you. Get you to understand. To forget about Vincent Milaeve. To give me a chance."

What??

"But aren't there others who know?" Sarah knew she was taking a chance asking this.

"Only that guy who works with you. He and Vincent went back to the old days. But he can probably be bought."

But Edgar couldn't be bought.

"And maybe my errand kid. But he can be bought and very easily frightened."

Dek? Perhaps he really was another victim.

They were marching evenly upward on the steps. Sarah was first. Matt was still a diagonal step behind, agitated as he told his story. She had to do something. Matt was a time-bomb waiting to go off.

He kept talking. "Vincent was corrupt. He counterfeited stock certificates. Years ago I even found some old engraving plates hidden in the basement. I told him I'd go to the lawyer with evidence and discredit him. It shouldn't have mattered. My name was on the will."

"You could have taken him to court."

"That's what I was going to do. But he asked to meet me. Said he had something to show me that would change everything. He said there was a place we could talk and we wouldn't be bothered. In a vacant school building his father had owned. You can't believe how shocked I was to find out you worked on that street."

Now she remembered that day at the crafts fair. The look on Matt's face when she told him about the location of her job. And his obvious unease the day he'd dropped off the envelope with the poster replicas for her.

"Vincent said he'd paid my delivery boy to make sure people would avoid the street almost anytime.

Especially at night."

So, Vincent was the one who paid Dek? And Dek worked for Matt.

"The old school building was empty. The church was shut. No one was around. I'd checked it all out a few days before. We met by the old school really late. He told me there were important documents stored in there and we needed to talk about them. He removed some bricks near the foundation of the building. Said it was where he'd left the key for safety." Matt caught his breath and continued. "But when Vincent reached inside, there was no key. He took out a gun. And he pointed it at me."

They reached the floor of the Zigeuner Café. Only a dim light was on. The walls, now empty of their vibrant posters, had a hollow look. Haunted. Remaining furniture and discarded restaurant items were strewn around. They would all be demolished along with the building.

Matt turned Sarah around to face him, still pointing the gun. But at least there was a little space between them. Mercifully, her ribs were free of the gun and her shoulder from his grasp.

"Then how did you…" Sarah faltered.

"He moved backward and lost his balance. He staggered and lost his grip on the gun. I grabbed it when it fell. I backed away, almost into the street. I… I didn't know what to do. I wanted to scare him. Then he got his footing and rushed at me…I panicked…and…"

Sarah swallowed hard. "I'm sorry, Matt. You need to tell the cops. It wasn't as if you planned to do this."

"It's too late. I waited too long. I need to put it behind me, Sarah. I really thought you liked me. I can give you such a nice life. Anything you want. The new place is so pretty. We could just forget about this."

Matt was going over the edge.

Gil was at the precinct, figuring that she was safely meeting Lorna for dinner who, by now, would have started to worry. Kelly was gone for the day. Mr. Butler could be anywhere. Gianni, too. Would Mrs. Butler and Edgar see her abandoned coat and shoulder bag and become alarmed? Would they call the precinct? Go there?

And what of May? She must have seen Matt drag her away. Yet she couldn't speak. She'd tried to tell Sarah, humming the notes of the song "Zigeuner," same as the name of the café. And when the cops questioned them after the murder, she'd said something that sounded like "aah." Probably trying to say "Matt," the sketch that brought such fear to her face tonight. What had May seen or suspected before and after Vincent's murder? If only Sarah had recognized the song May had been trying to hum all along or had shown May those sketches before tonight. The sketches that she'd left with May just now.

Matt grew more agitated, his face a mixture of pain and panic. Sarah remembered Cookie's comment about his sketch. That Sarah hadn't yet defined his face. That she was unsure about him. This was why.

His hands trembled badly now, the gun still pointed at her.

"Please, Matt. Don't do anything you'll regret. If you tell the cops, it'll be clear that you didn't plan to harm Vincent."

"You don't understand, Sarah," he said, his voice quavering. "Then I'll lose everything."

Again, money.

The remaining tables and chairs cast longer shadows now. The scattered glassware and empty bottles, old tablecloths, and trays looked like ancient relics, long forgotten. Maybe something could be used as a weapon. If only he would turn the gun away for an instant.

But now another shadow was moving. Not just the dim light flickering against the random objects in the room. Something more substantial. The shadow of a figure creeping into the room. Matt still faced Sarah, unaware of what was behind him.

A weathered floorboard creaked in the stillness.

Matt whirled and fired.

Chapter Thirty-Eight

Edgar crumpled to the ground.

Sarah screamed. She grabbed a small footstool and flew at Matt, but he moved too quickly. It only landed a glancing blow as they both toppled to the floor. The gun skittered from his hand. She grasped frantically for anything else to use as a weapon, but Matt shoved her sideways with an adrenaline-charged fury. Sarah's shoulder and cheekbone hit the wall, sending shockwaves through her body.

Matt struggled to his feet, gasping with anger, eyes feverishly searching in the dimness for his gun. "You're both really stupid." Rattling a half-open tray of cutlery, he grabbed a slender steak knife, the blade flashing in a sliver of light that seeped through the window.

Sarah crawled to Edgar, now slumped against the wall after a valiant attempt to stand and help. She snatched a discarded cloth from the corner and pressed it against his shoulder. In a moment, blood seeped through onto her hands.

"Sarah, I'm sorry." Edgar choked.

"It's okay…it's okay." Sarah kept pressing, trying to stop the bleeding.

Matt waved the knife, ignoring Edgar's wound. "You've put me in a terrible position."

"We've got to get him to a doctor." Sarah pleaded. "Now. Please, Matt. Now."

"You forget, Sarah. I'm the one with the weapon." Matt moved closer, brandishing the blade and edging toward the gun that was now in his sightline—and hers.

Sarah eyed it with hope. But Matt moved several steps, blocking any chance of her making a desperate grab.

She continued to press against Edgar's wound, uttering a silent prayer for both of them.

Then a shout cut through the air.

"Matt, are you there?" a familiar voice yelled from downstairs. "There's an old customer here wants to see you. To say goodbye before you move."

Everything halted in a moment of stunned silence.

Finally, Matt shouted. "Not now."

But the voice persisted. "What? I can't hear you. I'll bring him up. He said it's important."

Dek, the obnoxious teenager.

"No!" Matt shouted even louder, desperate.

But nothing was stopping the footsteps on the stairs.

Sarah wobbled to her feet. Matt was distracted. She needed to stop him. Warn the teenager. "He's got a knife and a gun," she yelled at the top of her lungs.

In one swift move, Matt swung and grabbed her, wrapping his free arm around her throat. His other hand still gripped the knife.

The footsteps stopped. But it was another voice that shouted now. Not Dek's. And it was another figure who appeared in the doorway.

"Drop the knife....*now*."

Gil.

No coat. Gun drawn, held out steady in both hands. Aimed right at Matt.

"Let her go." Gil spoke evenly, his eyes focused with intensity on Matt's face.

Matt moved the blade up to Sarah's throat.

"No. You drop your gun. On the floor. Or I'll kill her." He moved the knife closer, until she felt the harsh metal brush against her skin. Sarah held her breath.

Slowly, Gil put down the gun.

"Now, kick it into the corner."

Matt yanked Sarah even closer for emphasis. She gasped for air.

The gun slid over the wooden planked floor with the bumpy sound of an ancient roller coaster at a distance. Past the ledge with discarded bottles and glasses. Beyond a lone café table.

A beat of silence.

"You don't really want to hurt her." Gil spoke quietly, his eyes never leaving Matt's face. "It's me you're after...isn't it?"

Matt was silent. But Sarah felt an imperceptible shift in his body.

Gil slowly raised his hands. "Come over here. We can settle this. Just the two of us."

Sarah couldn't breathe. Gil was baiting him. Hoping Matt would come at him with the knife instead of hurting her. Trying to save her life. *But Gil was unarmed.*

The musty air in the abandoned café thickened and hung suspended. Faraway street noises faded to nothing.

The world was still.

Sarah sensed the movement a heartbeat before it happened.

Matt threw her aside abruptly and lunged.

Gil was ready, tackling Matt's left side hard, knocking him to the floor. But as Matt went down, he sliced Gil with the knife, still clutched in his right hand. A red stain crept down the side of Gil's shirt.

Matt rolled and staggered to his feet, ready to attack again.

In an instant though, fear flickered in his eyes at the harsh jolt of shattering glass on the nearby ledge.

Gil held the neck of a bottle he'd broken with practiced ease, its jagged half-remains as deadly as any knife.

Matt's face twisted in desperation. He rushed again, this time frantically leading with the knife. Gil smashed the knife from Matt's clutch with the broken bottle. Both weapons clattered to the floor as Gil delivered a gut-punch. Grappling, both men plunged to the ground.

Moments later, Gil slammed Matt face down, pinning his hands behind his back. Blood gushed from Matt's nose, lazily gathering in the crevices of the worn wooden planks.

Sarah struggled to her feet, shoulder and cheekbone throbbing. Noise thundered all around. Running footsteps. Shouting. Police. Distant sirens. People taken away…Matt…Edgar… And the rusty stench of blood mixed with dust was everywhere.

It all happened so fast, but it also felt like slow motion. A blur. Sarah heard her name called, as if through a long, vast tunnel. A strong arm held her close, a face pressed next to her chestnut hair. A familiar voice. "Sarah… Sarah… Thank God you're alive."

Chapter Thirty-Nine

"Brushie's still talkin' about the circus at the precinct that day." Harry Cahill gave a rare smile and lifted his wine glass, its contents shimmering in the candlelit glow of the charmingly set table. "To happy endings and even happier beginnings," he toasted before continuing.

"When I walked in that day, Brushie was at wit's end. What with the shoe guy talking and May waving those sketches. And that frantic Lorna person on the phone."

Sarah burst out laughing at the mention of Lorna's name.

"How did Lorna know how to find me anyway?" Gil looked amused, no doubt recalling walking by Sergeant Brushie's desk at the very instant Lorna's frantic phone call came in, minutes before the unlikely duo of Gianni and May burst through the precinct door.

"This is Lorna we're talking about. She'd already given me the third-degree about you. I'm surprised she didn't know your badge number, too." Sarah couldn't contain her amusement, thinking how for once, Lorna's curiosity about all things social had actually been helpful.

Gil laughed. "I'm flattered." Then he turned serious for a moment. "She was totally panicked when you didn't show up, and she'd commandeered the restaurant's phone and wouldn't let it go. While she was talking, Gianni and May were waving your sketches."

Harry Cahill chimed in. "Yeah. Evidently Gianni was just walking home from the subway when May was by his door, terribly upset. And she'd never even waved to him before this. When she showed him the sketches, he figured something really bad had happened."

"I had to give Lorna back to Brushie," said Gil, "because Gianni and May were into their story. But then Dek ran in terrified, like he was being chased, and started yelling that he saw Matt take you and he had a gun. I grabbed him and we ran."

"You sure got some fan club, Sarah. Even that snotty kid ended up helping," said Cahill. "Then Mary Butler flies in, hysterical, as if we hadn't heard enough of this from her before. I was barely able to figure out that your coat and bag were still at work, but not you, and that Edgar had dashed out the door without any explanation. So I mobilized the troops."

It was a week after the Zigeuner Café incident, and Harry Cahill had asked Gil and Sarah over to dinner at his apartment. Interrupting his story for a moment, he carried some serving dishes to the table. "Now, I need to mobilize dinner," he said, helping his guests to some lovely salmon, rice pilaf, and steamed escarole.

"Detective Cahill…" began Sarah.

"Harry," he corrected.

"Harry," replied Sarah with a smile. "This is wonderful…such a…" she hesitated.

"Shock," finished Gil with a laugh. "No one would ever guess that Harry likes to cook."

"Yeah, I'm just full of surprises." Harry was

enjoying this light banter. "Cooking was one of the positive things I got from my ex-wife." He grinned. "I figured this would be more relaxing than going to a restaurant while you're both healing up from those bruises and stitches."

"Thanks, Harry." Gil nodded. "And this is much better than any restaurant."

They chatted amiably during dinner. When it was time for coffee and dessert—chocolate cake, which Harry admitted he'd bought and not made—they returned to talking about the case.

"What amazed me was that so many people didn't tell you their whole stories," said Sarah. "No one wanted to admit they knew Milaeve's name."

"Happens more often than you'd think," said Gil. "People are afraid if they admit knowing something small, they'll be accused of something big. Sort of guilt by association."

"Take the Butlers, for instance," Harry said. "Mary Butler came forward to say she knew the name from her youth, but she stopped there. Then when you got her to come in with the rest of her story, she was scared."

"And then there was her husband," Gil continued. "After you and Kelly came to us with that file, we figured something was up and called him in to chat."

"Truthfully, we don't think he realized until recently that Vincent's father had been pumping money into the agency for years under a generic company name. But when he did, Lou Butler was afraid it would look bad, especially since they'd decided to fold their business."

Harry helped everyone to a second round of cake and more coffee as they continued dissecting the case.

"Poor Edgar," said Sarah. "I knew he had a backstory after talking with Gianni, but when he came to me to confess everything, I had no idea what was going to come out. And remember, I'd just had another confession from Mrs. Butler two days before."

Gil smiled at her. "You'd make a great cop, getting all those confessions."

"No way! It was really starting to get nerve-wracking. But I truly believed Edgar had gotten his life back on track. He wanted to tell you everything, but he needed one more piece of evidence. Basically, where Matt had stashed the gun."

"Sort of ironic, too," said Gil. "He took a bullet from the evidence he was looking for. And when he came to try and help you, Sarah, he didn't bring any weapon. He wanted to do it the noble way. In his mind, anyway. Divert Matt and give you a chance to run."

"Too bad the real Edgar couldn't see how decent his brother became."

"He's going home soon, right?" Harry asked.

"Very soon," said Gil. "He told us that he'll start a new job at another insurance firm, and he'll also be doing some charitable work with his lady friend. And guess who it's for? Father Haney. And here's some other good news. Old Mr. Milaeve really did own the church school building and rented it out for a while. Shortly before he died, he sold it as a donation for a charity project. So it won't be demolished after all. And it'll probably help the church."

"Vincent never went to the school, though," said Harry.

"No. Evidently it was easier to cut classes at public school, even as a young boy. He had a real problem with authority," said Sarah. "At least that's what Father Haney figured out from going through some old files. Vincent's parents weren't real churchgoers, but they supported both the church and the school. Their name was on a plaque inside the school. So there was some sort of connection. Oh, and that hollowed-out space under the bricks? I guess no one dreamed it would be a hiding place for a gun years later."

"Except for criminals or gangs." Harry invited them into the living room and poured brandy for each. "Which is how Vincent got a gun in the first place."

"Seems like Vincent's father was generous to a fault," Gil said. "He gave money to a lot of businesses and people. And evidently, he took to Matt like a grandson. We'll probably never know for sure if there was genuine affection on Matt's part or long-time currying of favor for an inheritance, or a bit of both. Whichever, Matt was going to inherit big, and when Vincent showed up, he had no intention of letting him get in the way."

"What's going to happen to Matt now?" asked Sarah.

"There's a slew of charges, some of which he might have avoided if he'd come to us immediately after he shot Vincent." Harry shook his head.

Sarah gave a sigh. "All for money. And then it just spiraled from there."

"And Matt's claim to that money and property is in jeopardy now," said Gil.

"What about Dek?" asked Sarah.

"He's just some fairly unknown kid who moved into the neighborhood after his mom got a divorce. He started making deliveries for Matt and a few others.

Your basic truant and wannabe wiseass," said Harry. "When Vincent came on the scene, he latched onto Dek and gave him a few bucks to run a few errands and randomly scare people off the street, particularly during off hours. He wanted access to the gun his supplier buried for him behind the bricks. Without an audience."

"But why wouldn't Vincent have just kept the gun?" asked Sarah.

"To avoid ever being caught with a weapon on him, and one that he had gotten through illegal connections." Harry continued. "And from what we gather, Matt took over and kept paying Dek to keep the street quiet. He also wanted free access to the gun which he'd stashed back in Vincent's hiding place at the school. And Dek soon got very nervous that something a lot more than a little harassment was going on. And by the way, Vincent actually staggered away after being shot, and it looks as if he did try to get into the church for help."

Gil shook his head. "Dek wasn't as tough as he wanted to appear. Matt had him follow you, too, but when you mentioned murder, he started to worry that Matt was guilty of something bad. Then, he saw you with Matt at the post office and the coffee shop and decided who you *were* and who you *knew*. He figured he could end up blamed for a crime or else murdered for something or other. By then, he didn't know how to get out of the situation. In the end, though, he had a real attack of conscience when he saw what Matt did to you, Sarah. And he readily agreed to yell up the stairs and distract Matt when he and I got there."

"So what will happen to Dek now?" Sarah was concerned for the teen who had, after all, sounded the alarm after Matt took her at gunpoint.

"Father Haney came forward and offered to work with him. Find out about his family. See if he can get him back in school. And I think Edgar's going to get involved, too."

Sarah was pleased. "At least something good will come out of all of this. Okay, but how exactly did Dek fit in with Jake?"

There was a moment of silence as Gil and Harry looked at each other.

"Dek met Jake when he was doing deliveries. Looked up to him and even got that same hand tattoo. Whether or not he knew about the arm tattoo, he figured Jake for being part of a gang, so he wanted in on that. Thought it would give him some sort of status. Street cred. Jake tried to ignore him. Discourage him." Gil paused.

Both men were weighing their words carefully.

Then Harry broke the silence. "Look, Sarah. We can't say too much. For your safety, the less you know, the better. Gil and I were only let in on things after you came to us with your story. It's out of our territory. But Jake isn't what he appears to be."

"Well, that's for sure," replied Sarah. "He seemed like a nice guy who worked at the flower shop until he scared me that night."

There was another silence.

"He *needed* to scare you away. Dek, too," said Harry quietly. "He had to look into things."

Now Gil spoke. "Jake *is* a nice person, Sarah, but he's part of a bigger picture. And that's probably more than enough to say now."

Gil looked closely at her. "We trust you, Sarah. But

we need to keep everyone safe."

Sarah's eyes widened.

So Jake was probably undercover or an informant. Something to do with gangs and guns and more?

"Okay. I get it," she said. "Best to only say that the flowers in the shop are nice?"

Both Gil and Harry nodded.

There was a brief pause. Sarah took a small sip of her brandy. It was warm and relaxing, and time to change the subject.

"I've sure gotten a lot of phone calls and visits in the past few days," said Sarah.

"Why am I not surprised?" Harry grinned. "I thought most everyone you knew called or showed up at the precinct and in the hospital waiting room."

The three of them laughed, breaking up the previously somber turn of conversation.

"The Butlers seem relieved," said Sarah. "Their building's been sold. They knew it was coming, but the timing was strange, just around the time Vincent was murdered. And, no, it wasn't one of old Mr. Milaeve's properties. They thought about relocating the agency somewhere else in the city and disagreed about it for a while. But then they felt they needed a change. So they're moving near their nephew in Florida. They're not old enough to retire, but they'll pitch in with the nephew's business. And it's not insurance. It's selling real estate."

"There's got to be some insurance tied up in that," said Gil.

"True. But they seem happy and that's what counts." Sarah smiled. "Everyone seems to be going somewhere. Gianni said he's finally going to move out near his one son. He said it's time."

"He's probably right," said Harry.

"Yeah," agreed Sarah. "And I know he's going to miss his shop and everything there. But as Mr. Butler said, everything's changing. I'm making a few nice sketches of Gianni's shop and of him and framing them as a Christmas gift. A little memento of the old street. I'll do the same for the Butlers with the office and the building."

"That's nice, Sarah."

"Kelly's got a new job. And it looks like I'm going to have one, too. I had to postpone my second formal interview till next week. When I explained why, the woman was nice about it and basically told me that the job is mine if I want it."

"Congratulations," Harry said. "So what's doing with Christmas for you two?"

"We've got dinners and parties at Gil's sister Amanda's and with my best friend Cookie's family," said Sarah. "Oh, and you remember Lorna?"

"Couldn't forget her." Harry laughed.

"Well, we're getting together with her and her fiancé over the holidays, too," said Sarah with a smile. "How about you, Harry?"

"I get to spend Christmas with Harry, Jr. So that'll be good."

They quietly sipped their brandy and contemplated upcoming Christmas plans.

"We're all busy people," said Harry. "What about May?"

Sarah smiled broadly as she answered. "That's one of my favorite Christmas stories."

Chapter Forty

A plump Christmas tree in the cozy parlor sparkled with tiny lights and a sprinkling of exquisite ornaments. Several old-fashioned chairs were set into little conversational groups.

When Sarah and Gil walked in, May's face lit up, brightening the entire room. They each gave her a warm hug. She led them over to her cousin, Helen, and the four of them sat down together.

"May, it's so good to see you." Sarah then turned to Helen. "I'm Sarah and this is Gil. We're May's friends."

Bridget Grady had wanted to make progress for May by Christmas. It was now Christmas Eve, and May and Helen were just settled in a new residence for women. Bridget had more than made progress. She'd created a miracle.

The address that Gianni found was a key factor. It led to an old family of seamstresses who helped them locate May and her cousin. They'd known both of them as well as May's mother, Julia Kieran. When May wasn't on the steps of the church, she went home to where she lived with her cousin. But both women had health issues, and during and after the huge blackout in the summer, their small rental rooms had bad problems and caused May such overwhelming anxiety that she sought out the neighborhood of her youth for some comfort.

Bridget's team, with Father Haney's help, found this newly created residence project through the church. Comfortable, good food, and good care. Safety, too. And Bridget would have plenty of opportunity to work with May and a couple of other women there. She'd help them and further her own research project at the same time. And now their little ad-hoc team was expanding; they'd bring in additional medical and social resources. It had the potential to grow bigger and reach out to more people over time.

"Merry Christmas," said Gil, removing some wrapped gifts they'd brought for the women. Both May and Helen eagerly opened the little gifts from Amelia's Crafty Crafts shop along with some bakery treats. There was also a little radio for each so they could listen to music, maybe even some of those songs on the station that Aunt Addie had loved so much. Same as Gil's dad and, of course, Sarah, too.

Once the two women were more settled in, Bridget and the staff said it would be great if Sarah and Gil and others could take them out for an afternoon or for a holiday. They already had invitations waiting.

When it was almost time to leave, Gil took each woman's hand, still as gentle as he'd been with May and Sarah when they were at the church and being questioned on that chilly day of the murder. Now, he wished May and Helen a beautiful Christmas and promised that he and Sarah would visit again soon.

Next, Sarah said goodbye to Helen and then kneeled down next to May. She removed her velvet scarf—the one from Aunt Addie with the embroidered flowers that May had always been so drawn to right

297

from the beginning. Perhaps May's mother had created scarves just like this one in the past. Or even May herself. And somehow the scarf had been the start of a bond between May and Sarah.

Now, Sarah placed the velvet scarf around May's shoulders and kissed her on the cheek.

"For you, May."

A word about the author…

Caryl Janis has been a fan of mysteries since childhood and finally decided to write one of her own. *To Sketch a Killer* is her first published mystery novel. She is a freelance musician and nonfiction author who enjoys theater, museums, and spending time with family and friends.